Whortle's Hope

The Deptford Mouselets

Whortle's Hope

ROBIN JARVIS

Hodder Children's Books

A division of Hachette Children's Books

Chapters

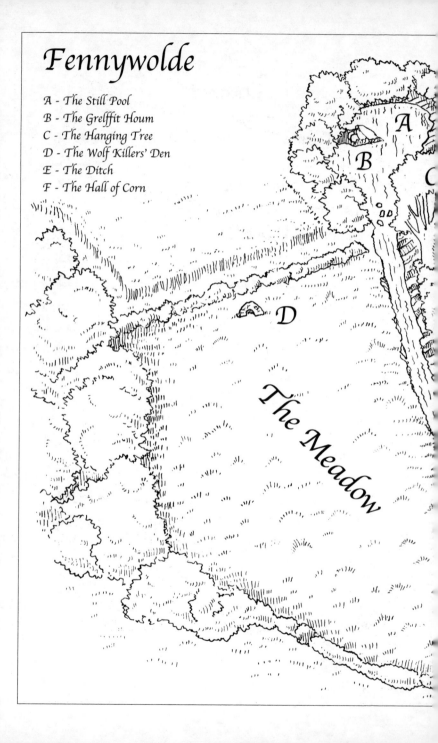

Fennywolde

A

B

C

D

The Meadow

The Cornfield

F

The Long Hedge

E

G

1

Five Friends

I t was a beautiful afternoon in early summer. The sky was as blue and as clean as anyone could wish and, in that forgotten corner of the countryside known as Fennywolde, the barleycorn was already growing high.

Fennywolde is not an important place. No great battles were ever fought or won there. No lost kingdoms or fortresses have been ploughed into the soil and the only gold to be found glints in the fur of those who call it home.

Yet, long ago, a band of warriors did make their way to this picturesque spot. Leaving the horrors of a terrible war behind them, a weary army of woodland animals, led by that courageous mouse of great renown, Captain Fenlyn Purfote, looked upon this little land and knew it was the sanctuary they had been seeking. Far away from the evils they had been fighting, they settled here and, during the long years of peace that followed, they and their descendants flourished.

Little had changed since that glad time. To the east of the ditch that cut through the gentle landscape, the earth had been tilled and corn now grew, but in the lower meadow the swaying grasses were still crowded with wild flowers and the bees droned lazily above as they had always done.

In the summer, the cornfield became home to many fieldmice. But in the winter they escaped the cold by retreating into ancient tunnels dug into the ditch's steep bank and under the roots of the elms, which shaded the gurgling water on its way to the still pool.

For one small fieldmouse the best week of his life was about to commence – one charged with magic, adventure and difficult choices.

But that morning it began in a very ordinary way. He came hurrying through the snug passageways of the winter quarters, scolding himself as he ran.

'You're late!' He tutted crossly. 'And today of all days.

I'm a great big daft dozy lummox!'

Whortle Nep, or Young Whortle as he was called, to avoid any confusion between Whortle, his father and Old Whortle his grandfather, hurried out of the tunnels, and into the delicious fresh air.

He scampered along the edge of the ditch, as fast as his little mousey legs would carry him. He had been daydreaming in his winter bedchamber and had forgotten what the time was. He often lost himself in his own fanciful world and his friends joked with him about it. But today a meeting was taking place that he did not want to miss.

Hopping over the stepping-stones, he crossed over the ditch and into the meadow. He hurried on, puffing and panting along one of the many mouse-trodden paths that crisscrossed it.

'And so!' a loud voice called out from behind a screen of wild grasses. 'May the best mouse win!'

A babble of excited voices erupted.

Disregarding the path in his eagerness, Young Whortle took a more direct route by diving through the wall of grass to his right – emerging in a little clearing filled with fieldmice.

They were chattering and discussing what had just been announced.

At the front, on a raised mound of earth, one of the elders was nodding and smiling. He was Mr Woodruffe, one of Fennywolde's most distinguished inhabitants. He was talking to a young mouse called William Scuttle, whom most called Twit because they thought he was a bit simple.

Although they were the same age, Twit was not one of Young Whortle's special friends and he looked searchingly in the crowd for them.

There they were, over in the far corner. He squeezed his way through the assembly to join them.

'Oh sorry!' he said, when he stepped heavily on someone's tail.

The startled mouse squeaked in surprise. It was Mrs Sedge, the mother of a pretty mouse maid called Alison. All the boys liked Alison. She was the loveliest girl in Fennywolde and their ears flushed bright pink when she turned her smile on them. Her mother, however, was a plump creature with a piggy nose who was fond of complaining to the parents of those mouse children she did not approve of.

'Did I squash it?' Young Whortle asked. 'I didn't mean to, honest.'

'Your eyes are never on the ground, Young Whortle Nep!' she grunted tersely as she rubbed her tail. 'Get along with you.'

'Yes, Missus Sedge!' he said, backing away – only to blunder straight into someone else.

'Watch where thou goeth, boy!' barked a stern voice behind him.

Young Whortle winced. He knew who that was.

Slowly he turned around and there, glowering down, was Isaac Nettle. Mr Nettle was a very tall, grave and sombre member of the Fennywolde community. He was the local mousebrass-maker and therefore commanded great respect. His faith in the magical Green Mouse was the most important part of his life and sometimes, not even the problems of his own son, Jenkin, seemed to matter.

All the fieldmice, even Mr Woodruffe, were in awe of Isaac Nettle.

'If thou spent more time doing an honest day's graft with thine soft paws or studying the ways of the blessed Green,' Mr Nettle said sourly, 'thou wouldst have less time for loafing and dreaming. Clouds and rainbows are all that drift through thy silly head! No good will come of it.'

Young Whortle stammered an apology and hurried away before Mr Nettle could launch into a long lecture. Just about everyone in Fennywolde had had their ears droned into by him, at one point or other.

Moving more carefully through the gathering, Young Whortle finally joined his four best friends.

'What did I miss?' he asked anxiously.

They were still giggling at his run-in with Mr Nettle.

They were a jolly group who delighted in each other's company.

'You were lucky with Pricklenose just then!' exclaimed Figgy Bottom. 'I thought you were going to have Green sermons drummed into you for the rest of the day.'

'Thou shalt not smile nor mucketh about,' warned Hodge, mimicking Mr Nettle's pious tones. 'And if thou sniggereth, thy whiskers shalt surely droppeth on the floor, thy tail shrivel up and thine hind parts turn purple. Amen to that!'

The others chuckled. It was a very good impression.

'So where have you been?' asked Skinny Samuel. 'You been wool-gathering again? Dreamin' about some barmy tale of Old Todmore's, no doubt. One about ghosties again, I s'pose.'

'Well,' said Todkin flatly. 'You've missed what was announced.'

Young Whortle stared at them. 'What did I miss? What was said?'

'Only news of the biggest event of the Fennywolde calendar,' Todkin replied.

'I don't think we should tell him,' Figgy teased. 'If he couldn't be bothered to be here on time, he don't deserve to know.'

'Tell me,' Young Whortle demanded. 'When are they going to be held? What do we have to do? Tell me or I'll go right back to Nettle and tell him who threw that beetle at him, back in the spring.'

Everyone laughed at the memory.

Figgy was fascinated by insects, especially ugly ones, and enjoyed frightening others with them. A few months ago, he had found a particularly large and hideous long-horned beetle. It was such a scowling, bad-tempered creature that it strongly reminded him of Mr Nettle so he thought the two of them should be 'introduced'.

Climbing one of the elms, the five friends had concealed themselves on a low branch and waited a whole afternoon until the intended victim came striding beneath and then Figgy hurled the beetle down at him.

It was a perfect shot and no one had ever heard the mousebrass-maker use such unholy language before. How he howled and leaped into the air when the beetle bit him! Mr Nettle was furious for days afterwards but, fortunately for Figgy and the rest, he believed the insect had merely flown into him.

The youngsters had nearly made themselves sick with laughter that day and even now the memory of it could make them burst into sudden gurgling fits.

'So tell me!' Young Whortle insisted.

'The Fennywolde Games,' Samuel explained, 'are going to take place in seven days' time. Whoever wins them is going to be Head Sentry for the rest of the summer.'

'Until the scythe falls,' Hodge continued in his Mr Nettle voice. 'And then the Green's power departs from the land and I become more miserable and my vinegar face looks more like a slapped backside than ever – amen.'

'Head Sentry!' Young Whortle whistled. 'That'd be summat grand to be. Just like bein' a warrior, in the legends of Captain Fenny and almost as good as bein' King of the Field.'

'You and your knights and battles.' Todkin smiled. 'You believe any old yarn, you do.'

Young Whortle's eyes were twinkling with excitement. 'What did Mr Woodruffe say about the entrants?' he asked.

'Everyone with a mousebrass is eligible,' Todkin answered.

Young Whortle's paw clasped the brass amulet he wore around his neck. Not long ago he and his friends had come of age and had been given these important symbols of family, protection and destiny in a very solemn ceremony. They all wore them with pride.

'At last!' he cried.

'You're not thinking of entering, are you Neppy?' Figgy chortled in astonishment.

'Why shouldn't I?'

'Er . . . cos you're useless at running and jumping and all that stuff!'

The others had to agree with him.

'He's not wrong there,' Samuel said. 'You're really rank at them, Warty.'

Young Whortle frowned at them. 'Well this year,' he declared in a fiercely determined voice, 'I'm going to win those Games – I'm going to be Head Sentry!'

His friends were about to laugh again when they realised that he was completely serious. They stared at him in blank astonishment.

It was the sensible Todkin who spoke first.

'I think we need to call a meeting of our own,' he said gently.

Close to the northern edge of the meadow, near to the old hedge, the five fieldmice had constructed a little hut. It was made from woven twigs and straw and hidden by a camouflage of leaves. They grandly called themselves the Wolf Killers, which was Todkin's idea.

Of course, none of them had ever seen a wolf, let alone killed anything, but it sounded very bloodthirsty and glorious. The best suggestions of the others had been: the Five Pips (Hodge's idea), the Sons of Fenny (Young Whortle's), the Small Tigers (Samuel Gorse) and the Crawling Menace. The last proposal had come from Figgy who couldn't decide between that and the Stinky Cheeses, which no one else liked at all. They had pushed him into the ditch for even considering it.

So the Wolf Killers it was. Although, far from killing them, the fieldmice really wanted to identify themselves with wolves and often practised howling, because they had heard that's what wolves did.

The hut was their hide-out, their wolf's den, where they met to avoid their sisters or discuss secrets such as the beetle incident. Sometimes they indulged in private feasts there. No one else was allowed inside the den. This was their secret refuge, entered only by passwords.

The passwords that week were 'Keep yer paws off me conkers' and once each of them had uttered those important words they were allowed inside.

Todkin was rather good at drawing so he had decorated the inside with pictures of what he imagined a wolf looked like. They were long-legged shaggy monsters with sharp claws, yellow eyes and many rows of teeth and fangs. His friends were very pleased with his efforts and those images often loped through their dreams.

Skinny Samuel took a hazelnut cake from his satchel and began munching. He hated being so bony and this year he had promised himself to put on some weight. But no matter how much he ate, he always looked like a half-starved furry skeleton.

Young Whortle was obstinately refusing to listen to anything his friends tried to tell him, and everyone was talking at once.

'You got no chance against me in the swim or the rafting!' Figgy insisted. 'Last time you went on a raft, you chucked up your breakfast.'

'And you ain't never wanted to have a crack at vaultin' before,' Samuel put in, spraying cake crumbs everywhere. 'Said you was scared, you did.'

Hodge closed his eyes and nodded. 'Then there's the Slingshot.' he said darkly.

'Yes!' everyone chimed in. 'The Slingshot!'

Young Whortle folded his arms and the creases in his forehead deepened.

'Don't care,' he muttered.

Todkin rose and waved his paws, calling for order.

'Young Master Nep!' he began, assuming a schoolmaster-like tone. 'Let me take a few moments to remind you of the nature of the Games. Firstly, they last for three whole days. There are twelve events and each entrant must participate in six of them. In no particular order, these events are: the Ditch Vault, the Meadow Race, which is compulsory to all, the Raft Race, the Ditch Leap, Ditch Swim, Tree Climb, Wrestling, Slingshot, Barley Swing, Pebble Lift, High Jump and Tail Hang.'

'My tail can cling on to a cornstalk as good as anyone else's,' Young Whortle piped up. 'An' for longer than most as well, seein' as how I'm so light.'

'That's only one event,' Todkin told him. 'You can't lift no heavy stones, nor wrestle anything bigger than a butterfly.'

'My sister Dimsel could beat Neppy,' put in Figgy.

'Your Dimsel could beat the lot of us,' Todkin added.

Hodge cleared his throat and, in a grumpy, girlish voice that was spookily like Figgy's sister, said, 'Gimme some of that there cake, Sammy, or I'll twist yer arm off!'

Everyone shuddered and Samuel hastily passed across a chunk of cake.

Then Young Whortle said, 'I can do the Tree Climb faster than most as well.'

'That's two then,' Todkin agreed. 'But no one ever became Head Sentry winning just two.'

'I might be better at other things if I practise hard all this week.'

'You could practise till the oaks rot and fall down,' said Samuel, 'but you'll never jump any higher than folk like Jenkin.'

'Not my fault I'm small,' Young Whortle grumbled.

'We never said it was,' Todkin said kindly. 'But your titchiness also rules out the Ditch Leap and you need longer arms to be any good at the Barley Swing.'

'So what do that leave him?' Hodge asked in his own voice, for a change.

Todkin rocked back on his heels. 'Well, everyone has to run the Meadow Race so that leaves only three more to choose from the list, either the Ditch Vault, the Raft, Ditch Swim . . .'

'I may not be the fastest swimmer in Fennywolde,' Young Whortle protested, 'but I ain't the worst neither.'

'Don't forget the Slingshot,' Samuel said.

The others laughed once more because they knew their friend was quite possibly the worst at that event. In the history of Fennywolde there had never been anyone quite so bad. The last time he had tried it, both the stone and the slingshot went whizzing in the wrong direction.

Todkin coughed. 'I really think we had better forget that one.'

Young Whortle shifted uncomfortably. He wanted to win the Games more than anything, but it really did seem like an impossible dream.

'Out of us lot, I reckon I've got the best chance of winning the most events,' said Figgy.

'But you wouldn't want to be Head Sentry though, would you?' asked Hodge. 'It's a big responsibility.'

Figgy thought about it for a moment. 'You're right there,' he replied. 'It'd get in the way of me insect collectin'.'

'I s'pose I'll do well in the vaultin',' said Samuel, 'and mebbe the Barley Swing and the Ditch Leap too, but I don't reckon I stand a chance of winning the title.'

Hodge shrugged his shoulders. 'I ain't bad at running, but that's about it,' he admitted.

'And I don't want to enter it at all,' said Todkin. 'I'm far too busy as it is, what with sentry duty to do anyway. It's just one big bother to me.'

Young Whortle listened to them sadly and gave a wretched sniff.

'It's not fair,' he blurted. 'It's only a laugh to you, none of you cares who wins, but I do. I ain't never won nowt and I'm the one who's got no chance at all.'

His friends were stunned into silence. They saw how unhappy he was and realised just how much this meant to him. As Young Whortle stared miserably at t. they looked at each other and silently agreed.

'We wasteth the blessed Green's time!' Hodge declared, springing up and heading for the doorway.

'Right enough,' agreed Figgy. 'There's lots to do.'

'I'll go and find some poles,' said Samuel.

'And I've got to work out a timetable,' said Todkin.

Young Whortle glanced up at them.

'What are you doing?' he asked glumly.

His friends grinned at him and Figgy slapped him on the back.

'We're going to help you!' he announced. 'In every way we can. We've got one week to train you and by the end of it you'll be the best pole-vaulter, the best rafter, except for me obviously, and we must do something about your lousy swimming.'

Young Whortle leaped to his feet. 'Really?' he asked. 'You mean it?'

'Warty,' Skinny Samuel said. 'This year, I am going to get nice and fat, and you – are going to win the Fennywolde Games!'

2
The Training Begins

O peration Champion, as Todkin called it, began in earnest straight away.

To avoid being seen by curious observers, the Wolf Killers walked to the far side of the meadow where a clump of ancient and stately oaks marked Fennywolde's western border.

Skinny Samuel had fetched a long pole to practise vaulting but Todkin, who was the main coach, wanted to see Young Whortle's climbing skills first, before he tackled anything trickier.

And so they marched to the base of a tree and Young Whortle was told to race against Figgy and Hodge.

The fieldmice rubbed their paws together in readiness and peered up into the high branches. It was a magnificent oak and looked perfect for climbing. The bark offered plenty of footholds, so Young Whortle was extremely confident that he could race up there and be the first to the top.

Figgy was thinking just the same, whereas Hodge was merely scratching his ears.

'One, two, three – go!' Todkin cried.

With a whip of three tails, the fieldmice shot up the trunk. Young Whortle tore upwards, faster than anyone was expecting. Figgy and Hodge were still scrambling past the lower branches as he went scooting by the halfway point.

'Look at him whizz up there!' exclaimed Hodge.

'Singe me whiskers!' gasped Figgy. 'And there was me takin' it easy so as not to show him up – well not no more!'

And with a grunt of determination, he took off like a rocket.

Down on the ground, Todkin and Samuel stared up admiringly. Breathless with anticipation, they watched their friends tear up the oak's mighty trunk until the leaves hid them from view.

'Go on Warty,' Samuel shouted.

'That were impressive!' Todkin said, jotting down some notes on a piece of paper. 'If he were half as good at the other events, he'd win the Games – no problem.'

'I hope he can, I ain't never seen him so set on a thing before. Real anxious to be Head Sentry, he is.'

Todkin nodded and let out a regretful sigh. 'Those crazy stories Old Todmore tells,' he said. 'They've put all sorts of impossible ideas into his head.'

'Then it's up to us to make sure this one turns out true,' Samuel added firmly.

'Yes,' Todkin agreed.

High in the oak, Figgy Bottom was gaining fast. Young Whortle was only a short distance away but the top of the tree was very close.

His paws were a blur and in moments it was over. He

sat in a fork of the top-most, leafy twig – too out of breath to let out a victorious cheer.

The whole of Fennywolde and beyond stretched out in all directions and he gulped great gasps of the clean, fresh breeze.

'Shift over!' Figgy shouted as he came scrambling up.

The small mouse made room and the twig juddered as Figgy joined him.

'You been eatin' lightning pellets or summat?' Figgy asked. 'You flew up here like a ratwitch with a thistle up her bum.'

His friend grinned back at him. 'Do you think I could beat the rest in our field?' he asked.

Figgy smiled. 'No contest,' he assured him.

Young Whortle hugged himself and a delicious tingle travelled along his spine. He felt as pleased as if the coveted title was already won. The sun shone over his red and gold fur and he closed his eyes, imagining how proud his mother and father would be.

Just then the twig wobbled alarmingly and Hodge called up from beneath them, imitating the foolish, ever-cheerful Twit.

'Bless me, Neppy, if I'd knowed you two was so fast, I'd have growed a pair of wings.'

All three chuckled. Hodge's impressions of Twit, the mouse with 'no cheese upstairs', were always good for a giggle.

They were still chuckling happily when Todkin's

voice shouted from far below.

'You reached the top yet?'

'Yes!' Figgy called down. 'And Neppy beat both of us.'

'Well don't hang about – plenty more to do!'

A short while later they were all back on the ground and looking at the pole that Samuel had brought.

'I reckon we should let our champion try this next,' Figgy said.

'I want to see the Tail Hang first,' Todkin answered, consulting the timetable he had been preparing.

'That means traipsin' back to the cornfield. Makes sense to give him a try at this, seein' as how it's here and so are we. He'll have to have a go sooner or later and better it be sooner.'

Todkin's eyebrows wriggled and twisted. He hated having his schedule interrupted but in the end he said, 'Just a quick go with it then. Sammy – you show him how.'

Skinny Samuel picked up the pole as delicately as if it were a dancing partner and ran his paws along it. He was very good at pole-vaulting. Figgy often joked that he actually looked like a pole.

'What shall I jump over?' he asked.

'Try that big root over there,' Todkin told him.

Samuel nodded, closed one eye and jiggled his shoulders. Then he hopped from foot to foot, lashed his tail and darted off, the pole at his side.

'Humpa, wumpa, jumpa!' he cried.

Young Whortle and the others watched him race towards the tree root that bulged through the grass. Then he gave a yodelling yell, thrust the end of the pole into the soil and was catapulted up. He let go of the pole.

High into the air he soared, squealing happily. Then down he came, landing in a soft mattress of ivy.

'Think you can do that?' Figgy asked Young Whortle.

The small fieldmouse eyed the discarded pole uncertainly. 'Sammy makes it look so easy,' he muttered. 'But I ain't sure.'

'You don't have a choice,' Todkin told him firmly. 'You never know, you could be a natural.'

Hodge hurried to collect the pole and put it in his friend's reluctant paws.

It seemed terribly heavy. He doubted if he could run with it, never mind flip himself so high and so far.

Samuel Gorse came scampering back, beaming all over his face. He had thoroughly enjoyed himself.

'Won't be able to do that when I'm a porker,' he said,

patting his flat stomach. 'No, don't hold the pole in the middle. You need to keep your paws at one end – no, the other end.'

Young Whortle changed his grip until Sammy was happy with it.

'Now take a run,' he said.

The fieldmouse swallowed nervously and clamped his teeth together. The pole wobbled in his paws. It took all his meagre strength merely to lift it, but with a steely resolve he began trotting towards the tree root.

'Faster!' Samuel called. 'Faster, Warty!'

Young Whortle strained and pushed himself. Then the root was before him. He thrust out the pole but forgot to dig it into the ground. It flew from his paws, sailed over the root and whooshed through the air like an arrow, before crashing down and spearing the ivy.

Left behind, Young Whortle sprawled across the root, winded and gasping for breath. His first great leap had been no more than a feeble skip, followed by a belly-flop, and he flailed his arms and legs like one of Figgy's up-turned beetles.

Todkin and Sammy were the first to rush over to him, but the others were rolling in the grass, helpless with laughter.

'You all right?' Samuel asked. 'You busted anything?'

Young Whortle coughed and wheezed, then rolled off the root and fell on his back into the grass, clutching his tummy.

'Ow!' was all he eventually managed to utter.

Todkin made a large cross on his paper. 'Do you want to show us your Tail Hang now, then?'

They marched through the meadow and were soon standing at the edge of the long ditch. The water was gurgling lazily through it and Young Whortle shook his head as he gazed across at the steep bank on the far side.

'I'll never vault across that,' he spluttered.

'Don't think about it just now,' Figgy told him. 'Come, show us what else you're good at.'

They jumped along the stepping-stones. The water was shallow there but the mud beneath was thick and gluey. They scrambled up the high bank, and the cornfield lay before them.

For the fieldmice there was no better place in the world. In the summer their great field was everything: home and playground, larder and golden cathedral. In the winter they dreamed of it and were only truly happy sitting atop an ear of corn, viewing the surrounding ripe, rippling sea.

In the centre of that marvellous place they had already cleared an area to create the Hall of Corn and had built their snug, spherical nests in a ring around it.

To guard their homes was the duty of every boy mouse and they took that task very seriously. All boys wanted to be a sentry and share long shifts on look-out with their friends.

Young Whortle and his friends were not due to begin their shift until the early evening but they loved it so much that they usually spent most of their free time on duty anyway. Not many of the girl mice ever became sentries and most of the others sniffily declared that they had better things to do.

'Hello down there!' called a cheery voice from above.

Young Whortle and the others looked up; there, holding on to an ear of corn was Jenkin Nettle, smiling down at them.

Everyone liked Jenkin, but because of his stern father the other mouse children were shy of making friends with him. Only the pretty Alison Sedge ever sought him out. She didn't care what the bad-tempered Isaac said to her.

'You starting your shift early?' Jenkin asked.

'Not yet,' Todkin answered. 'We're seein' how good Young Whortle is at the Tail Hang.'

Jenkin raised his eyebrows and came slithering down the cornstalk.

'Is this for the Games?' he asked. 'Being on duty, I missed what was said at the meeting but everyone was real excited when they came back. Even Twit is going to enter.'

'Oh my!' Hodge said in Twit's voice. 'Don't start the Games just yet – I think I left me head at home.'

'Don't make fun of him,' Jenkin said.

The others stifled their laughter.

Although he was as young as the rest of them, Jenkin was mature beyond his years and there was often a very sad, faraway look in his eyes. His mother had died when he was a baby and living alone with that strict, stern father of his had taken its toll. At times he could be very grave and moody, but then he usually took himself off to some lonely spot. Not even Alison Sedge would dare disturb him.

Perhaps it was these solitary periods that gave him an understanding of Twit. He had a peculiar respect for that idiotic simpleton that none of the other youngsters could fathom, and Jenkin would never join in their mockery of him.

'You're in with a good chance,' Figgy piped up. 'What events are you going in for?'

Jenkin shrugged. 'I don't know yet,' he said. 'I like them all.'

'Bet you're good at 'em all as well,' Young Whortle said, more than a little enviously.

'Pretty good,' Jenkin answered. 'I'll need to practise some of them, though.'

'That's what we're doing now,' Samuel told him. 'We're putting Warty through his paces.'

Todkin tapped his notes impatiently. 'Let's crack on with it,' he announced. 'Choose your stalk and let's see the quality of your dangling.'

Young Whortle selected a fine, strong stem and swiftly raced up it. The tender, green ear of barleycorn bobbed and danced when he reached the top and he deftly wrapped his tail about the slender stalk.

'Ready?' Todkin shouted.

The fieldmouse tightened his tail's grip then let go with his paws and pitched forward. A moment later he was swinging upside down, like a small mouse pendant and giggling at the sensation.

Todkin cast a critical eye up at him. 'Not bad,' he said.

'Not bad?' Jenkin declared. 'He's brilliant!'

'Hanging technique is only one aspect of it,' Todkin reminded him. 'It's staying up there what counts.'

He jabbed a finger at Samuel, who stepped over to the stalk. This was the dangerous part. In the past, many mice had been injured taking part in the Tail Hang event. During the Games, piles of hay were heaped up beneath the competitors to cushion their fall, but there were always those who landed badly or missed the soft straw. Only three years ago Grommel, the door guard of the Hall of Corn, injured his back and the pain of it was still his chief topic of conversation. 'As sore as Grommel's back' had become a Fennywolde expression.

So, when Samuel tapped the stem, he did it very gently.

'Don't just tickle it!' Figgy scoffed. 'That wouldn't dislodge a dew-drop from Old Todmore's nose. Give it a good thump!'

Samuel made a fist and biffed the stalk with it.

The resulting tremor went wobbling all the way up to where Young Whortle was dangling. His little body jiggled and bobbed but he kept a firm hold with his tail and shouted, 'Ha – you'll have to do better than that!'

Todkin nodded to Figgy, who took over from the hesitant Samuel, gripped the cornstalk with both paws and gave it a good shake – more violently than anyone expected.

'Steady!' Sammy cried.

But the motion could not be checked and grew wilder as it travelled higher up the stalk.

Everyone stared.

The stem wagged and rocked and Young Whortle was flung back and forward and left and right, with tremendous force.

'What did you have to do it so fierce for, you idiot?' Jenkin asked Figgy. 'He'll be thrown off and hurt!'

Young Whortle let out a shrill, warbling squeal of fright as the stalk flailed round and round, out of control.

'He said he was best at this!' Figgy protested. 'I was only testing him.'

'If he breaks his neck, you try telling that to his mum and dad,' said Samuel.

Figgy grimaced and they all watched open-mouthed as their little friend switched and bounced above them.

Eventually the jerks and quivers began to ebb. Calm returned to the cornstalk and to everyone's relief, Young Whortle's tail was still bound tightly around it.

'Amazing!' Jenkin breathed.

'I never saw no one cling on so good as that!' Hodge exclaimed. 'He'll win this, for sure.'

Todkin added a great tick to his notes. 'I don't think we need to practise this event any more,' he announced. 'He's got it in the bag.'

'Well done, Warty!' Sammy called up. 'Warty . . . are you all right? You don't look well.'

Still hanging upside-down, Young Whortle had grown very pale and he uttered a wretched groan.

'He looks like he's going to . . .'

'Run!' Figgy yelled.

But it was too late. Young Whortle's breakfast rained down on top of them.

'Soooooooooooorry,' his plaintive voice burbled.

Wiping their eyes, his friends stomped off to wash themselves in the ditch.

They spent the rest of the afternoon splashing about in the water. The stretch that flowed beneath the three elms was just the right depth for fieldmice to swim.

At first, Todkin attempted to turn it into a training session but Figgy and Hodge were intent on having fun. The warm sunshine made the breath-catching coldness of the ditch inviting and they loved jumping off overhanging branches and swinging from ropes of plaited grass.

When he had washed himself, Jenkin was about to return to the field to resume sentry duty but the others were enjoying themselves so much that he was reluctant to leave.

Hodge had climbed onto Figgy's shoulders and Young Whortle was climbing on to Sammy's.

'Let Todkin get on yours,' Hodge told Jenkin. 'Then we can fight and joust each other.'

Jenkin grinned and soon they were shouting and laughing – pushing one another over in the water and having the best time. Worries and cares were cast aside. Young Whortle even forgot about the Games and, for the first time since he could remember, Jenkin's mind was not clouded by the dark fears that gnawed at him.

When they were exhausted and lay on the grassy bank, chuckling fitfully and squinting at the lazy clouds above, a soft, cooing voice interrupted them.

'What you daft boys a-doing of?'

Everyone turned and there, standing on the edge of the bank, was Alison Sedge.

The mouse maid was smiling down at them, the reflected light of the water flashing in her large eyes. She was undoubtedly the prettiest girl in Fennywolde, or in the whole wide world, for all they knew. The sunlight glowed in her honey-blonde hair and she had a way of tilting her head at you that was very disconcerting.

At her breast, her mousebrass glinted. It was the Sign of Grace and Beauty, a dainty bell suspended from a crescent moon. No one in Fennywolde had received one of those before and it came as a surprise to the fieldmice to learn that the dour, no-nonsense Isaac Nettle had even made it in his smithy.

Young Whortle and the others coughed and spluttered and jumped to their feet. Since getting her brass, Alison was different somehow. She used to be good company, for a girl, but now . . .

They didn't understand why, but they felt uncomfortable when she was around. She made them want to go for long walks with her on their own, to talk to her about things that never usually entered their heads.

Young Whortle felt particularly silly whenever he encountered her these days. Scarlet-eared, he always looked at the ground and kicked his tail, desperately wanting to be noticed yet dreading it at the same time. Figgy, on the other hand, showed off shamelessly in front of her and Hodge performed his best impressions. Even Samuel tried to push his stomach out and Todkin would gabble, listing all manner of facts, trying to appear clever and interesting.

Alison revelled in this new power she had over them and giggled to herself, seeing them so confounded and jostling for her attention.

Only Jenkin remained immune to her charms. He saw what she was doing and hoped she would grow out of it. Before the mousebrass ceremony that spring, he and Alison had been the best of friends. Since then she had become vain and flighty – the very things she had previously scorned. Now Jenkin felt there was no one he could talk to about his troubles.

'We was just larkin' about in the water,' Figgy told her. 'Watch me swing from this grass rope we made!'

'I can jump in from that branch way up there!' Samuel boasted.

'Did you know there are two types of newt living in our ditch?' Todkin prattled. 'The smooth brown newt and the palmate.'

Alison laughed. 'Well now,' she said. 'That be nice for them.'

'And in the still pool, yonder, there's the great-crested sort – they're much bigger!'

'Lor!' Hodge squeaked in his Twit voice. 'Bless my big flappy ears! What a lot of newty beauties there be!'

Young Whortle studied the grass at his feet and smiled bashfully.

'The crested ones look like baby dragons,' Todkin ended feebly. 'I've drawn 'em. We . . . we could go questing for one if you like, Alison?'

The girl chuckled.

'Would you slay a dragon for me, Todkin?' she teased.

Todkin blinked and struggled for something to say. 'I . . . I . . .' he stammered. 'No need to slay it, newts ain't dangerous, I like 'em and they're not as common as they was. They're doing their courting round about now and the misters do a funny dance for their ladies, me and you could . . . go and watch.'

'Maybe next time,' she answered. And with that she fixed her potent gaze on Jenkin.

'Saw your dad afore, lookin' for you, he were.'

Jenkin frowned.

'What did he want?'

The girl shrugged and twirled her bunches in her fingers.

'I dunno. Had a face on him that'd pickle blackberries, he did. I didn't stop to find out why. I've heard enough from him this past month to last me, not that I takes no notice.'

Jenkin nibbled his lip.

'I'd best go see what's up,' he muttered, scaling the bank and hastening into the cornfield.

Alison flicked her bunches over her shoulders and hurried after him. 'Wait for me, Jolly Jenkin,' she called.

There was a loud splash as Figgy swung out over the ditch and plunged into the water to impress her, but the girl had gone and he came wading back to the bank feeling cross and strangely bewildered. He threw a stone into the water, and then sat down, silent and out of sorts.

Todkin and the others looked at one another sheepishly. They didn't like what Alison did to them. Girls were supposed to be annoying, like Figgy's sister and her cronies. They weren't used to them casting mysterious spells that turned everyone into soppy loons.

'Operation Champion,' Todkin said, when they finally stopped glancing up at the bank to see if she would return. 'Let's get back to it.'

In the time that remained until supper, they concentrated on Young Whortle's training.

His style of swimming was called the ratty paddle, and was little more than thrashing his way through the water. Figgy tried to teach him the minnow wiggle instead, but Young Whortle's legs stubbornly refused to obey and continued to kick as wildly as ever.

At last, weary and with a long evening's shift on sentry duty ahead of them, they trudged back into the cornfield where their suppers were waiting.

The first day of Young Whortle's training had come to an end but the first of his magical nights was about to begin.

3

The Not Quite Phantoms

The stars shone brightly over Fennywolde and a breeze laden with the heavy scent of hawthorn blossom wafted through the barley.

Young Whortle and the others had been on duty all evening and when it was time to hand over to the next shift, Todkin announced it by giving his best wolf howl. At the top of the swaying barleycorn, his friends joined in. It was a strange, squeaky sort of sound. Only Hodge came anywhere near making the right noise and that was just through guesswork.

Climbing down the cornstalks the friends slowly made their way back to their families.

Before they parted, Todkin addressed them in his no-nonsense tone of voice.

'If Young Whortle's going to stand a chance with this dream of his, then we have to pull together and not get distracted by the likes of Alison Sedge.'

The others agreed.

'So, tomorrow,' he continued, 'I wants an early start from everyone. I'll think up some exercises to get young Master Nep in tip-top condition, starting first thing with a brisk jog. Hodge is best at running so he can take care of that. You two meet at our den just after dawn and us three will set about buildin' a raft for him to use in the Games. It'll have to be the best there is, so I'll sketch out some designs tonight and my timetable needs a bit of fine tuning, so I'll have to get cracking.'

They smacked their paws together in solidarity, then Samuel's stomach rumbled so loudly that any further talk was pointless and they sought their nests.

The Hall of Corn was bathed in pale, pearly moonlight. Every year the fieldmice toiled long and hard to clear the young barley shoots and create this marvel. At the end of each summer it had grown into a wonderful, high-walled palace with golden pillars.

Hundreds of ball-like nests were woven around the ripening barleycorn. They were lined with moss and deliciously comfortable to sleep in. That night, the glimmering glow of tiny lanterns illuminated many of the round entrances. It was a beautiful, welcoming sight and Sammy and the others could not wait to climb into their own soft beds.

But Young Whortle was restless and not ready for sleep just yet. Excitement still sparked inside him. The hope that had seemed so absurd that morning looked as though it might be within his reach after all.

He wanted to make the day last a bit longer and so, instead of going home, he ambled through the moonlit field, leaving the Hall of Corn and the glowing nests behind.

As he wandered, fanciful dreams filled his happy thoughts. He pictured himself winning all his events and tried to imagine the surprise on everyone's faces.

'Won't they be boggled by it!' he told himself. 'No one would expect such a thing to happen but I'll show 'em – aye, and that Alison. She'll have to notice me then, when I'm Head Sentry and I won't have to feel awkward and useless in front of her no more.'

His meandering steps brought him to the northern edge of the field, where the elms reared up, giant and deeply black against the starry sky.

He was about to turn back when his large ears caught the sound of strange voices, singing in the distance.

The fieldmouse cocked his head and listened. It was not like any song he knew.

Curious, he tiptoed closer to the ditch and looked out across the sea of darkness that the midnight meadow had become.

Down there, not too far away, three small, yellow-green lights were moving through the wild grasses.

At first he thought they were glow-worms but that didn't make any sense. They didn't fly and they certainly didn't sing, unless they only did those things when they thought no one was watching and listening.

Baffled, he crept down the bank and stealthily crossed the stepping-stones. As silent as a burglar, he entered the meadow and approached the mysterious lights.

Gradually he drew closer, but even though the voices were much clearer, he still could not understand what they were singing. It was some odd language he had never heard before.

The eerie, wavering lights floated through the tall grasses. They were larger than he had at first thought and cast a ghastly, almost deathly glow about them. Suddenly Young Whortle had a terrible thought – what if they were ghosts?

He stifled a yelp, and froze.

Why hadn't he realised that before? Old Todmore was always telling stories of phantoms that prowled through the night, hunting for the unwary. The one about the blood-sucking Nachtag, the Midnight Death Hag, was particularly horrible and had always given Young Whortle nightmares. She was supposed to haunt the barren ploughed fields only in the winter, but remembering that fact didn't make him feel any better.

He swallowed nervously and wondered whether it would be safer to creep quietly back to the cornfield, or make a panicky dash for it.

Before he could decide, one of the orbs of light came flying through the grass in front and its spectral radiance fell full upon him.

'Cartho Magga!' called a voice in surprise. 'Wotty pundle mindi?'

'Get off!' Young Whortle cried, flapping his arms before him and stumbling backwards. 'You can't drink my blood nor crunch my bones. Get away – I tells you! I got me a brass and that means the Green Mouse protects me – so stick that up where the stars don't twinkle!'

Then, not looking where he was going, he tripped

and fell, and the apparition bore down on him.

Young Whortle squeaked in terror and the bleak light flooded his tearful eyes.

The unearthly glare pressed close, circling over him. Then the unknown voice spoke again but this time it was laughing, deep and heartily and not at all what he imagined a supernatural horror would sound like.

'Yoon rimpi-too,' it called. 'Pidd–diddenhol rimpi-too.'

Other voices called in answer and Young Whortle sat up, his curiosity conquering his fear. The weird light lifted away and relief and embarrassment washed over him when he realised that it was just an unusual, globe-shaped lantern made of dimpled, emerald-coloured glass. It was attached by a silver chain to a tall staff and he leaned forward to try and see who wielded it.

A large, wide shape lumbered into view. It was three times as tall as the fieldmouse and wrapped in a hooded cloak.

'What you doing scaring honest folk out of their skins in the middle of the night?' Young Whortle demanded.

Although he had never seen one before, he suspected that this creature was more than likely a rat and he had always been told that you had to be very stern with them.

'Where you from and where does you think you're going? This be our meadow so don't get no ideas about moving in,' he warned.

The stranger stooped to peer at him and within the deep shadow of its hood, a pair of sharp eyes glittered.

'Chilpi ranna,' it called, glancing back to where the other two lanterns were still bobbing in the darkness. 'Willibald, Firgild – ranna ranna.'

The lights came sailing forward and two other bulky, cloaked shapes loomed behind them.

'You'd best be on your way as well,' Young Whortle said crossly. 'Fennywolde ain't big enough for your kind, we don't want no rat folks round here.'

At this the large creatures burst into laughter.

They spoke quickly amongst themselves. Then the first cleared his throat and said, 'We are not rats, little rimpi-too, or at least not the sort you mean.'

'Well you ain't tadpoles neither,' the fieldmouse retorted. 'So, what are you then? Going about all swaddled up like you was spies or footpads, 'tain't the way nice folks behave.'

The strangers planted their staffs on the ground and, as the lanterns swung above their heads, they swept their hoods back and Young Whortle finally got a good look at them.

They had blunt faces with small features. Their eyes were bright but tiny and their ears were almost hidden in coarse, shaggy fur which would have made their mouths invisible if they had not been twitching with amusement.

A thin band of silver that glowed beneath the lantern light glinted on their brows. These newcomers were unlike anything Young Whortle had ever seen or heard of before.

They looked as he imagined kings might be in old legends and he realised that it was not his place to order the comings and goings of such lordly creatures. Whoever they were, they were far above the command or curiosity of a humble fieldmouse.

At once he felt ashamed of his rudeness and lowered his gaze, noticing as he did that each of them had a bag slung over one shoulder, stuffed with leaves and plants.

'Bit late for picking flowers,' he observed shyly.

'They are herbs,' one replied with a gentle smile. 'We have come forth to forage for those secret blooms which only moths ever visit and the sun never sees.'

'Why for?'

The three creatures grinned indulgently and whispered to one another before answering.

'First tell us why such a small rimpi-too . . .'

'I think, Brother,' one of the others interrupted, 'in his tongue, the word is *mouse*.'

'Ah, yes – I had forgotten, although if there was ever a more perfect example of a rimpi-too then surely it is the one before us now.'

'A plucky and sprightly fellow, to be sure.'

'So, little mouse, why are you abroad this night? Should you not be curled up and dreaming? Although, it is nigh on an age since we had dealings with the dwellers of Fenlynfeld, perhaps this is their habit now?'

Young Whortle looked at each of them.

'No, there's just me,' he said. 'Everyone else is tucked up, 'ceptin' the lads on night duty.'

'So what lured you out here with neither lamp nor candle?'

'I was doing some thinking and I does that best when walking. Then I heard you and saw your lights so I came to see what was happening and find out what you was. I still don't know. For a second I thought you was ghosties and phantoms.'

The strangers shook with laughter and their lanterns trembled, making the night shadows dance around them.

'But how brave and intrepid!' one of them exclaimed. 'To come seek out such frightful apparitions on your own!'

'Surely the valour of Fenlyn Purfote still runs true in your land. That is a glad discovery.'

'Cap'n Fenny?' the fieldmouse chimed in. 'Oh I knows all the tales of him and his band of warriors what came and settled here. Heard them tales a hundred times or more, I have – an' I believe 'em too. Todkin says they're just old twaddly stories but I spent my whole life a-listening and wishin' and . . .'

Young Whortle faltered and looked back at the ground.

'And?'

'Oh nothin'. It's daft.'

'Tell us.'

'I just wish I'd been born back then. To see them battles and fight against the badd'uns what filled the woods where they come from. Must've been summat real excitin', that must. There's no adventures no more, no magic – nowt thrillin' to look forward to. I just want summat special to happen to me, just the once.'

The first of the strangers smiled at him. 'What is your name, little rimpi-too?' he asked.

'Whortle Nep,' he replied. 'Though it's Young Whortle to most.'

'A thrice blessing upon you, Young Whortle. Know now that we are not rats.'

'Or phantoms.'

'At least not yet.'

'Not quite yet.'

'We are the Millagaroo.'

'Or, water voles in your speech.'

They bowed low and touched their brows in a gesture of greeting.

'I am Woppenfrake, Minister to the Glinty Water,' said the first.

'And I am Firgild – Guardian of Forgotten Secrets,' said another.

'Which leaves I, Willibald of the Gilded Dawn,' said the third.

Young Whortle touched his forelock in return. 'Evenin',' he answered. 'Them's rum names, an' no mistake.'

'We find the names of your kind equally peculiar,' Firgild told him.

The other two water voles nodded in agreement.

'But we must return to the Grelffit Houm,' he continued. 'We have gathered enough for our needs.'

'What's a Grelffit Houm?' Young Whortle asked.

Firgild tapped his forehead as he searched for the correct word in the speech of the fieldmice; then consulted his companions.

'I think it is – *burrow hall*,' Woppenfrake suggested doubtfully. 'But that is a very rudimentary name for so hallowed and ancient a site as the Grelffit Houm, wherein lies the sacred chamber of Fenlendis.'

'You got a burrow?' cried Young Whortle. 'We have tunnels in the winter. I likes it underground. Are your diggings far? I never heard of no water voles dwelling close by.'

The three strangers glanced at one another and their eyes brimmed with amusement.

'Walk with us, Young Whortle Nep, and we shall show you.'

'Oh I'd like to,' the fieldmouse replied, with a regretful shake of the head. 'But I got to get meself up real early in the mornin' so I can't do no more tramping about tonight.'

Suppressing their chuckles, the water voles promised they would not keep him away from his nest for too much longer.

'You are the first mouse we have met since the paths of our peoples were divided,' Firgild said. 'It would honour us greatly if you would stay by us for the shortest while. There is much we would learn from you and perhaps you also shall learn something.'

Young Whortle got to his feet and brushed the dust from his tail. 'A body would be downright bad-mannered to refuse,' he said brightly. 'I'll step by you for a way then – lead on.'

The water voles lifted their lantern staffs and began walking northward through the meadow, with the small fieldmouse at their side.

'Tell us,' Willibald began. 'That tale your friend disbelieves, how does it run in your land?'

'The one about Captain Fenny?'

'The very same.'

Young Whortle took a considering breath and clasped his paws behind his back. He wasn't very good at relating stories but he tried to recall how Old Todmore told them.

'Was a fearful long time ago,' he began. 'When evil fiends filled the untamed forests with darkness and horror. Branches of trees dripped wi' blood and no goodly folk were safe, for the heathen worshippers of the terrible rat god, Hobb, were great in number and if you didn't join 'em – you was killed and served up to their infernal master, with your skin pulled off.'

He paused to see how that had gone down.

The three water voles were gazing up at the stars. Were they even listening to him?

He wasn't sure whether to continue. Then, to his astonishment Woppenfrake began to sing:

> *Tread not into the fearsome night*
> *But pull the covers high,*
> *Step not into the wild dark wood*
> *For the Hobbers are dancing nigh.*

Willibald and Firgild halted and lowered their lanterns. Both of them shivered and the shadow of a fear passed over their faces.

'Never did I think to hear that voiced aloud again,' Firgild muttered.

'And I would have preferred not to hear it now,' Willibald added, casting a questioning look at Woppenfrake.

Woppenfrake leaned on his staff, the spectral green light gleaming in his eyes.

'We have prayed these many long years for those words never to be repeated in this world,' he said starkly. 'And yet we three know what is stirring, the flames we saw crackle when we were young shall burn again.'

Young Whortle looked at the ground, feeling a little uncomfortable. Something was passing between the three of them that he did not understand. The mirth had died in their faces and they had grown grim and pensive.

And then the moment passed and they shook themselves.

'Forgive us, Master Nep,' Woppenfrake declared, the humour returning to his voice. 'Pray resume your tale. What do you know of the bold Captain Fenny?'

He swung his lantern around and they began walking once more.

'Well . . .' the fieldmouse said, sorry that he had ever started the story in the first place. 'Before we come here, a whole bunch of woodlanders, all manner of types – not just us mice, but moles an' shrews and weasels, hedgepigs an' a lot besides, took refuge in a big hill in a forest far away. They was safe there from Hobb's filthy crew, till one day a princess of the black squirrels comes, chased by the enemy and Cap'n Fenny marches with her to a green country where a huge battle takes place, 'tween the forces of the Green Mouse and the devils of Hobb. That war was awful and gruesome but in the end, Fenny won through – wrestling Hobb hisself back into the endless Pit. Then the Cap'n takes the woodlanders off in search of somewhere peaceful, someplace quiet with no need for knives and swords. 'Twas here they came and this is where they stopped. The other folks went their own ways but us mice, we stuck with our field and that's where we be to this very day.'

The water voles smiled and nodded.

'Indeed,' Firgild murmured. ''Twas here they came and here they stopped. A most blessed corner of the world, where roots dig deep and terrors were laid to rest.'

'Or so it seemed,' Woppenfrake added.

Willibald pondered the tale and gave a toothy grin. 'A trifle garbled and inaccurate in places,' he told the fieldmouse. 'But yet a most enlightening tale, nevertheless.'

They had walked as far as the trees that surrounded the still pool, the large pond that was fed by the ditch and Young Whortle decided that was where he should say goodbye.

'I can't carry on,' he told them. 'I got to jog round the meadow at first light and the yawns have caught me.'

'Will you not see the Grelffit Houm?' Willibald asked.

'No further fer me this night,' the fieldmouse answered firmly. 'Remember, I'll have to traipse back through them there fields on my own.'

'But we are not travelling way over there,' Woppenfrake said. 'Our destination is already reached – the entrance to the Grelffit Houm lies in these trees.'

'By our pool?' Young Whortle cried in surprise. 'No!' And again the water voles laughed.

'Your pool?' Firgild chortled. 'The Glinty Water belongs to no one, not even its in-dwelling spirit would make such a claim. What strange fancies you have.'

'But we ain't never come across you afore. How long you been hidin' out there?'

'Hiding?' Woppenfrake said. 'Keeping ourselves to ourselves perhaps, but not hiding. We have done nothing to be ashamed of. If only everyone could claim the same. If you are certain you will not accompany us to the Grelffit Houm then we must bid you farewell and leave you now.'

Young Whortle twitched his mouth to the side. 'S'pose I could come and have a quick peep at it,' he said. 'Then I'd have to go straight home.'

The water voles smiled.

'Then follow,' they told him.

Holding their lamps before them, they pressed into the undergrowth which lay beneath the trees that grew around the pond.

Nettles and foxgloves towered high on every side but the water voles brushed them aside with their staffs and walked beneath the dangling, mournful branches of a great willow tree. Reeds replaced nettles as the path dipped down to the water's edge and, keeping the pond on their right, they pushed on a little further till they reached a slope of smooth boulders embedded deep in the ground.

Young Whortle recognised the place. It was where he and his friends had slid down and played around many times, so he wondered why the three cloaked strangers had halted in front of it now.

Woppenfrake reached out with his staff and gave one of the large stones a firm tap.

'Rindimmion!' he called. 'Ranna – affel wundy.'

To Young Whortle's amazement, there came a faint rasping sound of rock against rock and the boulder sank backwards, into the slope. A corridor of candle-light spilled out towards him, and a tunnel leading down into the ground was revealed.

'Smack me longways!' he exclaimed. 'A secret road into the earth. Well I never did! I wish Old Todmore were here to see it. He reckons he knows everything about Fennywolde but he don't know about this.'

'I should not think there is any in your field who is aware of this place,' Firgild said. 'It has long been forgotten.'

'Welcome to the Grelffit Houm,' Willibald announced, 'where we have dwelled since the great

Captain Fenlyn Purfote marched his battle-weary company from the great war against the cult of Hobb.'

'Will you venture within and see our chambers, young Master Nep?'

The fieldmouse clapped his paws together. 'You try stoppin' me!' he declared.

And so the water voles led him into the stone passageway and the boulder rolled shut behind them.

4
Inside the Grelffit Houm

Woppenfrake and his brothers blew out the flames in their lanterns and leaned the staffs against the walls. Then, down the steep way they guided Young Whortle.

The fieldmouse gazed about him in wonder.

Candles were blazing cheerfully and the walls were covered in bright paintings. Images of animals, trees and birds crowded every space; even the ceiling was covered with clouds and moons, bats and stars. Admiring the artistry and patience that had gone into the work, he reached out with his little fingers and traced the wiggling progress of a river that flowed alongside him.

There was nothing like this in the winter tunnels of the fieldmice. Isaac Nettle would never allow anything so wantonly colourful and frivolous.

'It ain't like bein' underground at all,' Young Whortle said. 'You'd never get the glooms down here with this lively blaze of pictures swirlin' round you. Them's so clever, must've took ever such a long time.'

Firgild beamed at him. 'Indeed it did,' he admitted. 'And it was only completed last year, although there is one more panel I have yet to paint.'

59

'Which bits did you do?' Young Whortle asked.

Willibald spoke up. 'This is wholly my brother's work, no other helped him. Neither I nor Woppenfrake can draw so much as a stick badger but he has always been the artist of the family.'

The fieldmouse stared around him. They had descended quite some way and the murals showed no sign of ending. It was almost impossible to believe that a single paw could have achieved so much in one lifetime.

Before he could exclaim in surprise, the tunnel curved round and the floor became level. Then, abruptly, the narrow way led to an arched opening. The three water voles passed through it and Young Whortle pattered after them, only to stagger to a standstill in shock and disbelief.

He found himself in a cavernous chamber, lit by countless tongues of flame leaping from glazed jars. It was the greatest spectacle he had ever seen and his mouth fell open as he gazed upon it.

Being a simple country mouse who had not travelled anywhere, he had never dreamed that such a magnificent place could exist. It was immense and made him feel even smaller than usual. Great pillars of stone, with the shapes of running beasts carved around them, supported the lofty ceiling and here too, every surface was covered in vibrant paintings. Faded banners and pennants were strung about the top of the stout columns and the warm air of the flames wafted them gently, causing a constant movement high overhead.

'You are the first, if you'll pardon the term, *outsider*, to visit our humble abode for many long years,' Willibald said.

The fieldmouse rubbed his eyes and gawped about him. It was some time before he could find his voice again.

The water voles regarded him with amusement.

'I hope your silence signals that you like our homely dwelling,' Woppenfrake ventured.

'Nowhere near as cosy as one of your delightful, round nests,' Firgild said. 'But it is what we're accustomed to.'

Young Whortle began to nod his head slowly and before long was wagging it briskly and gurgling with delight.

''Tis the most,' he spluttered, 'the best – the – oh my, mightiest, most magic thing I ever did see!'

The water voles looked away modestly. Then they busied themselves in removing their cloaks and hanging them on pegs jutting from the nearest pillar. The bags of herbs they placed on a circular table around the column.

'And now some refreshment for our honoured guest,' Woppenfrake announced. 'Let us give him a draught of our best vintage and answer some of the questions that no doubt are raging within him.'

With a polite wave of their paws they ushered Young

Whortle to the centre of the huge chamber, where a welcoming fire crackled in a hearth chiselled into the rocky floor.

Wooden stools, topped with over-stuffed cushions surrounded it and the water voles bade their guest to sit while they poured a clear, amber-coloured liquid from a large jug into four bowls.

Young Whortle clambered on to a seat. It was a bit high for him but once he was settled and comfortable, he lifted his eyes and they danced around the chamber, soaking up every detail.

The images were so intricately drawn and intertwined and there were so many of them that, sitting some distance away, unless you studied them, they became a blur of abstract shapes and colour.

Young Whortle focused on a particular section and stared at it. To his astonishment, what he saw there was not at all pretty. Among the pastoral scenes of trees and flowers, there were great battles and, shifting his gaze around he discovered that terrible conflicts between squirrels and bats swarmed over the entire wall. The bats wore frightening masks and gauntlets spiked with long knives and the squirrels bore shields and swords and cruel-looking spears. Pictures of death and murder were plentiful and the rivers of scarlet blood contrasted strongly with the green of the painted grass.

'That's a lot of red,' he whispered to himself.

He was so engrossed that when Willibald offered him the drink, he had to do it twice.

'Oh, sorry,' Young Whortle cried, whisking his attention back to the fireside and taking the bowl in his paws.

'I were just noticin' the fightin' up there and over there, and across there. Poor bodies with no heads and some with no arms and bats with swords in 'em or wings hacked off.'

'The war between the squirrels and bats was very savage,' Willibald said sorrowfully. 'And neither side knew that the pagan gods of the rats were the real enemy, not till it was nearly too late.'

'You got any pictures of wolves?' the fieldmouse asked suddenly.

Firgild blinked at him in amused surprise.

'No, there are no wolves on these walls. Although there were many in the forest of old who followed the Raith Sidhe. It took many squirrel arrows to fell those terrible beasts. Why do you ask?'

'Me an' my pals got wolf pictures in our den,' Young Whortle answered proudly.

He lifted the bowl to his nose.

'What be this? Smells like honey an' berries.'

'A refreshing beverage,' Willibald answered. 'A trifle more pleasing than the blackberry ferment your folk used to drink.'

'Oh we still does that,' Young Whortle replied with a chuckle. 'But only when Mister Nettle ain't lookin'!'

He took a sip of the liquid and it was so delicious

that, before he could stop himself, he had drained the bowl completely.

'That were like summer rain and happy tears and the excitement of Mousebrass Day – all made swiggable!' he cried, smacking his lips.

Willibald poured him another bowlful but begged him to drink it more slowly.

The fieldmouse did his best but it made him feel so contented that it took a great deal of effort not to knock it back in one guzzling go.

To stop himself from appearing greedy, he put the bowl on his knee and regarded the huge chamber once more.

'So who did the paintings in here, then?' he asked. 'Must've taken crowds of folk ages and them twiddly bits at the top can't have been easy to tackle.'

His three hosts were smiling at him.

'Crowds of folk?' they said.

'Yes,' Young Whortle told them. 'The rest of your kind. Them what were here before you, and the others what live here.'

'We are the only water voles here,' Woppenfrake said. 'There are just we three.'

'What about your mum and dad?'

'They . . . departed a long time ago.'

'Well, aunties, uncles – annoying cousins what borrow things and don't give 'em back?'

The water voles shook their heads.

'But the pictures!' Young Whortle persisted.

'Someone must've done them.'

Woppenfrake waved a paw around the walls.

'Can you not see the same brush-strokes here as in the passage?' he asked. 'This also is the fruit of Firgild's labour.'

The fieldmouse scowled at him. 'You're pullin' my tail,' he said. 'There ain't no way any single body could do all this, not in a whole lifetime.'

'Not in a normal lifetime, no,' Willibald said softly.

'Little rimpi-too,' Woppenfrake began in a gentle voice. 'Do you not yet understand? We three have been here since the beginning.'

'The beginning of what?' the fieldmouse asked in confusion.

'Since the day *He* brought us from the horror and terror of war,' Firgild answered.

Young Whortle shifted uncomfortably. 'I doesn't know what you be on about,' he said, 'but don't try and make a twit of me – we already got one of them in our field and we don't need a second.'

The brothers looked blankly at one another.

'It is difficult for him to understand,' Firgild said.

'Perhaps he could be shown?' Woppenfrake suggested.

'But how much?' asked Willibald. 'Not all?'

Woppenfrake tutted and shook his forefinger. 'Oh no, not all. No one must know all, that would never do and we would fail in our trust if we did such a thing. No, a little, show him a little.'

'Yes, a little,' Firgild said brightly. 'As Guardian of Forgotten Secrets, I believe we can show him a little. Come, Master Nep! Let us reward your faith in those so-called myths that your friend Todkin pours so much scorn upon.'

Rising, they led the fieldmouse further into the chamber, to where a tapestry was draped across an alcove in the wall.

'My brother is the illuminator of our world,' Woppenfrake said, indicating the skilful stitch-work. 'How drab and ashen it would be without him. How would we have managed throughout these long years?'

Firgild bowed at the compliment then drew the tapestry aside, revealing a doorway. 'And how draughty it would have been,' he added.

Leaving the chamber of the Grelffit Houm behind, they entered a short passageway, the end of which was covered by another tapestry.

The water voles halted before it.

'Tell us,' Willibald began. 'When your Captain Fenny came to this land with his warriors, what happened then?'

Young Whortle frowned. 'I already told you that,' he said. 'Us mice settled and lived in our field.'

His hosts shook their heads. 'Not straight away,' Firgild corrected him. 'The creatures who made that journey spent their first night down here – in the caves that were waiting for them.'

The fieldmouse's frown became a scowl. 'I never

heard Old Todmore tell of that,' he said.

'No doubt he is unaware of the fact,' Woppenfrake replied. 'Memories fade and fail and time buries the truth beneath the falling years. Come – be the first of your kind to look on the true history of their ancestors and know that those dusty fireside stories actually happened.'

He pulled the tapestry aside and Young Whortle stepped into the room beyond.

It was large and long but, in here, there were no murals or tapestries,

Mounted on the walls and arranged row upon row on wide benches and tiered trestles were weapons – hundreds and hundreds of ancient weapons.

Stunned, Young Whortle moved forward hesitantly. It was proving to be a night of surprises.

With round, incredulous eyes, he stared at the endless display of swords and knives that formed fan-shaped patterns on the wall, between thickets of longbows, halberds and pikestaffs. More weapons lay on the trestles: maces and axes were placed in front of myriad shields and at every ten paces there were great jars filled with feathered arrows. Countless helmets, fashioned for various animals, lined the floor. Some had pointed visors to protect long snouts, others curved cheek protectors and most had ear guards of jointed metal plates.

'What . . . what be this place?' he asked in a tiny voice.

The water voles had remained by the doorway but now they followed him in.

'It is the armoury,' Firgild told him. 'The weapon hoard of Fenny's warriors. This is where they laid them and here they have remained.'

Young Whortle drew a great breath and blinked at the bright reflections that bounced off the polished blades surrounding him.

'But they gleam and glint like they was new from the forge. Like they was only put here yesterday.'

Willibald cleared his throat. 'Firgild has spent the years painting every inch of the Grelffit Houm,' he said. 'And my task was to preserve this hoard. Every day I burnish armour and shield and make certain the swords are kept sharper than a kestrel's glance.'

Unable to contain himself any longer, Young Whortle let out a gleeful yell and capered around in a circle.

'I knew it were true!' he crowed. 'I knew it – I knew it!'

The water voles laughed to see him so delighted.

When his initial exuberance had subsided, the fieldmouse ran along the length of the armoury, not knowing what to look at first.

'Can I touch them?' he called. 'Can I pick 'em up?'

'They will not break, if that is what you fear,' Woppenfrake answered. 'But have a care, their bites are deep.'

'And is Cap'n Fenny's famous sword here?'

He clasped his paws together and recited the rhyme he had heard so often, sitting before Old Todmore the storyteller:

'And in the rout naught shone brighter
than the mighty blade of great Ratbiter.'

Willibald beamed indulgently. 'No,' he said. 'That sword is not here, but there are many others to see.'

Young Whortle tried to pick up a magnificent blade but his paws were too small to close about the hilt and he was nowhere near strong enough to lift it. With a grunt of disappointment, he chose a dagger instead and jabbed the air with it before dashing away to put a small helm on his head and swap the dagger for a mouse-sized spear.

'If I'd been in them battles,' he shouted, sounding fierce, 'I'd have impaled plenty of them dirty Hobbers.'

Blissfully happy, he jumped to and fro, thrusting the spear into imaginary enemies.

After a while he stopped, and his shoulders sagged.

'But all that were way back in history,' he murmured forlornly. 'I won't never see anything as excitin', there's just sentry duty for the likes o' me now.'

The water voles watched him return the spear and helm to their rightful places and a mischievous grin lit up Firgild's face.

'Reckon I'd best get goin' then,' Young Whortle said. 'I got this early start, see.'

'So you keep telling us,' Firgild said, smiling. 'But, before you depart . . .'

He crossed to one of the trestles and took up a brightly-polished brass horn, saying, 'Master Nep, this is the very instrument that sounded the clarion call of the woodlanders on their arrival at the great battle – when the need of the squirrels and bats was greatest. The last time it rang out was upon the blessed sunrise that saw Captain Fenny come to this land. It has remained silent ever since. See if you have enough breath in you to summon its voice once more.'

He passed the horn to the fieldmouse whose knees buckled when he took it in his paws. It was a heavy, cumbersome object which must have been used by a creature much larger than himself.

'Dunno if I'll be able,' he said. 'But I'll give it a go.'

Taking a deep breath, he put it to his lips and blew.

Nothing happened, not even a faint noise like a sparrow's sneeze.

'Try again,' Firgild prompted.

Young Whortle took an even deeper breath and applied himself.

This time a feeble *PARP* stuttered from the horn.

'No good!' he wheezed in defeat. ''Twere made for bigger lungs than mine.'

'One final attempt,' Firgild encouraged.

'There ain't much point,' Young Whortle said. 'But if you're so set on it . . .'

Gripping the instrument tightly, he inflated his

chest as far as it would
go and, with his eyes
clamped shut, he blasted
down the mouthpiece.

A blaring note thundered
around the armoury, the
swords resonated in answer
and the arrows rattled in the jars.

Firgild glanced over to his brothers and they nodded
for him to proceed.

Silently, he crept behind the fieldmouse and drew a
sign of power in the air above his head. The silver band
on the water vole's brow flashed with light and the air
shimmered.

It was done.

Young Whortle kept the sonorous note trumpeting
for as long as he could, then he drew back, feeling
light-headed and cold, but very pleased with himself.

A strong breeze was blowing through his fur. With a
shiver, he opened his eyes.

The armoury had disappeared. He was no longer
underground, but standing on a grassy hill. The stars
were blazing overhead and the night was filled with a
harsh, raucous din. A reek of burning choked the air
and glowing embers were whirling on the wind.

Bewildered, he stared around him. Armour-clad
figures pressed close on either side while behind,
marching up the hill to join them, were hordes more.
Every sort of woodland animal he could think of was

there. He saw the bitter glint of sword blades in their paws and each face was set sombre and deadly. After them came a host of squirrels bearing fluttering banners and singing a song of war.

Young Whortle hardly dared blink or breathe. 'Must be ten thousand or more,' he whispered.

Dragging his eyes from that glorious sight, he turned away and looked down the hill to the wooded stretch of land that lay between them, and a wide, winding river.

A fierce battle had been raging down there. The Children of the Raith Sidhe, the forces of Hobb, were fighting the beleaguered squirrels of Greenreach. They were hideous, hate-filled creatures: wild beasts who revelled in carnage, who licked their knives and swords after each kill. But the battle was not confined to the ground. Overhead, evil rooks and gore crows were circling and swooping, attacking and slaughtering the bats who flew against them. Hot blood streaked the air like rain, followed by the bodies of murdered bats that came crashing to the earth. It was a grisly, horrifying spectacle.

'Pull out me whiskers!' the fieldmouse gasped. 'I'm dreamin'!'

At that moment a sizzling cinder floated down and landed on his shoulder. He yelped when it singed him but knew then that this was not some fanciful imagining.

'It's real,' he murmured. 'I'm really here – slap-bang in the time of the big war!'

Any further exclamations of wonder were silenced when a figure came striding from the side and paraded in front of the woodland army, holding a sword high above his head.

It was a dark brown mouse, but the largest mouse that Young Whortle had ever seen. He was even taller than Mr Nettle. A silver helm, embellished with three woodpecker feathers was on his head and a leather jerkin protected his chest. On his left arm he carried a round wooden shield, displaying the device of a running hare leaping over the moon.

'Hearken to me!' his voice boomed out to his warriors. 'From peril we have come and into worse danger we now charge. Some of us will not return but if your hearts are quailing, I say to you – ignore them, what we do this night will echo down the ages. To rid the world of the Children of the Raith Sidhe – that is our duty. We must drive this festering evil, the Black Brotherhood of Hobbers, from the land and rid the dark of their terror. We must not fail in this and we shall not, for the Green Mouse will guide and watch over us!'

A tremendous shout thundered in answer.

'Fenny!' the army yelled. 'Fenny! Fenny! Fenny!'

Young Whortle's astonished cry was lost amid the roar. He was looking straight at the fabled hero of the fieldmice, the one who had given his name to their land, the hero of their oldest legends – Captain Fenlyn Purfote.

And, to the small fieldmouse's amazement, Captain
Fenny was staring straight back at him.

'How old are you lad?' he asked suddenly.

Young Whortle could only cough and splutter in
reply.

'Only just got your mousebrass, I'll warrant, from the looks of you,' Captain Fenny said. 'If that is your brass. Seem too short in years to be in the midst of this madness, but then that's what war is, a storm that sweeps all before it and tears up the tenderest shoots. What's your name?'

'Whortle Nep,' Young Whortle answered at last. 'An' this 'ere brass is mine own, right enough.'

A grim smile flashed across Captain Fenny's stern face. 'Then pick up your weapons, Soldier Nep,' he told him. 'Any moment now, the Hobbers down there are going to seethe up this hill like mad wasps and they won't take pity on a tiddly fellow such as you. If you don't kill them when they rampage at you, they'll stick your head on a pike and set a flame blazing in your skull to make a Hobb Lantern.'

Young Whortle shuddered.

At the foot of the hill the Hobbers were screaming in fury and many of them were already charging up the slope. Young Whortle's heart pounded fiercely in his breast when he saw their eyes shining red and cruel, and then beheld their ravening, yellow-fanged jaws.

He swallowed nervously. The fur on the back of his neck began to bristle and the palms of his paws grew clammy.

Captain Fenny glared down at the marauding creatures. 'This is it,' he muttered. 'Are you ready to fight, lad?'

Young Whortle looked up at him and his fear

drained away. Excitement and exhilaration took its place. He was standing on the edge of the most famous battle in history, next to the greatest mouse. How could he be afraid, he who had ached for adventure the whole of his life?

He cast his eyes down to his feet and saw there the spear he had been playing with in the armoury, as well as a shield just like the one Fenny bore.

Seizing them, he stuck out his chin and declared, 'Aye Sir! That I am.'

Captain Fenny raised his sword, the legendary *Ratbiter* and saluted him. Young Whortle felt as though he would explode with pride.

'Then unto victory we go,' Fenny cried to his army. 'Forward! In the name of the Blessed Green! Let's spill some Hobber blood!'

The woodlanders gave one final shout and rushed down the hill to meet the oncoming enemy. Young Whortle ran with them, yelling for all he was worth and grasping his spear tightly.

5

Doubts and Progress

'Neppy!' a voice called. 'Hey, Neppy!' Young Whortle was jolted awake. He stared around, confused and bewildered.

'Hobbers!' he gasped. 'You won't make a lantern out o' my bonce – you 'orrible filth!'

A shadow reared before him and the fieldmouse lunged at it, swinging his little fists with startling ferocity.

'Hey!' the voice protested. 'What's up with you?'

Young Whortle fell back. He landed in the soft moss of his bed and blinked away the last dregs of sleep. He was in his own snug little nest, back in Fennywolde and there was Hodge leaning in at the entrance, rubbing the side of his face ruefully.

'What did you hit me for? Who did you think I was?'

Young Whortle shook his head.

'Where did the battle go?' he cried. 'I were in the thick of it.'

His friend scowled at him.

'You and your daft dreams,' Hodge said crossly. 'I've been sat in our den ages, waitin' for you to turn up. An early start, we agreed on. I could've stopped in my own warm nest if I'd have known you was goin' to be so lazy.'

Young Whortle stared at him and his forehead crinkled as he tried to recall how he had returned home. Try as he might, he could not remember.

'It weren't no dream though,' he told himself. 'I know it weren't.'

Hodge pulled a wry face. 'Haul thy idle backside out of there,' he told him in his Isaac Nettle voice. 'Thou hast a jog to do.'

Befuddled and still very tired, Young Whortle clambered from the nest and the two fieldmice climbed down the corn stems it was built around.

The sun was not yet very high, so the Hall of Corn was still steeped in soft silver shadows. No one else was astir. The only sound was the morning birdsong, so they crept through the field exchanging whispered words.

'Todkin, Figgy and Sammy are down by the ditch,' Hodge told him. 'They're making a start on your raft. Do you want to go an' see his drawings for it before our run?'

Young Whortle was only half listening to him. In the cold light of day, the events of the night seemed utterly absurd and he was very angry with himself. How could he have imagined everything in such detail? Did the three water voles even exist, or had he dreamed them up as well?

'Mebbe there are two twits in this field after all,' he mumbled to himself, only to look up and find that Hodge was asking him a question.

'What have you done to your shoulder? Your fur's singed – looks like you burnt yourself.'

And with that, Young Whortle gave a whoop of delight. It was true – every bit of it.

Immediately, he set off northward, dashing happily through the cornfield.

'What you doing?' Hodge called after him. 'We're s'posed to run round the meadow, not here!'

But his friend did not answer and raced along, laughing and whooping.

'What's up with him today?' Hodge asked himself. 'Well, he can't out-run me, that's for sure.'

Chasing after him, he tore swiftly through the field – to see Young Whortle heading out towards the trees that surrounded the still pool.

'Why's he going in there?' he muttered.

Not pausing to look back and see if Hodge was even following him, Young Whortle dived between the nettles and foxgloves, then dodged around the huge reeds until, at last, he stood before the ridge of boulders that bulged from the grass.

Breathless, he strode over to the one he knew was the secret entrance to the water voles' magnificent burrow and hammered on it with his paws.

'Woppenfrake!' he cried. 'Firgild – Willibald! It's me, Whortle Nep! Let me in!'

He was still shouting when Hodge came bounding up.

'What are you doin'?' he asked. 'And why did you bolt off like that?'

Young Whortle spun around. 'This is where they

live!' he chattered excitedly. 'The water voles I met last night, they're behind this 'ere big stone. Oh, you should see it down there – puts our Hall to shame, it does.'

Hodge folded his arms and scowled. 'Have you turned loony overnight?' he asked dryly. 'I dunno what you're playin' at but you're not going to wriggle out of our jog that easy. There's no water voles live round here – everyone knows that. There's only us mice come here, 'specially Alison Sedge, so she can gawp at herself in the pond.'

Cupping his face in his paws, Hodge began to coo and sigh in the breathy way that Alison had recently adopted.

'Ooh, I be too purty for my own good, ain't no mousey wench to rival me, always shooin' off bees I is, cos I be sweeter'n honey. Ooh you naughty bees, keep off, I don't want my pollens pinched!'

'I'm not makin' this up,' Young Whortle said emphatically. 'Behind this rocky lump is a tunnel. Honest – I swears it.'

He resumed thumping the boulder and calling for the water voles while Hodge looked on, tutting sceptically.

Finally Young Whortle gave up and rested his bottom on the boulder instead.

'They do live down there,' he insisted. 'And they're magic too, proper magic! I'm not pretending. They know things, more'n we do, more than Mister

Woodruffe even. They magicked me PLOP into the past and must've magicked me back again – oh you should've seen it! It were the best tail-tingler ever, a real goggler, it were!'

Hodge forced himself to sound interested.

'Really?' he said breezily. 'Well maybe your new friends only show their whiskers above ground at night. So there'll be no more plopping any place for you till then, and no point hangin' around here neither. Let's get your training started. Todkin will tell Figgy to set his sister on us if we waste any more time and we don't want that.'

Young Whortle kicked at the soil with his heels. 'All right,' he agreed. 'I'll come back here later.'

Leaving the still pool behind them, they walked to the meadow where Hodge made his friend do some stretches before they began.

'Now, three times round,' he said. 'This ain't no race, just a warm-up so don't try going too fast. You wouldn't beat me anyhow.'

Young Whortle nodded but his mind was still full of the previous night's adventure and everything else seemed dull and colourless in comparison. Yet, when Hodge told him to run he obeyed and together they jogged through the wild grasses.

Around the meadow they went, but before they had completed three-quarters of the way, Young Whortle had to stop and catch his breath.

'You can't be tired already!' Hodge exclaimed.

'T . . . tired?' his friend puffed back at him. 'I'm jiggered. Can't we have a bite of breakfast before we trot any further?'

Hodge scratched an ear. 'You shouldn't run on a full stomach,' he said.

'Well, I definitely can't do anythin' on an empty one!' Young Whortle retorted.

'Oh all right, but let's go and see what Todkin and the others are doin' first. Though if you've got your breath back, let's at least run to the ditch.'

On the lower bank, Figgy Bottom and Skinny Samuel were dragging some large twigs along the ground for Todkin's inspection. The fieldmouse examined them closely, then shook his head.

'Too knobbly and irregular,' he decided. 'What's needed are some without all them wiggles so they can be tied together and make a good bit of deck. No sense having great big gaps between them. He'd only stick his feet down the holes and get disqualified.'

'But this is the best we could find,' Figgy grumbled. 'All the best stuff has already been snaffled. I reckon there's a few of the lads makin' new rafts this year. I saw a gang of them go up to the south hedge afore. Young Whortle ain't the only one wantin' to win these Games.'

Todkin narrowed his eyes. 'Then we'll have to cut some of our own. Sammy, go and ask your dad for a lend of his tools and we'll do this thing proper.'

By the time Hodge and Young Whortle found them, the three friends were hard at work. Figgy and Samuel were balanced on a branch in one of the elm trees. Each held one end of a long saw and was taking it in turns to push and pull the blade through the wood. Todkin stood below, calling instructions and giving advice as he danced in and out of the sawdust that drizzled down from above.

'What's this?' Young Whortle asked. 'You'll have Mister Nettle yellin' at you if he catches you cutting down good branches.'

'Can't be helped,' Todkin said, with a superior sniff. 'My design requires only the best materials.'

He took out his note-pad and showed Young Whortle several fanciful drawings of rafts that he had sketched out. Some were a trifle ambitious, with carved figureheads and three sails with rigging, while one even had a cannon that fired oak apples. His final

design, however, was quite simple. It was shaped rather like a smoothing iron, with a rail at the stern, a single mast rising from the centre and a square sail bearing a mouse's face wearing an eye patch.

'I call her the *Ditch Pirate*!' Todkin announced proudly.

'Hoy!' Samuel called down to him. 'It's Warty's raft – he should get to name it.'

'How's about the *Diseased Rat*?' suggested Figgy.

'The *Lusty Buccaneer*!' put in Todkin.

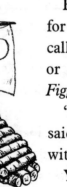

Hodge laughed. 'That's too fancy for a little raft!' he jeered. 'Why not call it after one of us – the *Jolly Hodger* or *Sammy's Sloop* – or what about *Figgy's Riggy*?'

'If you're going to be silly,' Todkin said huffily, 'there's no point going on with it.'

Young Whortle looked at the drawing again. The craft certainly looked as though it would skim through the water faster than Sammy could guzzle a pie and the dream of being Head Sentry burned inside him once more.

He tried to think of something appropriate, something magical and swift and at once he recalled the device carved on both Captain Fenny's shield and his own.

'Call it the *Silver Hare*,' he said softly.

The others smiled at him.

'*Silver Hare* it is!' they cheered.

Samuel and Figgy resumed sawing the branch while Todkin scribbled the title above his picture.

'So how did the jog go?' Todkin asked.

Hodge fell to the ground, clutching his stomach and gasping. 'I can't jog no more!' he groaned, sounding disturbingly like Young Whortle. 'I needs me breakfast and I only got little legs an' they're gettin' littler with every step!'

Young Whortle gave him a shove.

'I'm hungry, that's all,' he said defensively.

To his surprise Todkin prodded him in the tummy.

'You could do with losing that podge you're getting,' he said. 'You need to cut down this week if you're going to be of any use in the Games. I'll work out a healthy diet for you, starting now. Half a bowl of porridge for breakfast, but don't you go putting any honey on it.'

Young Whortle's face fell. 'I'll starve!' he protested.

'No you won't, that's plenty to keep you going till lunchtime, when you can have some healthy raw vegetables.'

Young Whortle was about to object even more strongly, but Todkin waved him away and told Hodge to go with him, to make sure he didn't cheat and over-indulge.

'Then you can get back to the meadow and continue the jog,' Todkin called after them. 'And when you've done that, I want to show you the exercises you've got to do three times a day.'

Young Whortle stomped off, groaning loudly.

Hodge joined him, chuckling, and made up a nonsense song on the spot.

> *'I'm a turnip weevil, an' weevilin's what I do.*
> *Gimme a luvverly turnip and I'll dig*
> *right in and chew.'*

The others laughed. Then Todkin cried out and had to leap aside as the half-sawn branch splintered, snapped and came crashing down.

'Oops!' Samuel shouted.

The three of them spent the rest of the morning chopping and sawing the felled branch into lengths. Then they carried them to the den where the difficult business of lashing them together commenced. It was hard work, especially for Figgy and Samuel, as Todkin preferred to order them about, instead of actually doing anything. The only muscles he strained were those in his face as he pulled critical expressions when he felt the others weren't doing it properly.

Once he had eaten a very unfilling breakfast, Young Whortle did his best to run around the meadow but kept stopping to catch his breath, much to Hodge's irritation.

'You won't stand a chance in the Games if you do that the whole time,' he told him. 'Even my gran could beat you and she's got a limp!'

Young Whortle struggled on but it was plain to Hodge that he would never be any good in the Meadow Race.

When lunchtime came, Young Whortle discovered just how determined Todkin was for his hideous diet plan to succeed. He had had a word with Mrs Nep and as a result she refused to give her son anything other than some diced carrot and one broad bean.

Young Whortle was appalled but there was no persuading her. Taking his meagre and unappetising food to the den, he was even more disgruntled to learn that Todkin expected him to perform the exercises he had devised before eating anything.

First there were tail stretches and twirls to make it stronger, just to ensure success in his best event. Then he had to hop on one leg to the count of a hundred before changing to the other leg. This was immediately followed by curling into a ball and rolling around a slalom course, made up of seats from the den. Quite what this was for, Young Whortle had no idea and Todkin couldn't furnish a very good reason for it, but said it was bound to do him good.

After that, there were star jumps and sit-ups, followed by a long head-stand.

By the time Young Whortle sat down to his meagre lunch, he felt a bit queasy and was almost too tired to eat.

Nibbling a slice of carrot, he tried to ignore Samuel, who was stuffing his face with great quantities of barley bread sandwiches filled with cheese and pickles. These were chased down with three beechnut cakes dripping with cream and honey.

'Wish I had a pot belly like yours,' Samuel told him between mouthfuls. 'Having to eat all this is a downright nuisance.'

'I'm sure,' Young Whortle replied stonily.

Figgy and Hodge bit their lips and had to look away.

When he was gnawing his broad bean, Young Whortle said, 'I met three water voles last night.'

Todkin looked up from his note-pad. 'Where?' he asked.

'Here in the meadow, but they live by the still pool.'

Hodge clicked his tongue and let out a sigh. 'He dreamed it,' he explained to the others.

'He must have,' declared Todkin. 'There's no water voles hereabouts.'

'They live in a big painted burrow called the Grelffit Houm!' Young Whortle insisted.

The others thought it best to take no notice of him.

'What we need for the raft is a great big sail,' Todkin said.

'I could ask my mum to sew us one,' Figgy suggested.

Hodge assumed a sly and secretive voice. 'Leave this

to me.' He cackled with a melodramatic twirl of his whiskers. 'I know where we can get one – mwahahahaha.'

Young Whortle finished his broad bean in silence. But suddenly he could not contain himself any longer and blurted out, 'They did magic and I met Captain Fenny!'

His friends stared at him for a moment. Young Whortle had always been full of stories and daydreams, but he had never made up such a ludicrous whopper before. They didn't know what to say.

'Let's get back to it,' Samuel suggested briskly and the awkward moment was broken.

The raft-builders returned to their work, while Hodge tried to get Young Whortle to run around the meadow again.

But the little fieldmouse was hurt and resentful that none of them believed him.

'I can't run any more,' he flatly declared. 'Don't make me. My feet feel like they're glued to the floor and my legs are aching and my back is starting to creak like Grommel's and besides – I'm not in the mood.'

Hodge had to admit defeat but the training was far from over that day. If Young Whortle didn't want to go running, there were plenty of other things he had to practise.

'You showed us yesterday how bad your vaulting is,' Todkin said. 'So Sammy can take you off to train you. Hodge can join me an' Figgy with the raft. Soon as this is done you've got to master this as well. There won't be no rest for you this week.'

'Come on, Warty!' Samuel said, feeling guilty for doubting his best friend but confused as to why he should be so passionate about such a blatant fib. 'I'll make you the best vaulter our field has ever seen. When we're done, you'll be somersaulting through clouds and soaring higher than larks.'

Hammering a nail, Figgy watched them depart.

'Neppy'll wear holes in his tongue if he keeps them tall stories coming,' he said. 'Fancy expectin' us to believe such a shocker! At least when I tell a bouncer I try and make it plausible.'

'He'll be having tea with the Green Mouse Himself next,' Hodge agreed. 'He's been real fired up about that barmy rubbish ever since he woke up.'

Todkin looked troubled.

'It's the worry of these Games,' he concluded. 'He's so desperate to prove himself, it's startin' to affect him.'

Figgy stopped his hammering. 'What do you reckon he'll do if he don't win?' he asked.

Todkin shrugged unhappily.

'I dunno, but it won't be good. Poor Young Whortle's pinning everything on being Head Sentry.'

'Then it's up to us to make sure he don't lose,' Hodge said, and Figgy resumed his hammering.

The afternoon saw the raft really take shape. One more morning's work would see it finished enough to try it on the water.

When it was time to return to the cornfield, they hid it behind their den, covering it with leaves.

'Just in case of saboteurs!' Hodge advised in a melodramatic voice.

'The other lads will be so jealous of her,' Figgy said.

'No one would be so mean as to wreck her on purpose though, would they?' Todkin asked.

'She *is* a beauty,' Figgy observed.

Todkin hastily threw some extra leaves over it and they made their way through the meadow, feeling very pleased with their labours.

Samuel, however, had not had the same degree of success with his pupil.

Young Whortle could not get the hang of pole-vaulting.

They had gone back to the oaks where no one could watch him practising. The last thing he wanted was for Alison Sedge to tease and mock his clumsy attempts.

Samuel was very patient with him. He did his best to coax and encourage. He would demonstrate and perform perfect vaults, then explain in detail how he had achieved them.

Young Whortle tried, but time and again the pole would hurtle from his paws and he would end up flat on his face. He had scraped his knees and grazed his paws and every muscle ached as never before.

'Some wolf killer,' he moaned despondently.

Fortunately Samuel was a better teacher than Hodge and never lost his temper, finding something constructive or hopeful to say about every failure, so Young Whortle never gave up.

Finally, when the sun began to dip in a reddening sky, he decided to make one final effort before going home.

'This is it Sammy,' he announced, gripping the pole with determination. 'This is the one.'

Taking long strides, he charged forward.

'That's right, Warty!' Sammy shouted. 'Now push it down!'

Young Whortle shoved the pole into the ground. It bowed then flipped upward. The fieldmouse clung on and was instantly wrenched into the air.

'Fantastic!' Samuel cheered.

A moment later, Young Whortle was lying in the ivy. He had not travelled very far at all but it was his first successful attempt and he felt as though he had performed a dazzling feat of athletic brilliance.

'I did it, Sammy!' he yelled in elation. 'I did it!'

Samuel hauled his friend to his feet and hugged him.

'That you did, Warty,' he cried. 'That you did, and you're gonna get even better at it.'

'Won't the others be amazed!'

'That they will!' Samuel laughed. 'That they will.'

6

The Dark Truth

In the Hall of Corn, the many mouse families were enjoying the evening sunshine. A rosy tint flooded the great space and everyone decided to eat outdoors.

Clean tablecloths were spread on the ground and delicious food placed upon them. The fieldmice were all chatting happily and tucking in by the time Young Whortle and Samuel arrived.

Todkin, Figgy and Hodge had claimed a cloth of their own from Hodge's mother and were munching a hearty supper of mushroom and onion pies, cheese and oatcakes and pear tart.

Young Whortle's eyes lit up when he saw the food. He had never been this hungry.

The other Wolf Killers were overjoyed to hear of his successful pole-vault, but when Todkin saw him reach out to take a fat wedge of pie, he brushed his paw away.

'No you don't,' he scolded. 'There's some dried apple and more broad beans here for you. Don't forget you have to do your exercises before you eat anything.'

Young Whortle uttered a wretched whimper.

'I'll be glad when these Games are over,' he said.

'Don't be so ungrateful,' Figgy chided, licking sticky crumbs of tart from his fingers. 'It's for your own good.'

'And don't get this cloth grubby,' Hodge warned. 'My mum don't know it yet, but she's just given us the sail for your raft – mwahahahaha!'

They talked excitedly about the *Silver Hare* and how they would test her tomorrow.

When Young Whortle finally got to eat his dreary supper, he did so with a grin on his face. He knew he was the luckiest mouse in Fennywolde to have such friends. He realised now how crazy his adventure with the water voles must have sounded to them, yet here they were doing everything they could to help him achieve his goal.

When the dusk deepened, lanterns were brought out and flickered into life. Somewhere in the Hall, a merry voice was raised in song and others joined in. Some of the children began a dance, while the rest gathered around an elderly, white-whiskered mouse smoking a pipe.

It was Old Todmore, the Fennywolde storyteller. He was the keeper of their history. Everything important that had every happened in that land was stored in his memory. Legends and lore had been handed down through his family, from mouth to ear through many generations. The stories were learned by heart and repeated without any elaboration, or fancy embroidery, as he put it.

Not only the very young sought him out. Every mouse in Fennywolde relished a cracking good yarn and before that night's sentry duty began, Young

Whortle left the others to visit Old Todmore's corner.

An audience of over a dozen mice had already assembled there, yet before Young Whortle could join them, a cheeky voice called out behind him.

'There goes Todmore's best ears, haven't you heard all them tales fifty times each, Neppy?'

Young Whortle turned to see three girls making faces at him.

It was the annoying trio led by Figgy's sister, Dimsel Bottom.

Dimsel, Iris Crowfoot and Lily Clover found just about everything hilariously funny and were vastly aggravating. They were as irksome as a flea-bite and always shrieked with laughter whenever they heard what the Wolf Killers were up to.

They didn't bother to call their gang anything, but now and again Dimsel would wind up her brother by telling him they had decided to be known by some mocking name, such as the Foxy Terrors, or the Killer Hunters, and would threaten to come and find his den and pull it down.

They never did, but the Wolf Killers were still wary of her and her two collaborators. In fact most of the boys in Fennywolde had reason to respect Dimsel Bottom – she was a dab paw at the Ratty Wrist-burn and had elevated arm-twisting and dead-legging to fiendishly expert levels.

'Evenin',' Young Whortle answered, wondering what schemes they were brewing.

Dimsel whispered something to her friends and they snickered, then she said, 'I heard our Figgy say you're going to try and win them Games.'

'What if I am?'

'What's a diddy thing like you want to be Head Sentry fer?'

'You wouldn't understand,' he replied. 'You're a daft girl.'

Dimsel and the others folded their arms and in a chorus trilled, 'Oooooooooh!'

Then she smirked and, with a waggle of her head, said, 'Well listen to this, Wet Nappy – us girls are going to enter the Games this year and we're going to win it.'

Young Whortle never knew when she was being serious.

'No you ain't,' he told her.

'You just watch us! You lads think you're so special with your jumping and climbing and all that rubbish. Ha – are you in for a shock. Wipe the floor with you, we will.'

Delighted to see his face fall, she spun around and sauntered away. Iris and Lily stuck their tongues out at him, and then followed her.

Young Whortle scowled and thought of several clever and caustic remarks he should have made, but it was too late now.

'Them girls is like a bad itch what never goes away and won't be scratched,' he muttered to himself.

'Alison Sedge is worse,' added a voice close by.

The fieldmouse glanced around and saw Jenkin Nettle leaning against a cornstalk.

Young Whortle brightened when he saw him but the creases returned to his forehead at once.

'What you done to your lip?' he asked.

Jenkin covered his mouth with his paw. His bottom lip was swollen and bruised.

'Was trying to match your tail hang of yesterday,' he explained. 'Only I didn't quite manage it – fell off and busted me lip open.'

'Nasty, is that.'

'Looks worse than it is.'

Young Whortle shrugged. Jenkin was even clumsier than he was. He was renowned for being accident-prone and was often nursing a cut or a black eye. He had broken more bones than anyone else in the field and it was a rare thing for him to be seen without a scab or a sling or several ripe bruises.

'So do you think they meant it?' Jenkin asked, blithely changing the subject.

'What, Dimsel and her cronies competing in the Games? I hopes not – but I wouldn't put it past 'em.'

Jenkin grimaced. 'It'd be real embarrassing to lose to any of them,' he said.

'Summat else to worry about,' Young Whortle groaned.

Jenkin licked his sore lip. 'I'd better put some extra practice in then,' he said. 'Right, I'm going to go do some long jumps before I turn in. See you tomorrow.'

With a wave of his paw he sprinted from the Hall, leaving Young Whortle alone.

'Flippin' Dimsel,' he grumbled. 'As if the Games aren't going to be difficult enough already.'

With a sigh he continued on his way to Old Todmore's corner and joined the audience.

They were still deciding what they wanted to hear.

With his paws clasped over the handle of his gnarled walking stick, Old Todmore puffed on his pipe and blew a stream of blue smoke over their heads.

'What'll it be tonight?' he asked.

'Tell us about the bad winter,' one of the youngsters

pleaded. 'When snow filled the ditch and the mice back then built ice castles in it – with frozen dunjuns!'

'No,' exclaimed another. 'I wants to know about the time when it were real foggy and snotty Missus Pindle got lost and climbed into the wrong nest and woke up in the morning next to a big fat toad!'

'And when she got over the fright,' someone else chipped in, 'she said its feet weren't nearly so cold as Mister Pindle's!'

Old Todmore sucked on the pipe, delighted to be the focus of their attention. Listening to the requests, he was considering what he should tell when he noticed Young Whortle Nep standing at the back of the eager crowd.

'Why, 'ere's me best listener,' he called out. 'And what would 'ee like this time, Master Nep? You must know all my yarns better'n me by now.'

Young Whortle grinned. He had sat at the feet of Old Todmore more evenings than he could count.

'Oh we all know what he wants to hear,' one of the little ones chirped. 'Everyone knows what his favourites are.'

The audience laughed and Old Todmore took the pipe from his mouth and chuckled with them.

'True enough,' he said. 'One about Captain Fenny, I'll bet.'

The smile faded from Young Whortle's face. A question had been smouldering inside him all day and suddenly it burst from his lips without warning.

'What happened to him?' he asked abruptly.

Old Todmore scratched his bristly white whiskers. 'Eh?' he asked. 'What do you mean?'

'Cap'n Fenny!' Young Whortle repeated, 'What happened to him? When he led the woodlanders here, your stories about him don't go no further.'

'That's cos his great deeds were done and we've had peace ever since.'

'So he just settled down and died of old age, then?'

A strange gleam flashed in the storyteller's eyes.

'What else?' he blustered evasively. 'What's bitten you this night, Young Whortle Nep? Don't you want to hear how he smote the Hobbers with *Ratbiter*, his famous sword? You never get weary of that one. You doesn't want to hear no list of his doings when he built his first nest.'

Everyone turned to look at Young Whortle. No one had ever asked that question before, they had not even thought about it.

'I might do at that,' he replied. 'When did he build his first nest? Were it the very same day they came marching here? Or were it the next? If so, where did they shelter? Not out in the open, surely?'

'Why, in the tunnels o' course,' Old Todmore answered.

'Our winter quarters?'

Some of the youngsters tittered. 'What other tunnels are there?' they said.

'But they can't have been dug in a day.'

The children shuffled restlessly. 'Hush,' they told him. 'Get away with you. We wants to hear funny stories.'

Young Whortle thought he caught a knowing glint in Old Todmore's eyes. Were there some tales the storyteller kept secret? Did he know about the water voles and the Greffit Houm? If he did, he certainly wasn't prepared to tell them.

'Missus Pindle and the Toad,' the old mouse began.

Young Whortle shook his head in disappointment and walked away. Through the misty veil of his pipe smoke, Old Todmore's eyes were glittering at him.

Sentry duty passed by uneventfully.

Sitting in the tops of the barley, the Wolf Killers called to one another as the world grew dim and dark about them.

Figgy was vexed that his sister had decided to compete. He knew her sole purpose was the pleasure of causing as much trouble and discomfort to as many of the lads as possible. Neither she nor Lily or Iris had any interest in being Head Sentry.

'If she weren't my sister,' he rumbled, 'I'd . . . well I'd be even ruder to her than I already am!'

'She's no serious threat to Warty's chances,' Samuel put in.

'I reckon she'll give up after the Meadow Race anyway,' Todkin added hopefully.

'No I won't!' Dimsel's voice cried out. 'I'm gonna kick your tails then give each of you a ruddy good thumping!'

The Wolf Killers gripped their corn stems tightly but the momentary fright was instantly dispelled when they realised it was only Hodge doing one of his impressions.

'Don't do that,' Todkin begged him. 'It's too like her.'

'I bet you just scared me out of any flab I might've

put on today,' Samuel whimpered.

'I wish your Dimsel was as clumsy as Jenkin,' Young Whortle said to Figgy. 'Then she might sprain her ankle or summat and that'd be the end of it.'

'That'd still leave us with Lily and Iris though,' Todkin mused.

Hodge snorted. 'Oh stop being so gloomy,' he cried. 'They're only girls. Can you imagine them doing the Ditch Vault or raftin'? As for the Barley Swing or the Tail Hang – they're useless! You might as well be scared of losing to Twit, as worrying about them!'

The night deepened and the waxing moon climbed among the stars. Staring up at it, Young Whortle guessed it would be at its fullest in a week's time – during the Games.

When their shift was over, the five friends clambered down, stretched and quickly ran over their plans for the morning as they strolled back home.

'Another dawn run for you,' Todkin told Young Whortle.

'And no stopping for breathers this time,' Hodge cut in.

Todkin continued. 'Figgy, Sammy an' me will get the *Silver Hare* ready for the water and you can spend the rest of the day on her.'

When they reached the Hall of Corn, they said goodnight and climbed into their nests. Every one of them was ready for sleep.

Presently, Young Whortle came scooting down again.

There would be no sleep for him that night, until he had found the water voles again.

Moving silently though the field, he headed towards the ditch to reach the still pool.

There was not a breath of a breeze – Fennywolde was slumbering soundly.

Young Whortle stepped briskly. He was looking forward to seeing Woppenfrake, Firgild and Willibald. There were so many things he wanted to ask them and he wondered if they would do any more magic.

Hastening his short strides, he passed into the long black shadow of the solitary yew tree and without thinking, began to whistle a jaunty tune.

'Who's there?' a stern voice thundered suddenly.

The fieldmouse halted. The tune died on his lips and he took a step backwards.

'Who's that askin' "who's there?"' he answered, peering into the impenetrable dark beneath the tree.

'You, is it!' snapped the voice. 'I mighta knowed. An' where be you a-goin' so late?'

Young Whortle relaxed. He recognised that voice, he ought to – he had heard it often enough.

'Mister Todmore!' he declared. 'What you doin' out of your nest?'

A glimmer of burning tobacco sizzled in the darkness. Old Todmore drew on his pipe, then came shuffling forward. Young Whortle heard his stick tapping the ground as he approached, but when the old mouse emerged from the shadows he hardly recognised him.

The contented, familiar face that he had so often stared up into during the telling of his favourite stories was drained and haggard, and fear flickered in his eyes.

'Mister Todmore!' Young Whortle cried. 'What's happened? You don't look well. You had a funny turn?'

He took the storyteller's paw. It was trembling.

'Let's you an' me go back to the Hall,' he said. 'We'll have you snug and safe in no time.'

The old mouse pulled his arm away and pounded his stick on the ground. 'Sit,' he demanded. 'I needs to sit.'

'Oh, all right. Here, there's a tussock. Sink yourself on there till you feels better.'

Old Todmore eased himself down, then signalled for the young mouse to do the same.

He took the pipe from his lips and inhaled a deep, calming breath.

Young Whortle said nothing, waiting for the storyteller to recover from whatever was the matter.

When Old Todmore's breaths grew easier, he regarded his best listener suspiciously.

'You and your questions,' he said gruffly. 'What did you have to ask me that fer, earlier this evenin'?'

'What?'

'About Fenny, and what he did after.'

Young Whortle hunched his shoulders. 'Was curious, is all,' he replied.

'I wonder,' Old Todmore muttered. 'There's summat changed about you, lad. You're not the Young Whortle you was yesterday.'

'I just got to thinking. There's a whole lot we don't know, a whole lot more about Fenny what's never told.'

The storyteller drummed his fingers on his walking stick.

'Could be good reason fer that,' he said darkly. 'Some things is best left unsaid. Not every tale can be repeated.'

'So you do know,' Young Whortle said softly.

Old Todmore nodded.

'Aye,' he whispered. 'I know. 'Tis a black story and one I tries not to think on often. But my dad, Green keep him, he made me larn it – just as he made me larn the rest. It's a thing none of us Todmores never told no other, but history is history and must be kept – no matter how dark it be.'

'Will you tell me?'

The storyteller returned the pipe to his mouth.

'That's better,' he said, taking several puffs. 'The shudders is passin'. I doesn't come to this part o' the field if I can help it. But sometimes I has to, to remember the tale in full and look on where it happened. But always it gets me churned up and curdles me innards.'

Young Whortle stared at him.

'Where what happened?' he asked.

Old Todmore rested his chin on his paws and leaned forward.

'There ain't no tales of Cap'n Fenny's life here in Fennywolde,' he began slowly. 'Cos . . . he didn't have one.'

'I don't understand. What do you mean? Didn't he stay here then? Did he move on to somewhere else?'

The storyteller glanced across at the enormous yew tree and shivered.

'Captain Fenlyn come from the war against the pagan rat gods,' he began, 'bringin' his warrior folk with him. They was tired and they was sick of the fight but he would not let them settle nowhere till they reached this blessed spot of country. This was where he were meant to journey, this was where he had to trudge, though he passed through many other lands and fields just as ready for settlin' as this.'

He paused and closed his eyes.

Young Whortle had never heard this version of the arrival at Fennywolde before.

'So why here?' he asked.

'Cos he were led. 'Tweren't his judgement what brought the last of the woodland army 'ere. By star and moon and sacred signs they was guided, cos . . . cos they had a ratwitch with 'em.'

Young Whortle rocked backwards.

'A ratwitch?' he cried. 'But how . . . and why? They'd

just fought a war against the ratwitches and priests of Hobb. They was destroyed.'

'Ah, but Fenny didn't know she were a witch. She didn't look like no ordinary Hobber. Wise and blessed by the Green, he thought her to be, but all the time she were still doin' the biddin' of her unholy master. Usin' her arts, she brought the woodlanders here – to the still pool yonder, sayin' as how it were a sacred site that the Green Mouse Hisself had chosen fer them to dwell by. There was even caves in the banks there, and so the warriors finally laid their war gear down and thought the evil had been left behind. But it hadn't.'

A horrible chill crept over Young Whortle. Those caves were the Grelffit Houm.

'That first night,' Old Todmore continued, 'the witch showed her true nature. While the woodlanders slept sound under earth and stone, she did her witch's dance to call up the power of the evil rat gods an' take vengeance on their great enemy. So, by song and spell, she called Fenny to her.'

He broke off to glare at the narrow track that led to the trees screening the still pool.

'Down that very path he came. Like a sleepwalker, our brave Cap'n left them caves and she capered before him, weavin' her filthy magicks. There was nowt he could do to stop her, such was the strength of the Dark Ones who worked through her. Brightly shone her eyes, fierce and flaming as she sang that binding charm, keepin' him asleep, asleep but walking and in her thrall.'

Old Todmore ground his teeth together.

'Where was the Green Mouse then?' he growled. 'Why didn't He do owt to save him – him what had fought so long in His cause? To that there yew, she leads him and into his strong but sleeping paws she puts a rope.'

'A rope?' Young Whortle breathed. 'But . . . no.'

'Aye lad.' Old Todmore lifted his stick and pointed to the tree. 'See that branch there? Well, the great hero of the war, the mighty Fenlyn Purfote – our Cap'n Fenny, that's where he ended. No well-deserved, peaceful life in these quiet lands fer him, no blissful reward at the end of his valiant struggles. No, when the warriors woke next mornin', they found him swingin' from that accursed branch.'

Young Whortle hid his face and they sat together in sombre silence.

The small fieldmouse recalled the previous night, when he had seen the battle at Greenreach. The words Captain Fenny had said to him echoed once more in his mind and he saw again the blade of *Ratbiter* gleam and flash as the great hero saluted him.

An emptiness replaced the chill and he felt numb inside. Was that really how the wonderful saviour of the woodlanders had perished?

'And the ratwitch?' he murmured at last. 'What happened to her? Did they catch her?'

'Oh aye, still dancing she was, danced the whole night long under that yew an' her feet was blistered and shredded. Mad and ravin' she were – screechin' with it. The evil forces she'd summoned had burned her wits away.'

Young Whortle wiped his eyes. 'I'm glad,' he said with anger in his voice. 'She deserved worse!'

'She got worse,' the storyteller told him. 'An' that were the blackest deed ever seen in Fennywolde.'

'What?' Young Whortled yelled. 'Blacker than murderin' Cap'n Fenny? How could it be?'

Old Todmore stared at the ground. 'Just as you are now,' he said. 'An' a whole deal more, the grief and fury of the woodlanders, the friends of Fenny, was terrible. They grabbed that there ratwitch and built a great bonfire for her. Still laughing and shrieking, she were thrown into the flames.'

'Good riddance!' Young Whortle spat. 'Why is that a blacker deed? That's what you do with witches.'

'But blinded by their anger, the warriors did a hideous thing. Mebbe there was so much evil in her that she couldn't contain it and some leaked out and afflicted them. That's the only excuse I can find for what they did.'

'What . . . what did they do?'

Pain pinched the storyteller's face.

'They made the witch's children watch their mother burn,' he muttered.

Young Whortle leaped to his feet.

'The rat had children?' he cried.

Tears were brimming in Old Todmore's eyes.

'Aye,' he said, 'and they were innocents. They were no Hobbers. And so you see, there are some tales best left untold. Who would want to hear such a foul history? Your friends, your family, all the merry inhabitants of our cornfield, they do not need to know how our ancestors began their new lives here.'

'No,' Young Whortle agreed. 'And now I wish I had not heard it.'

He glanced at the yew tree, then looked away quickly.

'Well you have,' said the storyteller. 'So keep it buttoned away. Now give me your arm and help this creaking old mouse up.'

Young Whortle did so, then asked, 'What happened to the witch's children? Where did those young rats go?'

Old Todmore leaned heavily on his stick. 'Oh,' he began with a shake of his head. 'They kept away from the woodlanders as you could imagine.'

'There's no rats anywhere round here, so I s'pose they must've scarpered as soon as they could and gone far away.'

The storyteller scratched his whiskers with the stem of his pipe.

'When I said she were a ratwitch . . .' he said, 'that weren't strictly right. She weren't really no rat. Folk called her that, but she weren't and nor were her three young 'uns.'

Young Whortle stared at him. 'What was she then?' he asked. 'What were her children?'

'Water voles,' Old Todmore replied. 'But whatever happened to Woppenfrake, Firgild and Willibald, us Todmores never knew.'

7

Aboard the *Silver Hare*

Young Whortle stared at Old Todmore, aghast. For some time he was too shocked to say anything. Instead he helped the old mouse back to the cornfield and into his large nest that was close to the ground.

'Goodnight lad,' the storyteller said. 'Remember to keep that tale to yourself.'

Young Whortle nodded distractedly. Questions and accusations were firing in his brain and he was anxious to run to the still pool and demand answers.

It could not possibly be the same three water voles. They could not have lived for so many centuries. And yet, they had already proven to be in possession of magical powers. If they could transport him back to the time of the terrible war, then staving off death might be child's play for them.

He was determined to learn the truth but before he could rush back there, a soft lantern glow fell across him.

Whirling around, he saw his own father leaning out of his parents' nest, looking cross and impatient.

'What are you doing up?' Mr Nep hissed down at him. 'Don't you go pestering Old Todmore for stories at this forsaken time. Go to bed right now!'

Young Whortle opened his mouth to try and explain, but where would he start and how could he, without betraying Old Todmore's trust? So, without another word of protest, he climbed into his own nest.

He knew his father would stay awake a little while, listening for him, just in case he tried to sneak off. He also knew that his father's watch would not last long, so he would wait until he felt sure he had nodded off and then hurry to the still pool.

Sitting on his comfortable bed, Young Whortle gazed out of the round entrance to his nest and looked on the Hall of Corn, steeped in moonlight.

The peace that lay over Fennywolde now seemed too quiet, almost sinister, and anything could be hiding in the deep shadowy corners.

Young Whortle sank deeper into his bed. The strains and exertions of the day had taken their toll. His muscles were paining him and his head thumped with questions. He was sorely tired and he felt wretched and miserable. He would wait just a short while more. Soon he would go to the pool . . . soon.

He awoke with a start.

The pale morning was slanting in. Furious with himself for drifting off to sleep, the fieldmouse bolted from the nest and almost dropped the distance to the ground below.

Not pausing to see if anyone else was about, he

charged from the Hall and pelted through the cornfield.

Running beside the ditch, he couldn't bring himself to look up at the yew tree but sped past as quickly as possible and hurried into the trees beyond.

Soon he was standing before the boulder that formed the entrance to the Grelffit Houm, yelling and pounding his fists to be allowed in.

The great stone remained fixed in place and no water voles answered him.

Young Whortle buried his face in his paws and wept.

'Tonight I'll make sure I'll be here,' he vowed. 'I'm going to ask them three what really happened.'

Wiping his eyes, he picked himself up and trudged away. His thoughts were so jumbled and confused that he walked without purpose. So it was with a shock that he eventually realised he had wandered into the meadow and was now very close to the den.

Needing to be alone, he did not want to meet anybody, not even his friends. He was just about to turn around when a voice hailed him.

'Good!' called Hodge. 'You got here early today! Now, you ready for those exercises?'

Young Whortle groaned inwardly but there was nothing he could do or say to excuse himself. Besides, his friends were putting everything into helping him and he did not want to let them down. So his third day of training began.

By the time Hodge had finished running him

around the meadow, Todkin, Samuel and Figgy had got the raft ready for testing and when he returned to the den, they showed it to him proudly.

The midday sunlight was shining straight into the clearing before their hut and the small craft was almost glowing.

It was a perfect re-creation of Todkin's drawing, with a single mast standing tall in the centre and a Young Whortle-sized paddle tied to the rail at the back.

Recovering from a stitch in his side, Young Whortle gazed at the raft and loved it deeply.

The *Silver Hare* looked wonderful and he let out a gasp of admiration.

The others smiled to see him so impressed. The joy on his little face was reward enough for their labours – even the countless splinters and banged fingers were forgotten.

'She's the most beautiful craft I ever saw,' Young Whortle cried. 'Thank 'ee all – thank 'ee! You worked so hard.'

His friends looked at one another shyly.

Todkin coughed.

'The sail's not attached yet,' he explained. 'I'm going to paint something on it.'

'Mercy knows what my mam'll have to say about that,' Hodge added. 'It's her second best tablecloth – but that don't matter. Just so long as you win that there race.'

'How can I fail now?'

'We reckon the whole raft would look best painted green,' Samuel said. 'But it's up to you – we could do it blue if you prefer?'

'Green be just fine.'

Figgy rubbed his paws together. 'Then we'll slap the colour on after your practice. Let's get her to the ditch and hope she floats!'

'Course she'll float,' Todkin snorted, indignant and affronted by the idea that his design could be flawed in any way. 'You'll see.'

It took four of them to carry the raft through the meadow to the bank of the ditch. Todkin took command and guided them along, cleverly avoiding having to do any lifting.

The other Wolf Killers did not mind. They were just excited at trying her out on the water.

When they reached the bank, they laid the raft carefully on the ground. Then everyone, including Todkin, began easing her in. It was a gentle slope into the water but he did not want them to make any mistakes at this crucial stage.

'Steady there,' he called. 'Go easy on the starboard side, Hodge!'

Paddling out into the shallows, they pulled the *Silver Hare* with them.

Figgy bit his lip nervously. Was she too heavy? Had Todkin figured it wrong? Would she merely sink to the bottom?

When the underside of the raft caught on a stone, he

thought the worst. She was stuck and they would never be able to budge her. There she would have to remain, like some shipwrecked vessel hurled ashore by the merciless sea. A rotting hulk for future generations of fieldmice to wonder at.

But even as those gloomy thoughts flooded Figgy's mind, Hodge gave the raft a hefty heave and she slipped free.

Out across the ditch the *Silver Hare* went sailing, floating serenely on the calm waters.

'Yes!' Todkin cheered, punching the air and jumping up and down, making a terrific splash.

The others joined him and yelled at the top of their voices. Figgy did a somersault and drenched everyone.

'Now,' Sammy said. 'Get yourself on board, Cap'n Whortle.'

Young Whortle looked up at him in surprise. The name made him think of that other Captain, who had met his doom there so long ago.

'Go on,' Hodge urged. 'We wants to see you master her today.'

Young Whortle shook himself. He could not think of that horrible story. It would have to wait till later.

Fixing his eyes on his very own raft, he lunged through the water and swam across to her.

'He's still doing that useless ratty paddle,' Figgy mumbled to the others.

Some moments later, Young Whortle clambered on board. Then he promptly slipped and fell off again.

A spout of water swashed across the deck. After floundering and thrashing his arms, he tried to struggle on board once more.

The raft pitched and yawed, making it more difficult than he had anticipated. It smacked the water, causing unexpected waves to roll clean over his head and fill his large ears.

Spluttering, he scrabbled at the rail to pull himself up but the *Silver Hare* tipped and threatened to capsize.

With the waves breaking about their knees, his friends watched in growing disbelief.

'What's he doing?' Todkin murmured.

'Why doesn't he just get on?' Figgy asked. 'This is ridiculous.'

Samuel sighed. 'He's doing his best,' he said.

'His best is useless and downright embarrassing,' Hodge put in. 'How's he going to stand any chance at all if he can't even get on the ruddy thing?'

Young Whortle's atrocious efforts continued until his friends could stand no more, and they swam out to fetch him back.

Figgy stayed with the raft and, with one deft movement, climbed aboard.

Untying the paddle, he swept it through the water and expertly brought the vessel back to the bank.

'She handles lovely!' he declared.

Young Whortle watched him miserably and felt thoroughly ashamed of himself.

'Maybe we expected too much at once,' Samuel

announced. 'Why don't we have a bite to eat before starting again?'

Everyone agreed that was a good idea, especially Young Whortle, who had forgone breakfast yet again.

And so they sat on the bank in the warm sunshine while Hodge and Figgy ran to fetch all their lunches.

Young Whortle's rations were the same dreary morsels of raw vegetable as the day before, but he ate them without complaint and presently began to feel much better.

Refreshed by the food and cheered by their own light-hearted chatter, they returned their attention to the *Silver Hare*.

'Why don't you practise getting on and off, here where we can hold her steady for you?' Todkin said helpfully. 'Only till you get used to it.'

There was no other way and poor Young Whortle spent a humiliating time learning the best way to board his raft. But at the end of it he could haul himself on to the deck without too much difficulty. Then the real problems began.

The only other occasion when he had been rafting had made him seasick. So when he was finally aboard the *Silver Hare* he sat down smartly and hoped the same thing was not going to happen now.

His friends were still holding on to the sides, keeping it stable and they looked up at him encouragingly.

'Now pick up the paddle,' Figgy instructed. 'And

you'll need to budge yourself along a bit – you're too far back.'

'Yes,' Todkin said. 'Let's see how well you control her.'

Young Whortle's friends let go of the raft and waded to one side.

'Take her into the middle of the ditch,' Hodge suggested. 'Then do some right spins, followed by some left ones.'

Without their steadying paws keeping the raft level, Young Whortle felt his stomach flutter and start to heave. The undulating motion was just as he remembered, and he hated it.

'Don't just sit there,' Figgy shouted.

Young Whortle dared not move. Any slight shift of his weight caused the raft to rock even more. He closed his eyes, but that only made things worse.

His innards seemed to be swinging from side to side and his tummy was one large pendulum that swung the opposite way. It was like the Tail Hang the other day when he . . .

'He's gone very pale,' Figgy observed.

'What's the matter with him?' Hodge said crossly.

'He doesn't look well,' Samuel said.

They splashed forward to help but at that very moment Young Whortle lurched sideways and threw up all over them.

Figgy, Samuel and Hodge uttered mournful groans.

'That's the second time this week,' Figgy wailed.

'A waste of the good Green's bounty!' Hodge moaned, in his Mr Nettle voice.

Samuel only whimpered. He had received most of it.

Young Whortle looked at them apologetically but all he said was, 'You'd best shift cos I'm gonna hurl again!'

His friends shrieked and turned to flee, but it was too late and their backs soon matched their fronts.

Having read the warning signs just in time, Todkin had saved his own fur and had hastily waddled away.

Now, sitting safely on the bank and tutting at them, he reflected that they were going to be there an awfully long time, and made several adjustments to his timetable.

When evening came, they had not achieved very much. Young Whortle still felt grievously ill when he was aboard the raft and once there, clung desperately to the mast or the rail.

Pulling the *Silver Hare* from the water and back across the meadow, the Wolf Killers had much to think of. The same thoughts were coursing through their minds – Young Whortle was never going to win the Games.

For his sake, his friends endeavoured to be as hopeful as ever, but they could not wholly conceal their concerns.

It was far too late now to begin painting the raft. Besides, it would take her all night to dry out, so they decided to leave that task for the morning.

They returned to the cornfield in thoughtful silence. What were they to do?

Dispirited and feeling like a failure, Young Whortle ate his frugal supper with his parents, hardly listening to the news of their day. When they asked him what was the matter, he mumbled that he wasn't feeling very well and gave the same excuse when they asked why he had not gone to listen to Old Todmore, who was surrounded by eager listeners as usual.

When it was time for his sentry duty, he climbed a stalk a little distance away from his friends, in order to be alone. He sat there staring up at the darkening sky.

Night clouds were moving slowly across the heavens. His father had said that he smelled rain on the wind and he wondered if that could possibly be true.

An unpleasant feeling ached in his stomach but this time it was not sea-sickness. He was dreading the confrontation with the water voles. They had seemed so kind and friendly, and yet their mother had committed such a terrible crime.

Sitting atop their own barley stems, Todkin and the others watched him and were worried.

They knew him well enough to understand when he needed to be on his own, but they hated to see him so unhappy.

Swinging his stalk closer to Todkin's, Samuel said in a whisper, 'What can we do for him? There's not many days left till the Games begin and his training hasn't got very far.'

Todkin narrowed his eyes and gave Samuel a mysterious, shrewd look. 'I think I have a plan,' he replied.

'What is it?'

Todkin wagged a finger at him. 'It's not fully worked out yet,' he said. 'Let's see how Young Whortle fares tomorrow. I don't want to say anything till then.'

'All right,' agreed Hodge. 'But I hope it's a good plan. I don't want to see him more miserable than he is already.'

Todkin smiled sadly. 'None of us want that,' he said.

When the shift was over, they returned to their nests and once again, after a brief wait, Young Whortle sneaked away towards the still pool.

This time his feet were heavy and when the yew tree reared into view against the dark clouds he could not bear to look at it. Hastening through its shadow he ran the rest of the way and was soon standing before the boulders once more.

'I knowed you're in there!' his thin, wavering voice called out. 'Woppenfrake, Firgild – Willibald. I needs to talk to you!'

He waited but there was no reply.

Picking up a pebble he hammered the stone with it and called their names again.

Nothing.

Exasperated, he threw himself against the boulder and pushed it with all his might.

'Let me in!' he bawled. 'I got told – I know what

126

happened. Don't you try hidin' from me!'

But the boulder was too large for a small fieldmouse to move and the only answer was the rustling of the reeds behind him.

Desolate and forlorn, he slumped down and sat with his back against the entrance to the Grelffit Houm. Never in his short life had he felt so unhappy and confused.

Gradually, he became aware of strange noises coming from the other side of the still pool.

Lifting his head, he waggled his large ears and listened.

Someone was swimming in the pool. Whoever it was, they were certainly skilled in the water, for there were no splashing sounds, only the unmistakable slap as ripples washed against the banks. At first Young Whortle thought it was just a large fish, but then he heard the pouring drips and splashes of something climbing out.

Picking himself up, he darted away. Racing around the pool, he leaped through the reeds and jumped over the hollows – running far faster than he had ever done for Hodge during training. It was a good thing he knew that place so well by day, otherwise he would have stumbled and injured himself in the darkness.

Finally, when he knew he was approaching the right spot, he slowed to a stealthy walk and tiptoed through the grass, creeping ever closer to whoever it was.

He could already hear someone speaking. It was too

low and muttered to be able to make out who it was or what was being said. Then, creeping a little nearer, he peered through the undergrowth and saw three large shapes shaking themselves and wiping the wet from their ears – it was the water voles.

Without thinking, Young Whortle sprang forward, bursting through the reeds.

'So there you are!' he yelled fiercely. 'I finally found you – and I wants me some answers.'

The water voles stood there – astonished and dripping.

'The little rimpi-too,' Woppenfrake exclaimed, pleased but bewildered. 'What does he shout about? Why does he look so quarrelsome and angry?'

His brothers could not imagine.

'Perhaps Master Nep thinks we should not swim in the pool?' Firgild suggested.

'He did think it belonged to his own kind,' Willibald said, remembering.

The fieldmouse stormed up to them and glared at each one accusingly.

'Just tell me this,' he spat. 'Why did your mam kill our Cap'n Fenny?'

8

Virianna

The water voles stared back at Young Whortle for a moment and the bright twinkles in their eyes dimmed.

'What have you heard?' Woppenfrake asked in a hoarse whisper.

'Plenty!' the fieldmouse raged. 'That there mother of yours were nowt but a dirty, filthy Hobber! A lying witch who made Cap'n Fenny hang hisself from the yew tree.'

The water voles drew sharp breaths and stepped back as though he had hit them.

'I dares you to deny it!' Young Whortle ranted.

The brothers looked at one another and memories they had long buried came back to torment them.

Instinctively and as one, they reached out to clasp each other's paws and bowed their heads in sorrow.

'Aye,' Young Whortle shouted. 'You may well look guilty and ashamed for what she did. I wish I'd never clapped eyes on you! Why did you stick around anyway? Why didn't you run off? Were you hoping to finish the rest of us mice one day? Taken your time about it, haven't you? Well, I wants you gone from Fennywolde by sun up – you don't deserve to live in a land that bears his name! I hates you, all three.'

His impassioned speech over, he stood there, breathing hard – wrapped in righteous fury.

'Well?' he demanded when none of the water voles answered him.

Woppenfrake squeezed the paws of his brothers. A tear was rolling down the nose of Firgild and Willibald had covered his eyes. Woppenfrake picked up the cloaks that lay on the bank and wrapped them around their shoulders.

Then, when he had comforted them, he turned and said to the fieldmouse, 'So that is what the descendants of Fenlyn Purfote remember. I mourn for the darkness that has taken root in his land. Now much is understood and I cast my lingering doubts aside.'

Young Whortle shook a small fist at him. 'What you prattlin' about?' he cried. 'Go on, try an' deny your mam were a murderin' witch!'

Woppenfrake fastened his own cloak at his throat and pulled the hood over his head.

'The most harmful lies and the most hurtful, always contain a grain of truth,' he said. 'But nevertheless, lies they do remain.'

'So, you are denyin' it?'

'Little rimpi-too, walk with us back to the Grelffit Houm. I shall tell you the whole truth of that time.'

'And why should I believe anything a Hobber's child has to say?'

'Because we were there!'

'And our mother was no Hobber!' Firgild said sternly.

'I'll walk back with 'ee that way,' Young Whortle answered. 'But I doesn't want to go down into your burrow again.'

'You were not invited,' Firgild replied.

Woppenfrake waved his brother into silence, then turned to Young Whortle as they set off around the pool.

'Virianna,' he said with an ache in his voice. 'That was our mother's name and I swear unto you, by the moon-sent angel himself, that she was not in league with the forces of the Raith Sidhe.'

'She were a witch,' the fieldmouse insisted.

'Is the Starwife a witch?' asked Firgil. 'Is any wise female a witch? Just because they have been blessed by the Green and given strange and beautiful gifts, does not mean they use them for evil purposes.'

Woppenfrake continued. 'In the time of the terrible war, our mother had served the old Starwife, the squirrel queen, but our father had been killed by the forces of Hrethel, leader of the bats. We were still only small children when the true enemies were revealed and the Hobbers came surging from the forest. We showed you how nightmarish those horrors were.'

Young Whortle nodded. 'They was frightenin' right enough,' he said.

'At the moment Captain Fenny and his army appeared,' Woppenfrake resumed, 'we three were about to be hacked to pieces by a hideous gang of Hobbers. His arrival saved our lives. Those fiends left us and charged instead at Fenny and his warriors. So you see, our mother was eternally grateful to him and, when the battle was over and all the weeping was done, she swore herself to his service.'

Young Whortle scowled. 'Then why did she kill him?'

'I shall come to that. First you must understand why they journeyed to this place. Did you know it was our mother who brought your captain and the others here?'

'I was told summat of the kind, aye.'

Woppenfrake halted and turned to the pool. It was shimmering beneath the stars and not a ripple marred its glassy surface.

'That is why they came here,' he said. 'That beautiful, darkling water.'

'Our pool?' Young Whortle exclaimed, to the chagrin of the three brothers. 'Why for? There's nowt special about that smelly old pond.'

The water voles gasped at his words.

'Can memories really be so short?' Woppenfrake murmured.

'It is the poison of the present,' Willibald said. 'Important truths are forgotten. If the denizens of Fenlynfeld are not aware of the import of this holy site, then they are lost indeed.'

Still staring dreamily ahead, Woppenfrake said in a hushed and reverent voice, 'Long, long ago, Master

Nep, when the world was young and the Green Power hale and mighty, the very soil tingled with enchantment. Each seed that fell to the ground flourished and grew, there was no death or decay and darkness was not a thing to be feared. Across this earth were many sacred places, hallowed to He who brought forth the first bud and reared the first sapling and those shrines were charged with the oldest magic of all.'

'I heard them tales.' Young Whortle interrupted. 'But what they got to do with anything?'

Woppenfrake continued gazing at the night-shrouded water.

'Those sites were countless and diverse,' he resumed. 'Caves, trees, stones, secret groves, the tops of hills, the silent hearts of forests, rivers, streams and of course – pools.'

The fieldmouse folded his arms impatiently.

'You trying to tell me that our dank pond be an ancient an' holy shrine?' he cried in disbelief. 'You're crab apple crackers!'

'It is one of the last retreats of the Almighty Green,' Firgild said firmly. 'So few remain out there in the damaged, tarnished world. They have been uprooted, sullied or destroyed and their power broken. Our Glinty Water is one of the rare few that have survived and we have guarded it these many ages.'

'Since the day the woodlanders threw our mother on to the fire and murdered her,' Willibald added.

Young Whortle stamped his foot and his tail whisked behind him.

'I told 'ee afore,' he snapped. 'I ain't a twit! If you can't speak no sense nor give me no proper answers, then I ain't wastin' no more of my time with you!'

He was about to leave when Woppenfrake caught hold of his arm and drew him back.

'Abide awhile longer,' he said. 'You wanted to hear what really happened that first night, when Fenlyn Purfote perished?'

'That I do!' the fieldmouse replied.

'Then your wish will be granted, but you are so overrun with anger that I doubt you will believe any denial from us.'

He opened his cloak and reached into one of the deep pockets inside.

'With your own eyes shall you see,' the water vole told him. 'Though afterwards you may regret what they have witnessed.'

Before Young Whortle could question him or object, Woppenfrake took out a small green stone and cast it into the centre of the pool.

It landed with a faint plop, which shattered the flat surface and ever widening circles radiated towards the banks.

Young Whortle stared at them. The ripples were glimmering with a pale green light that sparkled and glittered, growing brighter as they grew larger.

They raced to the bank and broke with a flash and a

crackle of flame. For an instant the surrounding trees blazed with emerald fire and Young Whortle's eyes whirled in their sockets.

'Clobber me!' he breathed, astounded. ''Tis glarey, bright as midday in June!'

Behind him the water voles pulled up their hoods and retreated. They had no desire to look on this again and they slunk into the shadows.

Suddenly the magical light dimmed and the pond was plunged into darkness once more.

Young Whortle rubbed his eyes. Green dots still swam before them. As soon as they had readjusted to the night he looked around for Woppenfrake and the others, but they were nowhere to be seen.

Then he noticed the trees. They seemed smaller and younger and the pool appeared wider and less overgrown. Overhead the stars burned more keenly than he had ever seen them and the very air smelled cleaner and pulsed with life and vigour.

'Summat fishy goin' on here,' he muttered.

'Fish?' a robust voice called out. 'I know not if there be any fish in there, my fine, pygmy soldier. An abundance of frogs and newts I deem, but of fish I have my doubts.'

The fieldmouse turned. A large, dumpy shape was waddling backwards around the pool, stooped almost double and intent on what it was doing. Dragging a stick through the soil with one paw, it was sprinkling a silver powder into the resulting furrow with another.

Startled, Young Whortle jumped back.

The stranger paused in the unusual task, then looked up and regarded him for a moment.

Young Whortle drew a sharp breath. It was a water vole, but this was not one of the three brothers, this was a female.

She smiled at him, then emptied her paw of the last pinch of powder and straightened her back, letting out a grateful grunt.

'Bless my bonny bones, that be better. After such a

long day and our wearisome journey, I really should take better care but who else is there to do this, I ask thee? And done it must surely be.'

Young Whortle mouthed a faltering answer.

'Why . . . what . . . who . . .?' he stuttered.

The water vole rubbed her aching back and smiled at him again.

She had a pleasant, podgy face. Lines of care crinkled the corners of her soft brown eyes but though they were gentle, they were not safe or tame. They were like two embers containing a force and energy of their own, capable of igniting abruptly and kindling the coldest of spirits.

Leaves, twigs and beads were threaded into the long wispy hair that trailed and curled from her head and a silver necklace encircled her furry throat. Bulging bags of dark green velvet and tied bundles of sweet-scented herbs hung from a loose leather belt that kept slipping over her hips and on the forefinger of her right paw she wore a silver ring, set with a green stone that winked and glinted under the glancing starlight.

'But why interest thyself in fish at this late hour?' she asked him. 'Didst thou not cram thy fill at the regale earlier? And what would'st thou do with a catched fish anywise? Indeed, I wonder if there be any tiddler small enough for such a dwarfish rimpti-too as thou!'

'I . . . I doesn't want no fish,' Young Whortle said. 'I were just . . .'

'Thou should'st be abed, my pygmy soldier,' she advised with an abrupt shake of her head and a wag of her finger. 'Why, my three sons cannot be much younger than thee and they were tucked up long since.'

Young Whortle clenched his fist and reached for his mousebrass. 'It's you!' he cried. 'The ratwitch! You come back to haunt us?'

Virianna smacked her knees and laughed. 'I see the malady now,' she said. 'Thou hast revelled too deeply, that blackberry ferment is more potent than it seemeth.'

'You evil Hobbing ghost – get you gone. You worked enough evil when you was alive.'

With one paw on his brass and the other shooing the creature away, he moved forward, hoping to banish her.

The water vole dismissed him airily. 'Thy head will pound sorely on the morrow.' She tutted. 'There is much for thy folk to do. The digging of quarters in the banks of yonder ditch must begin. The caves of the Grelffit Houm cannot harbour thee for ever. That is a hallowed place, and I must make it ready for He who is to follow. Captain Fenlyn shall have need of all his woodlanders, so get thee to bed and sleep thy indulgence away.'

And then Young Whortle understood. She was no phantom: he had been sent back into the past a second time.

'Now, leave me about my business,' she told him,

dipping into one of the velvet bags at her waist and taking out a pawful of the silver powder. 'I must complete this spell ere midnight.'

Bending over, she returned to gouging her stick through the soil and sprinkling the trench with glittering dust, muttering an incantation under her breath.

'Stop!' Young Whortle yelled. 'I know what you're doin'! You're summonin' Fenny out so you can put the rope round his neck. Well I won't let you – you'll have to kill me first!'

Lunging at her, he snatched the velvet bag from her belt, then ran along the furrow she had made, kicking and scattering the glittering trail aside.

'No!' she shrieked. 'Thou witless fool! What madness hath seized thee?'

Young Whortle held the bag high over his head and sprang away from her.

'I might not be as fast as Hodge,' he called. 'But there's no way a fat lump like you can catch me. So that's an end to your murderous magicks and our Cap'n won't have to die. He'll live to the ripe ol' age he deserved!'

Virianna lumbered after him. 'What murder? What evil?' she cried. ''Twas a spell of protection I was weaving about this place, as I have done every night around each of our camps since we left Greenreach. Sword and arrow are not enough. There must be other defences. Purfote is the great enemy of the Raith Sidhe.

Though Hobb is defeated, there are the two others of the infernal triad still abroad – they will seek vengeance. Hath I not sensed them prowling close? 'Twas only my magic that shielded us from their wrath.'

'Go boil yer bum in a rusty kettle!' Young Whortle jeered. 'I ain't listenin'.'

'Give me the bag!' she demanded. 'I must complete the spell. So little time is left.'

'You want this?' the fieldmouse taunted, dangling the bag before him. 'Well you can go swim for it!'

Flinging his arm wide, he hurled the bag out over the pond. The silver powder twinkled and sparked as it spilled from the open neck, fizzing like a galaxy of tiny stars when it touched the water. The bag sank beneath the surface and Young Whortle danced a jig of victory.

'What hast thou done?' the water vole cried, aghast. 'That was our only armour against the dark forces of Mabb and Bauchan. What peril and calamity hast thou brought down upon us?'

Young Whortle faltered.

'Drop the play actin',' he told her.

But Virianna was backing away from him and drawing shapes and symbols in the air with her stick.

'Thou art an agent of the dark gods!' she exclaimed. 'The evil is already among us – I must go rouse the guards. Thou might be Bauchan himself in disguise.'

'Hoy!' Young Whortle snapped. 'Don't you go callin' me no nasty names, Missus – it's you what's the ratwitch and me what's saved the day.'

'Avaunt!'

'Sling your hook!'

'I command thee to depart, foul deceiver of the outer darkness!'

'Push off!'

'Architect of lies – begone!'

'Get stuffed, you saggy-bottomed, lardy hag.'

For several moments they glared at one another, then Virianna relaxed and lowered her stick. The anger and indignation which blazed in the field-mouse's eyes was genuine and no trick of the treacherous Bauchan.

'Thou art no Hobber.' She sighed. 'Yet thou art truly the biggest and sorriest quacking noddy in the five kingdoms. How can so much folly be wrapped in so tiny a body?'

'You sayin' I'm stupid? What is it about you and your family?'

Virianna ignored him, glanced up at the stars and sniffed the air.

'Midnight draws close,' she muttered. 'And we are defenceless. Green spare us from the fury of the Raith Sidhe.'

Her voice was so fearful that Young Whortle began to doubt his rash actions.

'Stop it,' he said.

'And yet,' she continued hurriedly, 'there must be power in this place to guard us, the in-dwelling spirit of the pool must have a virtue against our enemies. I must go and speak with it. I pray there is yet time – in the deep reaches untouched by time he dwells.'

She hurried to the water's edge and was just about to leap in when a black cloud moved across the heavens and Virianna froze.

In a strangled whisper she hissed, 'Too late – the terror comes!'

A bitterly cold breeze came gusting over the fields, growing stronger every moment, until it tore through the trees. Round and round the pool it blasted, screeching and howling.

Young Whortle's breath was torn from his lips and his ears flapped against his face. His fur was raked in every direction and he had to close his eyes against the tremendous force of the unnatural squall.

'What's happenin'?' he yelled above the din.

'The Raith Sidhe!' Virianna shouted back. 'They are upon us!'

Snatching a bundle of dried herbs in each fist, she threw her arms wide and cried out to him, 'Get behind me – hurry!'

Without hesitation, Young Whortle obeyed and the gale raged about them.

Facing into the tempest, her wispy hair whipping

around her, Virianna called out words of power.

Above them, branches creaked threateningly and torn leaves teemed through the thrashing storm. The surface of the pool spat and the foaming water was capped with white froth as violent waves crashed against the banks, lashing the fieldmouse and the water vole and drenching them to their skins.

'The way is barred unto thee!' Virianna proclaimed. 'By the might and majesty of the conquering Green – I order thee! I compel thee. Avaunt! Avaunt!'

The freezing wind screamed even louder. Young Whortle was almost lifted off the ground and he clutched tightly to the water vole's belt.

'Make it stop!' he shouted. 'Make it stop!'

Virianna called out more words of challenge and

command, but the supernatural force continued to scream around them. Then, suddenly, it sped around the pool, flattening the reeds in its rampaging progress.

And then it was gone.

At once the trees ceased their violent shaking and the ragged leaves twirled to the ground. The pool stopped churning and the huge waves collapsed into nothing.

With her hair sticking up in all directions, the water vole gazed slowly around – her whiskers twitching and jerking.

'You did it,' Young Whortle breathed. 'Whatever that invisible fright was – you sent it packing!'

Virianna's brows scrunched together and pushed down over her eyes.

'No,' she whispered, ''Twas too easy. The Raith Sidhe are not dispatched so simply. The malignance is still amongst us, canst thou not feel it?'

The fieldmouse peered into the darkness. He couldn't feel anything except the cold of his own wet fur.

Virianna flicked her small ears this way and that, listening for the slightest noise. After the tumult of the gale, all was deathly quiet.

'It must've gone,' Young Whortle insisted. 'There's not so much as a breath a-sighing through them leaves what are left. It be like the world is fast asleep now.'

'Or under an enchantment,' the water vole added.

''Tis too quiet and still. There's evil at work – and my bottom is not saggy!'

Stuffing the bundles of herbs back into her belt and hitching it higher, she snatched up her stick and took hold of Young Whortle's paw.

'Hurry!' she told him. 'We must hurry before it is too late.'

Pulling him after her, she hastened through the grass.

'Where we goin'?' he cried.

'To the Grelffit Houm,' she answered. 'Thither hath the evil gone!'

'Cap'n Fenny!' Young Whortle yelled.

Together they ran through the undergrowth, until at last the familiar sloping boulders reared before them. The great stone was not in place and the entrance was gaping open.

Two stout hedgehogs were outside but they were curled into balls and their spears lay in the grass beneath them.

'Who are they?' Young Whortle asked.

'Sentries of the watch,' Virianna told him. 'Awake! Thou art on guard. Awake, ye stupefied dolts!'

She prodded their prickly forms with her stick but they made no movement.

'Is they killed?' Young Whortle murmured.

'It is the Dark Forgetfulness,' Virianna said in a frightened voice. 'The Mournful Unwaking. Mabb is here.'

9

Spitting Against the Storm

T he fieldmouse stared into the tunnel. Flaming torches were thrust into the ground at intervals down the passage. The light flickered over the rough bare walls and he noticed, first with shock and then understanding, that they were plain and undecorated. Firgild would not get around to painting them for many years.

'We've got to go down an' save the Cap'n,' he said urgently, remembering why he was there.

'Yes,' Virianna said, with a worried scowl. 'And my children are down there also.'

Before they could move, a blast of bitter air roared up the tunnel and the torches guttered. Virianna and Young Whortle staggered back before it and the water vole put a protective arm around his shoulders.

'Stay by me,' she told him. 'This is a horror beyond the endurance of any rimpti-too.'

One by one the flames were extinguished and the sound of dragging footsteps came echoing up the darkening tunnel.

'What's that?' he asked.

'Mabb is coming,' she answered.

The footsteps drew closer, but they could see

nothing. A cloud of night swirled thickly within the passage, steadily advancing towards the entrance.

'Mabb,' Virianna hissed. 'Consort of Hobb.'

She reached into one of her velvet pouches and the black fog flowed purposefully nearer.

Virianna began muttering under her breath and threw what looked like green moss at the entrance.

'Thy Lord is defeated!' she declared suddenly. 'This is a site strong with powers older than thine. Get hence, Mistress Widow-wraith. The War is done and lost, go and be forgot, till the oaken prison rots and fails.'

Faint, mocking laughter drifted from the billowing darkness and Young Whortle's hackles rose. It was the most evil sound he had ever heard.

Then out of the tunnel the cloud came pouring. It was like a creature of smoke with tendrils of living, inky vapour that snaked through the air, grasping and groping their way forward.

Young Whortle shrank back but Virianna stood her ground.

'Return to thine emptiness,' she commanded. 'Let the victors enjoy their peace as is their right.'

The unnatural darkness spilled across the threshold.

Young Whortle was shaking. An aura of menace and terror floated before it and he ducked hastily as a serpentine finger of night threaded towards him.

The clumps of moss that Virianna had thrown down crackled into small green fires when the cloud moved over them but they quickly sputtered and died. That night the power of Mabb was too great to be denied.

The water vole continued undaunted, staring defiantly at the approaching darkness. She shouted her commands and called out every repelling incantation and spell of resistance she could remember, but her efforts were in vain.

Writhing and seething, the cloud reached her, undulating in front of her unflinching form and she braced herself, ready to be engulfed.

'Stand clear!' Young Whortle yelled.

But the fog did not wrap itself around her. For a moment it swelled and bulged threateningly before her face. Then it veered aside as if impelled by a fierce wind or driven by a single, indomitable will. It rolled silently away – passing along the muddy track towards the ditch.

'That were close!' the fieldmouse cried in relief. 'I thought it were goin' to swamp you and gobble you up.'

Virianna was breathing hard and staring into the distance where the cloud floated down the path.

'Mabb is bent on vengeance and destruction,' she murmured, lowering her eyes and looking at the ground. 'Yet why did She spare me? What vileness is She brewing?'

But Young Whortle was not listening.

'Don't matter!' he said. 'Now we're safe let's nip down and make sure the Cap'n is too.'

'Hold!' Virianna barked abruptly. 'No one is safe.

Look here – what canst thou see?'

The fieldmouse peered down at the soft mud. Where the cloud had passed there were the fresh imprints of a mouse's feet, a large mouse's feet.

'That murk had a purpose,' Virianna said. 'It is a cloak, a swaddling, smothering blind – conveying Mabb's great enemy to some evil doom.'

'Fenny!' Young Whortle whimpered. 'He were inside that noxious fog?'

She nodded slowly.

'Enslaved by some spell – or I know nothing of Mabb and Her craft. Fenlyn Purfote hath ne'er been in greater peril than at this very instant.'

'You're right!' Young Whortle exclaimed. 'The yew is down that track. He's going straight for the Hanging Tree!'

Breathlessly they ran along the bank, to where the sinister shape of the yew reared high into the midnight heavens.

The cloud of darkness had come to rest beneath it and, with a sickening lurch in his stomach, Young Whortle saw that it was whirling and unwinding. Bands of supernatural black mist were peeling away, twisting and coiling up into the air – forming a plume of fog that drifted between the branches.

As the skeins of vapour rose, the solid form that had been concealed within was gradually revealed.

Wearing a green cloak, fastened by a silver brooch in the shape of a leaping hare, was Captain Fenny.

The burly mouse's eyes were closed and it was clear he was fast asleep – lost in the Mournful Unwaking.

Young Whortle cried out in dismay and sprang forward, but Virianna pulled him back.

'Beware – thou fool!' she told him. 'This is Mabb's hour, when Her evil is at its height. Thou would'st be destroyed and thy spirit enslaved unto Her service.'

'But the Cap'n!' the fieldmouse protested.

Virianna stared at the sleeping hero. He was swaying slightly. Only a wisp of darkness remained about his waist and it was steadily coiling upward to join the rest of the supernatural cloud above.

'Do as I bid thee,' she whispered to Young Whortle. 'What are you going to do?'

'Try and keep that baneful force busy, so that ye may lead Fenlyn Purfote back to the pool – but make haste, for there will be but moments to achieve it. As soon as thou art there, push him in – head-first if thou must and leap in after. The virtue of that blessed water is thine only hope of protection now.'

Young Whortle was about to ask another question, but there was no time.

Virianna was looking up at the swollen blackness and in a clear, courageous voice, she called out, 'Mabb! Hear me! 'Tis I, Virianna – Daughter of Thamesis, Tender of the Hallowed Oak that is no more and Priestess of the Green. Many are the times thou hast tried to entice me whilst I slept, whispering in mine slumbering ear of the might and power thou would'st bestow if I were to betray my oath and do thy bidding. Never once did I hearken and always hath I struggled to thwart thee. A greater threat am I to the Raith Sidhe than this battle- worn warrior. If thou must wreak a vengeance, then direct it unto me.'

Glowering up at the black fog, she stuck out her jaw and waited.

Young Whortle chewed his lip anxiously.

Virianna gave a grim laugh.

'Can it be?' she cried. 'Is the Great Mabb, the Beldame of the Pit, afraid to confront me? Ho – what a night this is. What was I afeared of? Indeed, what terror is left in thee now? Hobb is the true power of the Unholy Three and without Him – thou art naught but a shifter of shadows and a causer of bad dreams. Why, any gripe in the guts can boast the same!'

She paused and held her breath in expectation. If that did not provoke the Rat Goddess, then nothing would.

Young Whortle glanced across at Captain Fenny, keying himself up to dart over and get him.

Above them the cloud was pulsing and rippling. Suddenly a flaming vein of crimson light streaked through it and, for an instant, they were all lit by an infernal glare. A sulphurous stink fouled the atmosphere.

Then, from the midst of that eerie smoke, a husky, growling voice spoke.

'Petty slave of root and water. I have not come for

you this night. Though you have ever tried to hinder the Three, your paltry efforts were but spitting against the storm. You are nothing. Run now, for Mabb is merciful. Leave the sleep visitor to her prey.'

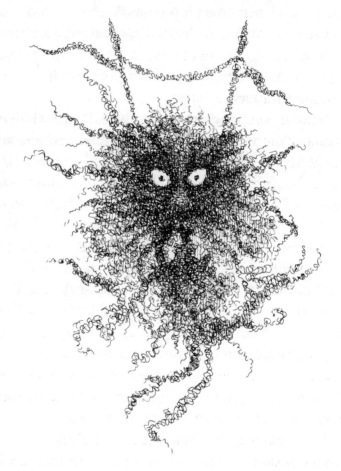

'Never!' Virianna snapped back. 'I challenge thee, Mabb! For thou knowest the significance of this sacred land, by star and moon and secret sign I found it. Here, upon this soil and sod, it is foretold that the final end shall be shaped – when Light and Dark do battle at last and the doom of all things is written until the world's last gasp. This ye know and from this the flames of thy heart quail, for the prophecy declares a God shall perish here. Will that God be thee, this very night?'

A tremendous rumble shook the living darkness and, in its heart, two points of golden light were blazing with fury.

'Mortal speck of bone and flesh!' the Goddess roared. 'You have earned my attention and you will suffer.'

The water vole chuckled bleakly. 'A contest twixt thee and me,' she said, rolling up imaginary sleeves and clapping her paws. 'Bring it hither!'

Another rumble thundered through the air and scarlet and purple flames ripped from the cloud.

Young Whortle dragged his eyes away. A fiery shape had crackled into being: an image of a tall rat woman wearing a high headdress that fluttered with the tattered ribbons of ancient war banners.

Mabb had appeared and from the thick, flame-rent vapour She descended, as a being formed from swirling shadow – shot through with infernal flame.

Virianna gripped her stick so tightly that her knuckles shone white. Her soft brown eyes looked with horror upon the terror of Mabb, but she did not cower or cringe.

On her finger the green stone of her ring flickered

with a light of its own and the water vole knew that the Green Mouse was with her.

'Guide and protect Thy humble servant,' she said under her breath.

'Your precious Green will not save you,' the voice of Mabb snarled from the shadow shape. 'The night is my realm.'

With that a sheet of scorching flame flew from the shadow's ethereal claws and the duel commenced. Virianna leaped aside, jumping down the ditch's high bank and the fires roared over her head.

Mabb flew after her. Another torrent of flame blistered through the darkness. This time Virianna was not swift enough and the hair smoked on her scalp.

Racing to the ditch, she threw water over herself to soothe the burns then turned to face the terrible spectre that was already bearing down on her.

Virianna held her stick before her like a sword. The ring on her finger blazed with emerald fire and at once the stick burst into flames.

Mabb came swooping down. Her darkness rushed into the hallowed fire and a horrendous shriek split the night.

Green and scarlet flames flashed across the ditch, striving against each other and Mabb went shooting upward, screeching in fury.

Virianna staggered back, stumbling into the running water.

'Go now,' she said to herself, desperately willing the

fieldmouse to seize this chance and take Captain Fenny to safety.

Suddenly the nightmare of Mabb came streaking down once more.

Virianna thrust the blazing stick upward and a beacon of bright flame crackled high above her.

It soared into the night and burst through Mabb's plummeting shadow.

The surrounding countryside shook with the screams. Purple lightnings jagged along the ditch and the dark shape of the Rat Goddess exploded.

Beneath the yew tree, Young Whortle had run to Captain Fenny's side and was shaking him roughly.

'Wake up!' he hissed at him. 'Wake up, Cap'n!'

But the large mouse remained lost in Mabb's enchantment and could not escape it.

Young Whortle took hold of his arm and pulled.

'This way,' he told him. 'Follow me to the pond. Come on . . . this way.'

Half dragged, half stumbling, the sleeping Fenlyn Purfote lurched after him.

The screams and rages of Mabb resounded in Young Whortle's ears but he dared not look back. He helped Captain Fenny on to the muddy track and hurriedly made for the still pool.

Mabb's shredded shape whooshed through the tree tops, manifesting back into Her fearful form and, with a blood-curdling cry, She came rushing down for another attack.

Ankle deep in the ditch's water, Virianna clenched her teeth and waited. The Green Mouse would protect her and she realised too late that she ought to have trusted to Him and stayed by Captain Fenny. Now they were separated, she would have to hold to her plan and pray that it worked.

Then Mabb was upon her again.

The evil Goddess flew about her. Whenever Mabb's darkness touched the hallowed flames, She shrieked and her golden eyes burned with fury. The green fires spat and scalded and the resulting cries were filled with the hate and agony of battle.

'How's that for spitting against the storm?' Virianna shouted.

The shadow shape circled her more slowly and the eyes shrank into glowing dots as the Rat Goddess became consumed with anger and bent Her spite and loathing upon the water vole, seeking for ways to attack.

'The Three will never conquer,' Virianna told her. 'Life and light shall always be greater than thee.'

Mabb hissed. Then the eyes glimmered and shone more brightly than ever.

'I waste my time with you,' she growled. 'Shelter and skulk in the sanctuary of your squalid Green – my sport was not with you this night. The hero of Greenreach awaits me.'

The shadow shape rose and flew to the yew tree.

Virianna thought quickly. There had not been

enough time for the fieldmouse to take Captain Fenny to the sanctuary of the pool.

'Mabb!' she called out. 'What of the contest? Art thou so easily beaten?'

The Rat Goddess made no answer but when she found the base of the yew deserted, her wrath knew no equal and she rushed along the track, her scarlet fires streaming behind her.

Young Whortle had already reached the reeds and was urging the sleeping warrior mouse to follow.

'Not far now, Cap'n,' he said. 'A little way more and you're safe.'

At once the fury of Mabb cannoned into them. Before he knew what was happening, Young Whortle was hurled aside and Captain Fenny was snatched away. Back through the mud, the shadow shape hauled him and by the time Young Whortle scrambled to his feet to follow, Mabb had dragged her victim back to the Hanging Tree.

'No!' he yelled and darted forward.

Virianna had clambered up the bank of the ditch and was waiting when Mabb returned with Captain Fenny. The stick was still burning with green flames in her fist.

'Leave him!' she commanded.

'Never,' the shadow shape snapped. 'The Raith Sidhe must have vengeance. We demand a life!'

'Then take mine instead,' Virianna said grimly.

'Yours? But you hide behind your hated Green.'

The water vole lowered the stick and the magical flames licked up her arm. Then she hurled it away from her and it landed with a splash in the ditch below.

'A bargain,' she declared. 'My life for that of the noble Captain. Do you agree, Mabb?'

The shadow shape stirred and a grotesque laugh issued from it.

'Mabb agrees,' She said. 'If you renounce the protection of your Green Spirit, then one life only shall I take this night.'

'Swear it.'

'Mabb swears, by the horns of my Lord Hobb, you have my oath.'

Virianna bowed her head and slowly removed the silver ring from her finger. 'Then I renounce the guardianship of the Almighty Green,' she said in a broken voice.

Closing her eyes, she flung the ring after the stick. For a moment it shone briefly, glittering in the darkness until it fell into the water and vanished.

With a triumphant shout, Mabb stretched out her claws and swooped towards her.

When Young Whortle came running up the track, he saw only Virianna standing upon the high bank and Captain Fenny leaning against the bole of the yew with his chin on his chest. There was no sign of Mabb.

'Where is She?' he murmured. 'Where is that horror?'

He looked at Virianna. She was trembling. At first he thought it was fear but then, to his astonishment, he realised that she was laughing. Her shoulders were rocking with mirth and presently her whole body juddered and shook.

'Missus?' he ventured. 'Is you all right? What's gone on?'

He was about to run to her side when the water vole turned her face to him and Young Whortle caught his breath.

Virianna's eyes were blazing, shining with a fiery light and from her lips a horrible voice came echoing.

It was the voice of Mabb.

'You trusting fool,' She jeered, but She was not addressing him. She was speaking to Virianna whose body She had taken possession of.

'One life only I swore to take this night, but not yours. I came for the warrior and his life I claim. Did you really believe you were so important to the Raith Sidhe? No, claws other than mine shall end your worthless existence. The very vagabonds you have striven to protect will serve you your death.'

Her ensuing laughter was awful to hear.

Young Whortle shook his head and was about to race to Captain Fenny, when something slithered along the ground beside him.

It was a long length of strong rope. Summoned from the Grelffit Houm by Mabb's arts, it squirmed through the mud like a living snake, then reared up and swayed before Fenny's slumped form.

'No!' Young Whortle cried. 'Stop it.'

Only another laugh answered him and the possessed Virianna began to dance.

The rope rose into the air and the lower end curled tightly about the Captain's neck, tying itself in a knot above his head.

Virianna's slow, waltzing dance gained in speed until she was capering wildly around in circles and the voice of Mabb within her was laughing insanely.

Captain Fenny was hoisted off the ground and Young Whortle could bear it no more.

'Help!' he screamed. 'Help!'

A heavy paw touched him on the shoulder and the fieldmouse gave a startled shriek.

'You have seen enough,' Woppenfrake said gently. 'Come forward, Master Nep.'

Young Whortle stared up at the stout water vole and threw his arms around him.

'I'm so sorry,' he wailed. 'Forgive me. I didn't know. I thought it were your mam what killed our Fenny.'

'As did your ancestors,' Woppenfrake said softly. 'Mabb made certain of that. She did not leave our mother till they had thrown her onto the bonfire. Trust not the promises of the Raith Sidhe, little rimpi-too.'

Young Whortle glanced back at the yew tree, but only the night breezes moved through its branches. There was no sign of Captain Fenny or Virianna and the ground beneath his small feet was firm and dry. He was back in the present, yet the horror of the past pressed heavily on him.

'Go to your nest,' Woppenfrake said. 'There is rain on the air. Sleep and let the sound of it wash the fear from you.'

The fieldmouse nodded. More than anything he wanted to be in his own nest and try to forget what he had seen. He took a step towards the cornfield, then hesitated.

'Can . . . can I come and see you again?' he asked. 'Would I be welcome, after . . . after the nasty things I said?'

Woppenfrake was already walking back towards the still pool, the folds of his cloak flowing around him.

'My brothers and I will be glad to see you,' his voice called back.

Young Whortle smiled and ran to the edge of the cornfield. Then he halted once more and yelled, 'I liked your mam. She were a hero – just like Fenny!'

Woppenfrake faltered in his steps, then continued.

And the rain began.

10

Tears in Moonlight

Throughout the night the rain teemed down but Young Whortle slept soundly in his snug, dry nest. No fearsome visions of Mabb troubled his dreams and he awoke refreshed and eager for the day.

The rain was still drumming down when he popped his head out to view the dawn.

It was watery and grey. The sky was leaden and low and he knew the rain would continue for the rest of the morning.

A great drop of water sploshed on to his neck and he hastily withdrew into the nest once more.

'I won't get no trainin' done today,' he said ruefully. 'The lads won't be out in this and I doesn't fancy it neither.'

As he said it, he heard a gurgling giggle outside and he peered out once more, taking care not to push his nose out too far.

Down in the Hall of Corn, a solitary figure was jumping in the puddles and spinning around, arms outstretched – revelling in the downpour. With his face upturned he caught the raindrops in his mouth, delighted laughter gargling in his throat.

It was Twit.

He was rejoicing in the soaking weather, relishing the simple beauty of the world washed clean. To him the barley was bedecked with diamonds and he marvelled at the spectacle.

Young Whortle watched him cavorting from puddle to puddle and tutted to himself.

'Poor nutter,' he said.

Just then a female voice called out across the Hall. It was Twit's mother demanding that he get out of the wet.

Young Whortle curled up and hugged his knees. Twit's mother was a town mouse and he wondered if that was the reason her son had turned out so stupid.

The rest of the morning was spent under cover. No one did much of anything if it meant getting drenched and only a few zealous sentries took up their posts.

By mid-afternoon the sky had brightened and the rain had become a light drizzle.

Some brave souls ventured out. Isaac Nettle was seen striding through the barley, his face stern and grave as usual. Mr Woodruffe inspected any damage the rain had caused but this was very minor. Josiah Down's nest had fallen apart and he and his family had been forced to take shelter with the Crowfoots. Josiah was renowned for the shoddy workmanship of his nest building, so this came as no surprise to anyone. The only cause for concern was Granny Bottom, who unwisely stepped into a patch of thick mud and promptly sank up to her waist. She had to be rescued by three of the strongest mice and, instead of thanking them, gave each a smart slap for handling her so roughly and in her view, 'with a want of decency'.

Gradually life in the cornfield returned to normal and, by the early evening, the sullen clouds had rolled away, to reveal a spectacular sunset that bode well for the following day.

Young Whortle had tried to perform as many of his exercises as possible. Naturally, he did not roll around the floor, for the ground in places had become a quagmire, but he did his best and adhered to his wretched diet throughout the day. He did not see anything of his friends and so before it was time for them to begin their own sentry duty, he set off for the meadow to see if they were in the den.

On the way, he saw a crowd of curious mice gathered on the bank of the ditch – exclaiming and muttering. The rain had swelled the waters, which were foaming and tumbling faster than the onlookers had ever seen.

'It's so high,' they cried.

'The stepping-stones are completely covered.'

'If it rises any more, it'll spill over the lower bank and flood the meadow.'

It was all terribly worrying, but passionately

interesting and they lingered to speculate on the worst possible outcomes.

'There'll be no Fennywolde Games if it don't subside,' Grommel observed.

'And what about our pond?' gasped Widow Mayweed. 'If that overflows it'll drown our own field and the barley will rot.'

With this thought uppermost, they hurried along the track to look at the still pool and Young Whortle went with them.

He knew there was no genuine cause for alarm. The water would return to its usual levels but everyone secretly enjoyed contemplating such disasters. Besides, because he was unable to use the stepping-stones, this was the long way round to the meadow and the only route to the den of the Wolf Killers.

When the fieldmice reached the pool, they let out squeals of surprise.

It had swallowed its banks and was twice its normal size. The water's edge now lapped against the surrounding trees and the bordering reeds were completely engulfed.

Everybody's mild apprehensions suddenly became definite fears. Frightened discussions broke out.

'We'll be drownded!'

'Swept away as we sleep!'

'And I've already got a rotten cold.'

'I never did see so much of the wet stuff – 'tis playing havoc with me bladder.'

Young Whortle left them fretting. Alison Sedge's mother was amongst them and she was picking quarrels with whoever would listen.

There was no immediate danger. Although the pond had encroached upon the trees, there was still a distance to go before it posed any serious threat to the cornfield.

Picking his way around the edge, he made his way to the sloping boulders that formed the entrance to the Grelffit Houm. To his consternation, he saw that the water had risen around them and they now jutted out into the expansive pool like a craggy headland.

'I hope them water voles is all right,' he murmured.

Apart from swimming across to them, there was no way of reaching the stones to find out. Besides, he doubted if Woppenfrake and the others would answer his calls so early in the evening anyway.

'I'll try later,' he told himself. 'When everyone is asleep.'

And with that he hopped away, scurrying through the trees and out into the meadow.

When he reached the den he found his four friends already there. They were examining the raft and shaking their heads.

'Hello,' Todkin hailed him. 'We was just seein' how she fared after all that rain. No chance of us painting her tonight, the wood's too wet.'

Figgy chewed the inside of his cheek. 'She'll never dry out if we stow her behind the den again. We'll have to leave her here in the open and hope it don't pour again.'

'An' that your sister don't come sniffin' round,' Hodge put in.

Todkin squinted at the glorious sunset. 'Should be dry enough tomorrow,' he said. 'Today were a wash-out in every sense. My schedule didn't allow for that. We'll have to work twice as hard to try and catch up.'

They all agreed. There were now only three days left until the first day of the Fennywolde Games and Young Whortle promised not to complain, no matter how many times Hodge made him run around the meadow.

It was already time for their shift in the cornfield, so they left the raft and strolled back, talking lightly of the day's events and laughing when Figgy described the outrage and indignation of his grandmother. She was determined not to be rescued the next time she became trapped in a mire, he told them, and would rather sink than be dredged out by mice who had no respect for a genteel lady of advanced years.

As they chatted and chuckled, Young Whortle desperately wanted to tell them of his harrowing experience the previous night. But he knew they would not believe him so he remained quiet. Only Samuel noticed his silence and when their sentry duty began, he chose to climb a stalk close to his best friend and waited to tackle him about it.

Presently, when they had enjoyed the balmy airs and

admired the swaying corn ears, he said, 'Warty, what's up?'

Young Whortle tightened the grip of his tail about the barley stalk and avoided his friend's questioning eye.

'Nowt,' he fibbed. 'Just thinkin' on the Games and how I'll do.'

Samuel regarded him sadly. He knew that was not true and was hurt to be excluded.

Young Whortle caught the injured expression on his friend's face and felt mean. He had never lied to Sammy before.

'You wouldn't believe me if I told you,' he cried. 'So it's best you don't ask.'

Samuel was shocked at the outburst and did not know how to respond.

He stared out across the rippling corn, now pearled with moonlight, and thought deeply.

At length he said, 'Is it to do with them water voles you were on about the other day?'

Young Whortle scowled and made no answer.

His friend persisted. 'We been best pals since we was tykes. There's nowt that rattles in my head what you don't know about and till this week 'twere the same the other way round.'

'A lot's happened this week.'

Samuel looked down at the ground below then fidgeted with his whiskers, winding them around his fingers as he clumsily sought for the right words.

'Warty,' he mumbled at last. 'You's more like a brother to me – in fact you're more a part of me than me own skinny ribs. If you tell me summat's true, I promise I'll believe it – no matter how outlandish or fantastic. I'd be a lousy sort of friend not to.'

Young Whortle stared across at him and a huge grin lit his face.

'Green bless you, Sammy,' he said.

The rest of the shift was spent telling him everything that had happened. Throughout it all Samuel Gorse remained quiet and attentive. He didn't interrupt or scoff sceptically, as any of the others would have done.

When Young Whortle finished, Sammy merely scratched his ears and said, 'No wonder you're so tired in the daytime and been so crummy at the training sessions, with all that lot goin' on.'

'Then you don't think I'm dreamin' or makin' it up?'

'I trusts you Warty,' he said squarely. 'If you say you been poppin' back to ancient times, fighting Hobbers an' tryin' to save Cap'n Fenny then I don't have to believe you – I knows it happened, just as you said it did.'

Young Whortle sniffed and rubbed his eyes.

'There is one thing though,' Sammy began.

'What?'

'If them water voles of yours is so magic, could they make me fat?'

★

When the shift finished, Figgy, Hodge and Todkin returned to the Hall of Corn but Young Whortle and Samuel set off for the still pool to find the mysterious sons of Virianna.

The water was still high and had crept past the trees. In the shadow of the branches, the two fieldmice blundered over the squelching ground until they were suddenly ankle-deep in water.

'It's bigger than it were afore,' Young Whortle said, springing back.

'You don't think it will swamp our field, do you?' Sammy asked.

'Woppenfrake wouldn't let that happen. Besides, he says it's one of the ancient shrines. Strong magicks are in this 'ere Glinty Water.'

'In our old pond?' Samuel said in surprise. 'Who'd have thought that?'

'Ssshhh!' Young Whortle told him. 'They doesn't like us calling it "our pond".'

'Whose is it then? Theirs?'

'No . . . I dunno. There's something lives deep down. But I don't think it belongs to him or her – or just plain it.'

They skirted around the water until they could see the sloping boulders rearing solid and black above the calm, mirrored surface of the moon-glimmering pool.

'It's an island now,' Young Whortle groaned with disappointment.

'Certainly looks magic,' Samuel breathed. 'Like a

forgotten kingdom over the silver sea.'

'You're dreamier than I am,' his friend chuckled, giving him a shove. 'How we goin' to reach it, though?'

'I doesn't fancy a swim at this time of night,' Samuel grumbled. 'And your raft is too heavy for the two of us to lug over here on our own. Why don't you shout your new friends' names? They might hear you – there could be another way out of them tunnels you told me about.'

Young Whortle thought it was worth a try, so he cupped his paws around his mouth and was about to call out, when they both heard a sound that caused them to forget the water voles for a moment.

Somewhere close by, someone was sobbing.

'Who's that?' Samuel whispered.

Young Whortle shrugged.

It was a wretched, desolate sound, filled with despair and they glanced at one another uncertainly.

'Don't sound like Woppenfrake or Firglid, or Willibald,' he said softly. 'Though they do have more to be sad about than most.'

'Let's go and see, then,' Samuel suggested. 'It's coming from over there. Maybe it'll lead to another frightening time in the past.'

Cautiously, they tiptoed towards the unhappy sound. They did not have far to go, merely around one of the trees – to where an old fallen branch leaned out across the pool.

The two friends halted. The gnarled, broken bough

was silhouetted against the reflected moonlight and sitting upon it, hunched over and cradling his head in his arms was a fieldmouse.

Tiny ripples disrupted the pond's shimmering surface as hot tears tumbled from the hidden face.

The unknown mouse was so wrapped up in his unhappiness that he was oblivious of the two friends who were watching.

Young Whortle and Samuel did not know what to do and began to grow uncomfortable. They felt like intruders, spying on a private misery. This was no magical adventure, just a glimpse into someone's secret grief and they wished they had not come here.

'We'd best go,' Samuel murmured. 'Sounds like there's a lot of snivellin' still to come. If he's not careful it'll be his blubbin' fault the pond spills over, not the rain.'

He turned to depart but Young Whortle caught his arm.

'We can't go,' he hissed. 'Whoever that be, needs our help.'

'Big noses only get squeezed,' Sammy replied, repeating a favourite saying of his mother's. ''Tain't none of our business, Warty.'

Young Whortle frowned. 'Well I wouldn't like to think of one of our friends being so sad and lonely,' he muttered. 'I'm going to try.'

Edging forward, he stole towards the branch and, taking a deep breath, cleared his throat loudly.

At once the figure looked up.

'Who's that?' it demanded. 'Who's there?'

Samuel and Young Whortle opened their mouths in surprise. They recognised that voice.

'Jenkin . . .?' Young Whortle exclaimed. 'Be that you?'

Jenkin Nettle turned away hastily.

'Leave me alone,' he shouted.

'What's the matter? What's wrong?'

'Just go.'

Young Whortle looked at Samuel. They knew Jenkin had strange moods and would often take himself off to sit them out, but they had no idea he was so desperately unhappy.

Young Whortle tried again. 'Can we help?'

Jenkin's response was fierce and filled with anger.

'Why don't you ever listen to me?' he snapped. 'Why can't you understand what I tell you? Why won't you leave me in peace? I don't want to see your face ever again – I'm sick of the sight of you! I hate you! I wish you'd never been born!'

The vehemence of Jenkin's outburst was so brutal and unexpected, that Young Whortle flinched and flattened his ears against his head.

Spluttering with outrage, Sammy leaped forward in his defence and was about to yell some insults of his own at Jenkin, when Young Whortle stopped him.

'Leave it,' he begged. 'He don't know what he's saying.'

Reluctantly Samuel bit his tongue and allowed himself to be led away.

'*Jolly* Jenkin – my crusty batflaps!' he fumed. 'He's just as nasty as his dad – worse even.'

Young Whortle said nothing. He glanced over his shoulder to take one last look at the figure sitting astride the fallen branch. Jenkin had buried his head in his paws again and the jerky movement of his shoulders showed that he was crying once more.

He did not understand what the matter was, but he felt certain Jenkin's anger had not really been directed at him. He was confused and he wished he were cleverer. If Todkin had been there, he would have handled it differently.

'I tell you this, Warty,' Samuel continued, still cross and seething. 'There's no way we're going to let that snotty Jenkin beat you in the Games. I wants you to win them more than ever now, and as soon as I tell the others – they will too. You're going to be Head Sentry, if it's the last thing we do.'

11

Swearing the Oath

The promise of the ravishing sunset was delivered the following morning. It was going to be a day drenched in sunshine and the breeze was as warm as midsummer.

A thick blanket of fog had risen with the dawn and carpeted the ground. When Young Whortle peeped out from his nest, he itched to go running through it.

Chewing on his dreary breakfast, he scrambled down and dived into the mist. The white vapour reached up to his chin and he charged backwards and forwards, ploughing through the mist, his large ears scooping up great eddying waves.

It was tremendous fun and he zipped around the Hall to fetch his friends. Soon they were all chasing one another through the field, hiding in the mist and leaping out unexpectedly.

When the brilliant sun finally burned the fog away, the five friends took the long way round to their den, ambling along leisurely. Young Whortle laughed more than he had done for days, but when Samuel began telling the others about their unpleasant encounter with Jenkin, he sighed and wished to forget the whole thing.

Figgy and Hodge were angry on his behalf and wanted to find Jenkin straight away and demand an apology. Todkin, however, looked thoughtful and tapped his fingers together.

'I wonder what lay behind that, then?' he said. 'There's more to it than we know.'

'Well I'm with Sammy on this,' Figgy declared. 'Jenkin don't deserve to win the Games.'

'By the great Green's grizzly bits!' Hodge proclaimed in Isaac Nettle's voice. ''Twould seem a brain the size of a gnat's danglers runs in his family.'

'Explains why he always felt sorry for Twit,' Figgy added.

'We don't have time for any of that now,' Todkin interrupted, changing the subject. 'I've worked out a new timetable. There's a lot to squeeze in, to make up for yesterday. First off, Young Whortle does his exercises, then Hodge takes him for his run, then he spends a few hours with Sammy at the pole-vault. If the levels have gone down and it's safe, Figgy can teach him how to swim the minnow wiggle properly this afternoon and, if this sun keeps blazing, the raft will be dry in no time – we can paint her and practise on her all tomorrow . . .'

Suddenly his voice dwindled into nothing and he halted.

The others stumbled to a standstill and stared in front of them.

They had reached their den but, to their dismay,

there was no raft basking in the sunshine outside it – the *Silver Hare* had gone.

'It's been pinched!' Figgy cried. 'Who'd do such a scummy thing?'

Hodge ran behind the hut to check it hadn't somehow found its way back there overnight.

'Empty!' he wailed.

The fieldmice stared at one another unhappily.

'All that work,' Samuel groaned. "Tain't fair.'

'You don't think Jenkin did it, do you?' Hodge asked. 'Do you reckon he's that much of a loony?'

Young Whortle sat down on the warm grass, crushed and dejected. It was such an unkind thing to do and it made him feel sick, to think that anyone could be so spiteful.

As the others ranted and uttered cries of disbelief, Todkin came forward and inspected the ground for clues.

'That raft was far too heavy for a single mouse to lift,' he said. 'Jenkin couldn't have done it without help.'

'His horrible dad?' Figgy suggested.

Todkin rubbed his chin thoughtfully.

'Old Prickle-knickers might be misery on a stick,' he said. 'But this would go against his precious Green Laws. No – he wouldn't have done it. In fact I doubt if even Jenkin was involved. Look at those footprints, they're quite small and there's at least three different sets.'

'Who, then?' Hodge asked.

Todkin narrowed his eyes and ran through the possible suspects in his mind. It really didn't take very long and he could have kicked himself for not thinking of them straight away. In a trice he darted inside the hut.

'Come here!' he shouted to the rest.

The others followed him in.

Todkin's wonderful wolf drawings had been torn down and, in their place, on one of his own sheets of paper – was a notice written in a brash and spiky scrawl. It read:

We foxed the wolf killers!
Thanks for the raft, mouldy-brains.
D. I. L.

'Dimsel!' Young Whortle exclaimed.

'And Iris and Lily,' Todkin observed.

'The scabby dollops!' Hodge cried.

Figgy screwed up his face and ripped the notice into tiny scraps.

'Right!' he fumed, throwing the pieces on the floor and stamping on them. 'I'm not having my own sister scupper Neppy's chances. This is war!'

Furious and hungry for battle, they stormed from the den and marched through the meadow in single file.

Dimsel and her cronies were known to laze their days away somewhere by the Long Hedge at the southern border of the cornfield. The Wolf Killers never went there, they liked to keep as much distance from them as possible but now they were determined to seek them out and rescue the *Silver Hare*.

'What if they've chopped it to bits?' Young Whortle asked.

Todkin shook his head. 'They won't do that, they'll want it for their own try at the Raft Race.'

'They've probably painted it pink by now,' Hodge grumbled. 'And wrapped flowers round it as well.'

'This is Dimsel we're talking about,' Figgy reminded him. 'It won't be pink. Stuck all over with hedgehog spikes more like – with brambles and thistles for good measure.'

'My poor raft,' Young Whortle lamented.

The Long Hedge was laden with hawthorn blossom and looked like a high snowdrift. Insects buzzed in and out and the scent was rich and heavy. Beneath the hedge the grassy slopes were more crowded than the fieldmice expected. Everyone who was taking part in the Raft Race was putting the finishing touches to their handiwork.

Todkin regarded them critically but soon satisfied himself that they were all inferior to the *Silver Hare*.

The Burdock brothers had made two jaunty-looking vessels for themselves. Each was painted sky blue and flew bright red flags. The brothers were very pleased with their efforts but as a consequence of an earlier quarrel, they, too, were covered with splashes of paint.

Shrubby Raggit had built a very rickety contraption that would undoubtedly sink right away, if it ever made it to the ditch without falling apart. As the Wolf Killers strode by, he stood on the deck and the whole thing collapsed around him.

'Fourth time today,' he muttered in vexation.

'Never mind Shrubby!' a happy voice called out. 'I'll come and give you a helping paw, soon as I done finished mine.'

The cheery volunteer was Twit. He and his father were close to completing work on his entry and Todkin was astonished to see how good it was.

'Hullo, lads!' Twit greeted them with a hearty wave. 'Ain't she grand? Just wait till you sees her glide over the water.'

'What's she called?' Samuel asked.

Twit puffed out his little chest and gave the mast a loving pat.

'This 'ere's the *Scuttleboat*,' he announced proudly.

Hodge sniggered into his palm. 'Wouldn't the *Daft Raft* be a better name?' he chuckled.

'Oh no,' Twit replied with a puzzled expression. 'That wouldn't make no sense. It's cos we're called Scuttle, see.'

'Willum, lad,' his father said gently. 'They know that. Hodge is teasing you.'

Twit looked baffled, then broke into infectious giggles. It was a joyous sound, devoid of any ill-feeling.

'You rascals!' he laughed.

The Wolf Killers continued on their way and Elijah Scuttle gave his son an affectionate smile. He and his wife knew how special Twit was, even if nobody else did.

Young Whortle and the others passed several other craft in various stages of completion, but there was still no sign of Dimsel. The grassy bank was overgrown in places and clumps of cow parsley reared up like dense, snow-capped forests that had to be navigated around.

As the five friends approached another of these obstacles they heard a loud hammering coming from the far side of it.

'Could be Dimsel making alterations,' Figgy whispered.

'My design is perfect and don't need changing,' Todkin said.

'Let's creep up and see,' Young Whortle suggested. 'If it is her and her crew, we can surprise 'em.'

'I'll count to three,' Todkin said. 'And we'll rush them.'

'Watch out for her fists,' Figgy warned. 'She's got a punch on her that cracks conkers.'

'An' don't let her grab your wrists,' Samuel added. 'She can twist yer arm up round yer shoulders, fast as lightnin'. Don't half hurt, that do.'

'She bites sometimes too.'

'She's really horrible, your sister,' Hodge told Figgy.

'I know,' he said glumly.

The Wolf Killers steeled themselves and Young Whortle found himself wondering how he could charge recklessly into an army of evil Hobbers and yet be nervous and afraid of encountering one mouse maiden and her two friends.

'Wish I had my spear with me,' he murmured to himself.

'One . . .' Todkin whispered. 'Two . . . three.'

The five friends dashed around the cow parsley, then slithered to a stop.

The hammering ceased. But it was not Dimsel and her gang – it was Jenkin Nettle.

He was busily fixing a seat on to his own small raft and, when Young Whortle and the others came barging up, he straightened and slowly laid the hammer down.

For several moments they were all too surprised to say anything. Jenkin stared at each of them in turn.

Figgy, Samuel and Hodge glared at him with hostile looks of their own. Todkin studied him with curious interest and, feeling awkward, Young Whortle glanced at the ground.

'We, we thought you was Dimsel,' he muttered falteringly. 'She's gone and robbed my raft.'

Jenkin removed the three iron nails he held in his mouth and licked his lower lip. It was still swollen and bruised.

'Well I'm not,' he said. 'And this is my raft, as you can see.'

Samuel could not keep it bottled up any longer. 'Ain't you got nowt else to say?' he exploded.

'Yes,' Figgy joined in. 'How about sorry?'

'Weren't no call for what you said to Warty last night,' Sammy continued.

Jenkin turned away from them. 'I got a right to be left on my own,' he said coldly. 'I warned you but you wouldn't listen. You shouldn't go stickin' your whiskers where they're not welcome.'

'We was only trying to help,' Samuel retorted. 'We won't bother next time.'

'Yes!' Figgy agreed with a snap of his fingers. 'We've had enough of you. Your head could fall off and we wouldn't care.'

'Leave me alone then,' Jenkin said.

Hodge pulled a disgusted expression and, in his most witheringly accurate Isaac Nettle voice, said, 'Verily this witless dolt is not worthy of our holy nose pickings, much less our pious attention. Let us go and sing Green hymns to our belly button fluff.'

The effect the impression had on Jenkin was startling. His temper flared and he snatched up the hammer.

'Don't you dare make fun of my father!' he raged, lunging forward and wielding the hammer threateningly. 'Don't you dare!'

Hodge's eyes flashed back at him and he yelled out an insulting song he had composed the last time Isaac Nettle had lectured him.

> *'Who's the fella what makes the brasses*
> *And doles them out to lads an' lasses?*
> *Is he a smiler or is he a hero?*
> *Nah, it's Nettle – the sour-faced zero.'*

Jenkin's ears turned a fierce red and the hammer trembled in his fist.

'Take that back,' he demanded. 'He's better than the lot of you put together.'

Hodge was about to yell the next verse when Jenkin

punched him in the chest. At once Figgy and Samuel pounced and pushed him to the ground. Todkin took the hammer from the boy's paw and threw it out of reach.

'Stop it,' Young Whortle implored them. 'We shouldn't be fightin'. We was friends yesterday. Stop it.'

Jenkin thumped Figgy in the stomach, then he and Samuel rolled on the ground, kicking and wrangling.

'What's this then?' an amused voice called suddenly.

The fighting ceased and everyone looked down the bank – to where Alison Sedge had appeared from around the cow parsley.

The girl was fanning herself with a large hawthorn leaf and there was blossom in her hair.

'Mornin' boys,' she said, breathy and drawling. ' 'Tis so hot today I feels all floppy. My heart's a-beatin' so fast – I'm afeard it'll fly clean out of my chest. You put yer paw there, Hodge, and see if it ain't true.'

Frozen in their aggressive attitudes, Young Whortle and the others stared at her. Then they recovered. Samuel and Jenkin picked themselves up and Figgy staggered to his feet, rubbing his stomach ruefully.

A practised smile slipped on to Alison's face. 'Was you bad boys a-fightin'?' she asked with a laugh. 'Were it about me?'

'No, it weren't,' Jenkin told her curtly.

Alison shrugged.

'The Burdock brothers were feudin' over me afore,' she boasted. 'I was goin' to go fer a special walk with one but the silly babies are covered in paint now so I ain't going nowhere with neither.'

She directed her most effective glance at her audience and heaved a sigh. 'So I got no one to walk with me. Not unless one of you would be so gallant?'

For the first time since she had perfected her arts, not one of the boys leaped at the chance of being her escort and she touched her mousebrass to make sure it was still there.

'How about you, Todkin?' she asked. 'The still pool would be delicious an' cool right now and you could show me them newts you like so much.'

Todkin looked at his friends. None of them were in the mood for Alison's enchantments today.

'Maybe later,' he found himself saying. 'We got to go find Dimsel and rescue Young Whortle's raft.'

'You and your stupid games.' She smiled, showing how grand she was by not taking offence. 'I'll stop here and bother Jenkin instead.'

The Wolf Killers muttered their apologies and departed, exchanging resentful looks with Jenkin.

Isaac Nettle's son waited till they had disappeared from view, then relaxed and slumped on to the seat of his raft.

His lip was bleeding again and he licked it gingerly.

Alison watched him and her beautiful eyes were full of pity and compassion.

'Never was a mouse as clumsy as you,' she said gently and with meaning. 'My lovely, lost, fat-lipped Jolly Jenkin. Gormless you are too. You should never chase friends away – them's good lads, they are. Don't take your anger out on them, 'tain't fair.'

Jenkin put the nails back into his mouth and cast around for the hammer.

'You know nothing,' he told her.

'Happen I don't. And I won't tell no one what I don't know neither.'

Their eyes met. They understood each other far too well for any pretence.

'I dunno what to do,' he muttered in a broken whisper.

'Get away from this place, Jenkin,' she said. ' 'Tis the only way.'

He shook his head.

'I can't.'

Alison wanted to say that she would go with him, but she held back. The moment passed and she was to regret it for the rest of her life.

Sweeping her bunches over her shoulders, she returned to safer topics.

'What you callin' your raft? How 'bout you names her after me?'

Jenkin laughed in spite of himself.

'The *Saucy Smack*?' he suggested.

'The *Lovely Alison*.'

'Not likely – besides, my dad's picked the name already.'

Alison nodded slowly.

'Of course he has,' she said.

Young Whortle and the others spent the rest of the morning searching for Dimsel and her cronies but they were nowhere to be found. When everyone gathered in the Hall of Corn for lunch, those three were the only mice absent.

Figgy asked his mother if she had seen her but was reminded that Dimsel was a law unto herself and did as she pleased. Mr and Mrs Bottom had given up trying to tell her what to do a long time ago. No information could be gleaned from the Crowfoots or the Clover family either, so the Wolf Killers ate their meal in the lowest of spirits.

'Do we try and make another raft?' Samuel asked, in between great mouthfuls of cheese and herb pie.

'It'll never be as good as the *Silver Hare*,' Figgy reflected gloomily. 'But I reckons we'll have to.'

'And we'd have to take turns sleepin' in the den to guard it,' Hodge warned. 'Otherwise they'll pinch that raft as well.'

Todkin frowned. 'We need a new den too. That one's no good now Dimsel's gang know where it is. They'll be raiding us all the time and making a blessed nuisance of themselves.'

He consulted his timetable and scribbled some figures down. 'A whole morning wasted,' he said. 'And Young Whortle's done no training. He'll have to skip the run and spend a couple of hours with Sammy at the pole-vaulting. The rest of us will get more wood for another raft.'

And so, after lunch, Samuel and Young Whortle made their way to the oaks beyond the meadow and began.

The lesson went terribly. Young Whortle was worse than ever and failed to manage one proper jump.

Samuel tried his best to coach and advise him but even his patience was sorely tested that hot afternoon.

When Young Whortle lay gasping on his back for the umpteenth time and Sammy was searching for new ways to encourage him, they were suddenly disturbed by the sound of raucous guffaws coming from the tree above.

They looked up and there was Dimsel Bottom, lolling on a branch, helpless with laughter. Iris and

Lily were with her and they, too, were shrieking with cruel glee at Young Whortle's ludicrous attempts.

'Hey!' Samuel shouted at them. 'Where's our raft? What you done with it? Give it back!'

It was some time before the girls could answer without collapsing in fits of hoots and giggles again.

Eventually, Dimsel said, 'That rubbish raft is where you won't never find it.'

'You're s'posed to make your own for the race,' Sammy countered. 'We'll tell Woodruffe and you'll be disqualified.'

Dimsel gave a squeal of mock fear. 'Oooooh I be sooooo scared,' she jeered. 'You go do that and make yerself look even more dumb than you is. We got our own raft, see – made it ourselves and it's better'n your scrappy bonfire-in-waiting.'

'Tell us where ours is, right now!' Samuel yelled.

The girls just laughed all the more.

'Skellington Sammy's gettin' awful cross!' Lily squawked.

'Does your ribs clank together when you get angry, Sammy?' Iris asked.

'Shut up!' Young Whortle bawled. 'Why is you so mean?'

'Cos we are,' Dimsel answered tartly. 'We're wild and savage and scary. If you want to know where your precious raft is, why don't you come up here and make us tell you?'

'I'd like to see them try!' Iris laughed. 'Bony Sammy

191

and Titchy Neppy. Oh I'm wettin' meself already.'

'Why don't we go get them instead?' Lily suggested. 'We could bash them good and proper.'

Dimsel thought that was an excellent idea and started scrambling down the oak tree.

'I'm gonna play tunes on your ribs, Sammy!' she called. 'An twist Wet Nappy's arms so hard he'll think they're on backwards!'

'Get them!' Lily and Iris chanted, climbing after her.

Samuel and Young Whortle could only turn tail and run. Dimsel was perfectly capable of making good her threats and they fled into the meadow as fast as they could go.

'Wolf Killers?' Dimsel bellowed. 'You sorry lot couldn't fight a dandelion!'

Jumping to the ground, she held her aching sides and laughed some more.

'Let's chase 'em,' her friends urged.

But Dimsel shook her head. She enjoyed terrorising her brother's friends but didn't really want to run after them, especially on such a blazing afternoon.

'Let's go and finish making our own secret den comfy,' she said. 'Those dozy boys will never find it.'

And they ran off through the trees, revelling in the glorious carefree day and thinking of the fun they would have in those still to come.

Figgy and Hodge were hard at work sawing branches by the ditch when Young Whortle and Samuel came running up. As usual, Todkin was supervising.

'You decided on a run anyway,' said Hodge brightly. 'That's good.'

Samuel and Young Whortle had to wait to get their breaths back before they could answer.

'Dimsel were after us,' Young Whortle panted. 'She won't say where our raft is.'

'Needs to be taught a good lesson, she does,' Figgy scowled.

'But who'd be brave enough to try?' Todkin asked.

'Not me,' confessed Hodge. 'And none of you is, neither.'

Resigned to the fact they would never see the *Silver Hare* again, they continued collecting enough wood for another.

The flowing waters of the ditch had returned to their normal level so Young Whortle spent the remainder of the afternoon with Figgy, trying to learn the minnow wiggle.

And the day slid slowly into evening.

Much later, after their shift on sentry duty, a secret, emergency meeting of the Wolf Killers convened in the den.

Todkin had painted his most ferocious-looking wolf monster yet and had written 'Keep out' in red letters between its claws. He was fixing this new sign above the entrance when the others arrived.

'That won't stop my sister,' Figgy said flatly.

Within the hut a small candle was flickering. Todkin

followed Figgy inside and stood before his friends. Three grave and sombre faces looked back at him. Young Whortle was not amongst them. He had not been invited and knew nothing about this meeting.

Todkin remained standing and put his paws behind his back as he got straight to business.

'We all know why we're here,' he said, in his most grown-up and no-nonsense tone of voice. 'Operation Champion – it started out as a bit of a lark and to help our Young Whortle, but things have changed. We got enemies now, an' it could turn ugly.'

'Already is ugly,' Hodge put in. 'Specially Dimsel.'

Figgy agreed. 'With her against us,' he said, 'and determined to ruin Neppy's chances, it can only get worse. Then there's Jenkin. No telling what he'll do next.'

'But we made a promise to Warty we'd help him win,' Samuel interrupted. 'We can't give up now.'

'How was Young Whortle at the pole-vault today?' Todkin asked.

Sammy shuffled his feet and stared at the candle flame. 'None too good,' he admitted.

'Be honest, he was downright dreadful, wasn't he?'

'Worse even than that,' Sammy said, feeling horribly disloyal.

Todkin turned to Figgy.

'And how were his swimming?'

Figgy held his nose in answer.

'There you are then,' Todkin announced. 'Let's face

it, our little friend stinks at most of the events. He don't have a hope of winning and being Head Sentry. He's going to make a complete idiot of himself.'

The others agreed.

'It'll break his heart,' Samuel said. 'He wants to win so much, it means everything to him.'

A mysterious and crafty smile appeared on Todkin's face. 'Then it's up to us to ensure that he does,' he told them.

The three fieldmice looked at him blankly.

'What do you mean?' Hodge asked. 'We can't do any more than we already have and that got us nowhere. He's just downright useless.'

Todkin's eyebrows twitched upward.

'That's because we were playing by the rules,' he said darkly. 'That is about to change. I propose we commence – Operation Foul.'

'Ooh,' said Figgy and Hodge together.

'What's that, then?' Samuel asked.

Todkin peered outside in case anyone was spying on them, then said, in a conspiratorial whisper, 'Operation Foul is every low, sneaky, dirty, cheating trick we can think of. From now on we stop at nothing to make sure Young Whortle wins through.'

'I likes the sound of that,' Figgy said, nodding.

'The Almighty Green helps those who nobble the competition,' Hodge chuckled.

Samuel shook his head.

'Warty'll never agree,' he objected.

The others rolled their eyes in exasperation.

'That's why he's not here!' Todkin groaned. 'He's not supposed to know. He'll think he's won on his own and only us four will know different.'

'Ahh . . . Oh, but isn't that lying to him? I doesn't want to do that.'

'You'll live with it.'

'Think how upset Neppy'll be when he loses if we don't,' Figgy told him.

Samuel tried to imagine his best friend finishing last in the Games.

'All right,' he relented. 'Operation Foul it is.'

'That's settled then!' Todkin said, grinning. 'There's no doubt about it no more, Young Whortle's going to win – we're going to make sure of it.'

Taking hold of his mousebrass with one paw and reaching out with the other, he instructed the others to do the same. They obeyed and took hold of his free paw with their own. Only the gravest of oaths were ever sworn this way. The candle flame fluttered and their shadows danced high and black around them.

'Repeat after me,' Todkin began. 'We, The Wolf Killers, do solemnly swear, with the Great Green Mouse Himself as our witness, to be the baddest mice our field has ever known. Whoever gets in our way will be shown no mercy. We vow that no underhand trick will be too mean and no lie too wicked. Let our hearts be like stones, let our minds be filled with a single purpose – for our dear friend Young Whortle's sake

and, if we fail, then . . . may we all be cursed and
doomed.'

'Steady on!' spluttered Samuel.

'It's all or nothing,' Todkin told him sternly. 'Too
late to turn back now.'

So Samuel repeated the terrible words.

'Amen to that,' said Hodge.

'Here's to cheating!' Figgy cheered, and the dreadful
pact was made.

A gust of wind blew into the hut. The candle flame
jittered and was extinguished and they were plunged
into darkness.

12

The Most Welcoming friends

Even as Operation Foul was being planned and discussed, Young Whortle was making his nightly journey towards the pond. The moon was bright once more and he hoped the pool had receded from the boulders so that he could visit the water voles.

As he passed through the trees, he went as quietly as he could in case Jenkin was about. He did not want to meet him here again. But the area around the still pool was silent and deserted.

Why had everything changed in his field? Everyone was suddenly so unpleasant and unfriendly. There had never been anything like that fight this afternoon and it troubled the small fieldmouse greatly. What he really needed right now, most of all, was a good long talk with Woppenfrake and his brothers.

The ground grew soft beneath his feet and water seeped up between his toes. The pond was still flooded and brimming and the entrance to the Grelffit Houm was an unreachable island.

Greatly disappointed, Young Whortle was about to turn away when a familiar voice called out.

'Master Nep, stay!'

The fieldmouse stared at the shadow-wrapped

boulders. A shape was moving in front of them, a large bulky shape.

There was the faintest of splashes and the mirrored moonlight wobbled on the water as a water vole came slicing through the pond. Within moments he had reached the shore and rose from the shallows, the silver band around his forehead glinting and gleaming.

It was Woppenfrake and he smiled at Young Whortle as he bowed in greeting.

'It has been many years since the Glinty Water was so greatly increased,' he said. 'Is it not a singular sight, to inspire and inflate the heart?'

'Certainly big enough,' the fieldmouse answered. 'Everyone was afeared it'd break out and flood our field.'

Woppenfrake chortled. 'There was no cause for alarm,' he said. 'Although it has leaked down into the Greffit Houm and spoiled some of Firgild's painting. Even now he and Willibald are busy with buckets and mops but my duties lie with the Glinty Water. It must be at its greatest and look its best. The rain was summoned for just this purpose.'

'You made it rain?' Young Whortle asked in amazement.

'With the aid of my brothers.'

'Why, what's going to happen?'

The water vole's eyes glittered at him. 'Four nights hence,' he said. 'When the moon is fully round and ringed by fire, come here and you will see for yourself.'

'That I will.'

Woppenfrake's eyes continued to gleam and shine at him. 'But you are troubled,' he said. 'What clouds can dim such a merry fellow's spirits?'

Young Whortle hung his head and explained what was happening. He told Woppenfrake of Jenkin, the Games and his own silly hopes, of the stolen raft and how hard his best friends had worked in trying to help him. It took some time to tell everything and they wandered as he talked until at last they stopped by the very branch Jenkin had been sitting on the previous night.

'And the worst of it is,' the fieldmouse concluded, 'I'm afeared their efforts have been for nowt. I'm only good at the Tail Hang and climbing. What if I don't win? I'll have let 'em down.'

'They sound like good friends to have,' Woppenfrake said.

'The best.' Young Whortle nodded heartily. 'Real lucky I am – wish I could do somethin' special to thank 'em.'

Woppenfrake regarded him strangely for a moment. A secretive, amused light flickered briefly in his eyes. Then he said, 'And you say one of your friends has tried to teach you how to swim the . . . what did you call it?'

'Minnow wiggle.'

The water vole laughed out loud. 'You rimpi-toos are such absurd fellows. You have never understood the ways of the water.'

He looked out across the pond and clapped his paws together as a sudden idea gripped him.

'But of course,' he declared. 'Why did I not think on it before? Consider this, Master Nep, if you wished to fly, would you ask your friends, worthy though they are, to help you? No, you would seek the advice of a creature of the air, so why do you not do the same in this matter?'

Young Whortle was not sure he understood what he meant. 'There ain't no fish in the ditch,' he said. 'And I don't know fish-chat anyway.'

Woppenfrake stepped down the bank into the water and held out his paw.

'This way,' he said. 'Come, swim in the Glinty Water with one who has revelled in this blessed place for longer than most of the trees it gives life to.'

Then Young Whortle realised how greatly he was being honoured. Thrilled and excited, he took hold of Woppenfrake's paw and paddled into the pond.

After such a hot day, the water was cool but not cold. He eased himself deeper until it was up to his neck.

'Now,' Woppenfrake said, sliding backwards and floating as easily as a cork. 'Show me this wiggling of the minnows.'

Young Whortle took a breath then launched himself forward. There was a great splash for one so small and he thrashed his feet and flailed his arms.

At once Woppenfrake burst out laughing and begged him to stop.

'What are you doing?' he asked. 'Do you think the pond is a monster, to be attacked and battered so?'

Young Whortle shook his waterlogged ears.

'How do you mean?' he asked.

Remaining on his back, with his paws behind his head, Woppenfrake drifted gracefully around him, making only the slightest of flicking movements with his feet.

'Like all land dwellers, you have a terror of the water,' he said. 'You must remove that fear from your heart or you will not succeed, and that would be a tragedy.'

'I does get scared when I can't touch the bottom,' the fieldmouse confessed.

'But why? There is so much more to explore in the deeps and the upper world is not going to disappear while you are not in it.'

'Cos I doesn't want to drown!'

Woppenfrake tutted and meandered in circular patterns out across the pond.

'And yet you think naught of climbing an immense oak. Any fall from such a height would undoubtedly shatter your bones, yet that does not prevent you.'

Young Whortle had not considered that before.

'I never think about falling,' he said. 'I just likes clambering to the top.'

'Then bring no dread hither. Rejoice in this element. Respect it and it will reward you with such sights and gifts as can be found nowhere else.'

'Let me have another go,' Young Whortle said,

preparing to crash forward once more.

Woppenfrake stopped him.

'Before travelling through the Glinty Water, you must first be at peace with it. Lift your feet off the ground and surrender. Learn to trust. The water will love you back and carry you wherever you wish.'

The fieldmouse tried to do as he was bid but he panicked and whisked his arms wildly as he sank below the surface.

Woppenfrake sailed over, stood up and placed his paws behind Young Whortle.

'Fall back slowly and I will catch you,' he said. 'Have faith in the water's embrace.'

Young Whortle obeyed. He felt the strong paws supporting him and saw the stars twinkling high above. The water was all around and underneath. A delighted smile spread over his face: he felt wonderfully safe and secure.

'The water is a realm in itself,' Woppenfrake's soothing voice said. 'There are more creatures here than in your field, some so small you cannot see them, but they are there. You are never alone here: there are the nymphs of the damselfly, the water boatmen beetles whose rowing skill you could learn from, for your raft race, and pond skaters and water striders. The early dragonflies are already emerging and, in high summer, the air is filled with them, hanging in the heat like jewels. There is nothing still about the Still Pool, Master Nep – it teems and boils with life and, from it, all life springs.'

'Yes,' Young Whortle breathed. 'I ain't never felt so unfeared in it afore.'

'It is the most welcoming of friends,' Woppenfrake murmured. 'Whenever you feel alone and in need of comfort, it will embrace you. It is always here, waiting to greet and calm you and, in its caress, troubles can be washed away.'

Young Whortle dabbled his paws at his sides and gently moved his legs. The moon and stars turned in the heavens and he closed his eyes dreamily.

'Just like flyin'.' He sighed. 'Being lighter than thistledown and gustin' where the breeze blows me. I could float right over our field and beyond, out into the big world – maybe even to the town where Mrs Scuttle came from.'

'That's right,' Woppenfrake said warmly. 'Give yourself up to the water, no harm shall come to you. When you feel your burdens are too great to bear, come to the pool and it will receive them. It can hold more grief than either you or I.'

The fieldmouse was so perfectly contented and relaxed that he thought he must be falling asleep, for Woppenfrake's voice seemed to be drifting away.

''Tis simple with you holdin' me up,' he replied.

'Dunno if I could do it on me own.'

The water vole chuckled with delight. 'But you are, little rimpi-too, you are.'

Young Whortle opened his eyes and raised his head. Without realising, he had floated away from Woppenfrake and was now almost in the centre of the pond.

A momentary panic seized him but the sound of the water vole's laughter dispelled it immediately and he, too, began laughing.

There really was nothing to be afraid of, it was the easiest thing in the world. He experimented with different ways of wiggling his feet while slowly moving his legs.

Across and around the still pool he propelled himself, rolling over in the water and fearlessly letting it close around him.

Woppenfrake swam across to join him.

'Now, forget everything your friend tried to teach you,' he said. 'There is no single right method of journeying through the water. Think of the many inhabitants who make this their home; from wriggling tadpoles to the assured kicks of their parents, each travels their own best way and you must do the same.'

As if on cue, at that very instant a frog scudded past them. One of its bulging eyes winked at Young Whortle, then it dived down and vanished.

'Not elegant swimmers,' Woppenfrake conceded, 'but their technique serves them well. If only they were better guardians of their children.'

Young Whortle tried to emulate the way the frog had kicked its legs. He scooted forward in fits and starts, much to the water vole's merriment.

Reclining on his side as he glided along, Woppenfrake gestured with his fingers and muttered some words.

Suddenly the pond contained a new visitor as a small, ginger and gold frog, with bright amber eyes and a mousebrass around its squat neck, croaked with delight in Young Whortle's voice. Then, taking a deep breath, it plunged down to explore.

Soft silver moonbeams filtered from the world above, making everything appear ghostly and strange.

The pond was incredibly deep. The gentle banks sloped onto rocky shelves where forests of weed stirred as he swam by. Beyond them the rocks dipped sharply and the centre of the still pool was a steep shaft that no light ever reached. He wondered how far down it stretched but did not dare try and find out; besides, he was simply enjoying being part of this watery kingdom and, with a powerful thrust of his legs, he shot back to the surface.

His familiar mouse face broke into the air and Woppenfrake welcomed him back.

'The heart of the Glinty Water is no place for you to try and reach,' he warned. 'That is the home of the spirit of this ancient shrine.'

'I'd dearly love to meet him,' Young Whortle cried.

'Not this night,' Woppenfrake told him. 'But maybe – before the end.'

The moon inched across the sky.

Young Whortle's joyous exploration continued and Woppenfrake whispered more strange words.

The fieldmouse felt his body stretch and his arms shrivel into fins as his neck grew wider and his large ears disappeared.

'What am I?' he cried, with new fish-like lips. 'I feel like a snake.'

Woppenfrake chortled. 'You are an elver.'

'What's one of those?'

'A young eel, my friend.'

Young Whortle let out a shriek. Not having any shoulders, his mousebrass had slid down his serpentine shape and when his legs finally dwindled into nothing, the anti-owl charm slipped from him and sank into the deeps.

'My brass!' he yelped.

'You had best fetch it,' The water vole told him. 'Before it falls too far.'

The elver wriggled its slithery body in a confused coiling tangle, before pointing its head downwards and, with a flick of its tail, sped after the mousebrass.

Spinning slowly as it fell, the amulet glinted coldly until it passed beyond the reach of the moonlight.

Young Whortle saw it fade into the surrounding dark and, putting all his strength into the chase, whipped his new shape into blurring zigzags.

Woppenfrake was humming an old stoat ballad to himself when the elver reappeared with the mousebrass in its mouth.

'Well done,' he said. 'Now let me guard that for you, a fish has no use for such an ornament.'

'I thought I was an elver,' Young Whortle said as soon as the water vole had taken the mousebrass from him.

He lashed his long body, only to discover it had shrunk beneath him again and he was now a gleaming, copper-coloured fish with stripes of black and gold down his sides and a lustrous white belly.

'You are a minnow,' Woppenfrake told him. 'And a fine one at that.'

Young Whortle gave a shout of joy then raced off through the pond, darting through the weeds and zooming around the water vole. It wasn't a bit like Figgy's style of swimming and now he understood why Woppenfrake had laughed.

After a while, Woppenfrake trailed his fingers beneath the surface and stirred them around to call him back.

When Young Whortle returned, he tickled him under the chin and at once, the minnow sprouted arms and legs.

'What now?' he asked.

'Certain learned scholars would name you *trituris vulgaris*,' Woppenfrake answered.

'What's that?'

'Just a smooth newt.'

'Ha – wait till I tells Todkin!'

Laughing, Young Whortle sped off and the water vole resumed humming the ballad.

When the newt next appeared, it was with a burst of bubbles and Young Whortle could feel himself changing once more.

'What am I?' he cried eagerly.

Woppenfrake smiled.

'You are a *micromys minutus*,' he said.

'No kidding?' Young Whortle cried excitedly. 'What's one of them?'

'A fieldmouse, well, strictly speaking, a harvest mouse. In short – you are yourself.'

Young Whortle looked at his paws, then felt his large ears twang back into place. He was himself once more.

'Now,' Woppenfrake told him. 'Use all you have learned and invent your own method, suited to your strengths and skills.'

The fieldmouse nodded and quickly found that he could swim far better than Figgy. It was so much easier swimming in his true form, and he knew that from now on, he would spend as much time as possible in the ditch and the still pool.

Eventually, the water vole made his way to the shore and waited as a trail of Nep breath came popping towards him.

With a shout and a happy gasp, Young Whortle erupted from the pond and ran splashing to the bank. It was time to return to the Hall of Corn. He had spent so long in the water, his paws were wrinkled but his eyes were afire and his hopes aflame.

'There's no one in our field what can beat me now,' he declared. 'I'm goin' to win that race, faster'n any mouse ever did afore! Thank 'ee Woppenfrake – oh thank 'ee.'

'Remember always,' the water vole said as he replaced the mousebrass around the fieldmouse's neck. 'Travel your own best way, in all things, Master Nep.'

Young Whortle hugged him and promised to return tomorrow night to see Firgil and Willibald.

'And can I bring my friends too?' he asked. 'Sammy be dead keen to meet you.'

Wappenfrake was already wading back into the water.

'No, Master Nep,' he said. 'You alone were intrepid enough to discover my brothers and myself that first night, so you alone are welcome in the Grelffit Houm. That is the way it must be.'

The water vole swam off towards the island of boulders, where the entrance to the tunnels lay.

Watching him, Young Whortle suddenly felt very sad. He had wanted his friends to share these magical experiences with him. He felt guilty that they were not allowed to take part.

Woppenfrake must have guessed what he was thinking, for his voice called out, 'Do not grieve, my dear little rimpi-too. Your merry band of wolf killers shall not hunger for adventure. My brothers and I will furnish them with a special one, the like of which they shall never forget.'

Young Whortle grinned and he ran from the pond, skipping along the track towards the field. He wondered what Woppenfrake had meant and when it would happen.

He did not expect it to take place the very next day.

13

The Five Heroes

Another lovely day dawned.

Dimsel Bottom stretched her strong sinewy arms and leaped from her nest. Figgy's sister was not a beauty but she was certainly striking and, once encountered, never forgotten.

She was a solidly built mouse maiden with dark brown hair, brushed over a forehead that projected a little too far. Beneath that over-generous brow her eyes were small but quick and alert, which caused even her most good-natured smile to appear fierce. Sometimes even Isaac Nettle trod gingerly around her.

The usual life of a girl mouse was not for her. She had never been interested in what was normally expected of a daughter of Fennywolde and laughed at Alison Sedge, even though Alison was one of the few fieldmice who was not afraid of Dimsel. There existed an uneasy truce between them. Mistress Bottom might possess the brawn but Alison had subtler and more effective weapons – with no scruples about using them.

In the main though, whatever course Dimsel wanted to steer, she was sure to pursue it. Although she found it amusing to frighten and threaten her brother and his friends, and anyone else who took her fancy, such pleasures were merely fleeting diversions. She only took part in those daily events that truly interested her, shrugging off those she believed would waste her valuable time.

As she strode through the field and then the meadow, her thoughts were filled with the Fennywolde Games.

She had never really taken much notice of them before. The notion of being Head Sentry had always left her cold. It was a silliness reserved for boys but, after teasing Young Whortle Nep about it, the idea had grown on her.

Not once in the history of Fennywolde had a girl won the Games, or even taken part. Dimsel had never needed to prove she was equal to the boys: she had always known herself to be superior. If she were to win the title though, that really would be something. Everyone would know how excellent she was – not even simpering, scheming Alison could deny that. Besides, Dimsel would love to see Alison's face when she stole the glory right from under Jenkin Nettle's nose.

There was no other serious contender to threaten her ambition. The Burdock brothers really only competed against one another and could be counted on to squabble at some point and ruin their own chances. Young Whortle's atrocious attempts at pole-vaulting had proved there was nothing to fear from that quarter, and she almost regretted expending the energy it had taken to steal his raft. There were a few others whom she would have to keep a cautious eye on, but she was extremely confident. She was certain to win. As for Twit, she didn't give him any consideration at all – no one ever did.

Dimsel's two friends, Iris and Lily, were full of admiration for her and would help in any way they could. United, they made a formidable trio.

With her arms folded across her chest, Dimsel strode through the wild grasses of the meadow, chuckling to herself.

Dew was still sparkling underfoot; hanging in trembling sunbursts from languid shoots, it freckled slowly unfurling flowers with brilliance.

A mob of birds was making a confused and rowdy din in the sky and she gazed up, curiously. Something had alarmed them. They were swooping around in great circles, crying and squawking, calling out 'Danger!' and 'Flee!'

Dimsel glowered at them. She had no time for birds. They were silly creatures who only thought of food during the day and the best roosts in the evening. The slightest thing frightened them. Perhaps they had just spied her grandmother wearing the new sun hat she had made for herself yesterday.

'Now that be summat to be scared of,' she cackled.

The birds continued to cry and shriek and then she heard another sound.

Dimsel stopped and turned her head.

It was a noise she had never heard before. And the very strangeness of it caused her to look over her shoulder and peer through the grass and wild flowers to listen.

Something was snuffling along the ground, something far larger than any beast she had ever seen. Then, in the distance she saw a great, dark, four-legged shape prowling through the meadow. Its sharp shoulders cleared the tallest grasses and a great hairy tail swung left and right like a massive rudder.

Dimsel could not begin to guess what sort of monster it was, but she could imagine its slavering jaws and pictured a long, lolling tongue dragging along the grass.

Figgy's sister shuddered with relish and wondered where the creature was going and where it had come from. Did she dare to creep closer for a better view?

That test of her courage never came, for the huge hideous shape was already drawing closer. It was obviously following a scent, slavishly and ravenously tracking some poor wretch . . .

The girl's heart leaped to her throat as she realised – it was tracking her.

Dimsel opened her mouth to yell, but a cold wave of fear paralysed her and for vital moments, she was rooted to the spot. The great beast stalked ever nearer. Then, as the terror mounted within her and seemed to be whistling from her ears, she gave one desperate cry and spun around – running for her life.

Behind her she heard a deep, gargling snarl, followed by a ferocious, baying howl as the horror raised its enormous head and gave chase, snapping and biting the air.

Young Whortle and the others met outside their den and inspected the branches that had been collected the previous day.

'Take till nightfall to put this together,' Samuel observed. 'Maybe longer, and then we got to paint it.'

Figgy threw Todkin a secret glance that reminded him they had other things to do now they had sworn their oath.

Todkin shrugged. Building the raft was just as important. There was no way around it.

'I done my exercises already,' Young Whortle chirped. 'So I'm set for me run now. You ready, Hodge?'

Hodge did not seem very enthusiastic.

'You don't need me to set a pace no more,' he said. 'I'd be more use here. You go run round on your own.'

'Oh,' Young Whortle replied, his grin fading a little. 'Whatever you think best.'

His friends had been unusually quiet that morning, but he could not fathom why. It was as if they were hiding something from him. The small fieldmouse shook his head and rebuked himself. It was he who had something to hide. He had resolved not to tell them of his new-found prowess in the water. What a surprise they would get during the Ditch Swim. When Figgy tried to teach him the minnow wiggle again later that day, he had determined he would pretend to be even worse than usual. The thought made him snicker, but none of the others noticed.

With a wave, he set off on his run around the meadow.

When he was out of earshot, Todkin addressed the rest.

'Before we start work, I want to take down any ideas you've had for Operation Foul.'

He hurried to the hut to fetch his notepad but halted before the entrance.

'Curse your rotten sister!' he exclaimed to Figgy.

'What's she done now?' the others asked in unison.

Todkin pulled the new sign from above the entrance and held it out before him.

His wonderful, terrifying picture of a wolf had been carefully cut from the paper and only the words 'Keep Out' remained between the ragged holes where the claws had been.

'What she do that fer?' Figgy cried.

'It's a war of nerves,' Todkin said. 'She's tellin' us she can do whatever she likes, whenever she likes. Straight after the Games we got to find us a brand new den.'

'Your lovely painting,' Sammy lamented.

Todkin nodded. It had been one of his best.

Tearing the sign in two, he threw away the pieces and plodded dismally into the hut, only to come dashing out again – an amazed look on his face.

'Come and see!' he squeaked. 'Look in here! I doesn't believe it. Where'd they come from?'

The others followed him inside and let out cries of astonishment.

Five weapons were thrust in the ground, arranged in a row.

Figgy cooed in wonder. There were three beautiful swords with gleaming blades and jewelled pommels, a spear and a pikestaff adorned with a silver tassel.

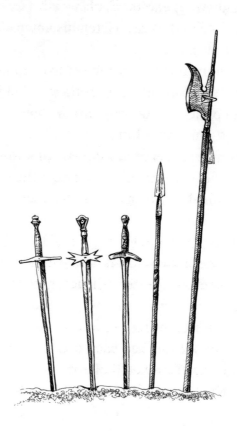

'Is they real?' Samuel asked, doubting his eyes.

Todkin reached out a wary finger and touched one of the bright blades.

'Real as you or me,' he breathed. 'An' sharp too.'

'How'd they get here?' Hodge asked. 'Where'd they come from?'

A broad grin split Sammy's face. 'It's Warty's mysterious voles,' he said. 'They put 'em here.'

'Don't be ridiculous,' Todkin scoffed. 'Them's just in his dreamy head.'

'How do you explain it, then?' the skinny mouse replied. 'Look at these things, they're ancient and special – anyone can tell that.'

'He's right,' agreed Hodge. 'They're more beautiful than anything Old Nettle ever made in his forge.'

Figgy took hold of a sword hilt and pulled the weapon from the soil. It was perfectly balanced and he took it outside to swipe it through the air.

Todkin and Hodge did the same, leaving Sammy with the pikestaff and spear. He took up both of them and left the den.

'What do you think they're for?' he asked.

Figgy and Hodge were already having a play fight and clanging the blades together – much to Todkin's annoyance.

'These aren't toys you know!' he said crossly. 'They're for killing and maiming. If you chop your arms off by accident you'll be sorry.'

Suddenly frantic shouts cut through the air and

Figgy and Hodge dropped their swords as if they were to blame.

To their surprise they saw Young Whortle pelting back along the path, his face stark with fear and with him, running for all she was worth, was Iris Crowfoot.

'Figgy!' he yelled. ' 'Tis Dimsel – oh my! What do we do?'

His friends stared at him, bewildered. Then they stared at Iris.

The girl was shaking and kept looking behind her. Her eyes were wide with horror.

'What's happened?' Figgy cried.

Young Whortle gulped his breaths down and jabbed a finger back along the path.

'I . . . I hadn't gone far when Iris come crashin' towards me, more frighted than anyone I ever did see in my life. She says there be summat up with your Dimsel, but I can't work out what.'

Iris would have sprung away and continued running if Hodge had not caught hold of her. She looked hunted and was anxious to escape.

'Leave me be,' she pleaded. 'Let me go. I got to warn everyone, oh it were awful – poor Dimsel.'

Figgy grabbed her by the shoulders. 'What do you mean 'poor Dimsel'?'

Iris began sobbing and tears flowed down her cheeks.

'The monster!' she cried. 'The monster's got her!'

The boys glanced at one another.

'What monster?' Todkin asked sternly. 'You're talking rubbish. There ain't no monsters.'

'But there is!' she squealed back. 'I were making my way to the new den we'd found when I saw it. Scrabbling at the soil and makin' them 'orrible noises. Its eyes were terrible, the worst things ever and there's poor Dimsel stuck down there an' it's tryin' to dig her out and eat her up.'

Iris was so genuinely terrified that they could not fail to believe it.

'Dimsel,' Figgy said quickly. 'I got to go and save her.'

He snatched up his sword again, then dashed off down the path.

'Hey!' bawled Hodge, running after him with his own sword in his paw.

Young Whortle blinked at the flashing blades. 'Where'd they come from?' he asked.

Then he saw the spear in Samuel's grasp and recognised it immediately.

'That's what I fought the Hobbers with,' he exclaimed.

'Then take it,' Sammy said, pushing it into his fist. 'Let's go and help Dimsel.'

They hurried away, leaving Todkin with Iris.

Todkin was impatient to follow them and he took hold of her trembling paw. 'You've got to show us where Dimsel is,' he said.

'Don't make me go back there!' she begged. 'You

ain't seen it – an' I doesn't want to see it again. Let me go and get help.'

'No time for that,' Todkin told her sharply. 'You're the only one knows where your den is. You have to come.'

Iris tore her paw from his grasp and backed away. 'Oh you'll find it all right,' she wept. 'An' that thing will find you!'

It was useless trying to argue with her, so Todkin ran after his friends as fast as he could, holding his bright sword before him.

Dimsel Bottom cowered on the floor of her den.

It was an old abandoned burrow dug by some small creature a long time ago. Situated directly beneath one of the great oaks beyond the meadow, it was a splendid discovery. No one would ever think of looking under those giant roots and she, Lily and Iris had spent the past few days, sweeping out the debris that had accumulated inside and making it even more comfortable and suited to their needs.

Nobody had a den like this – it was perfect. So, when the monster had pursued her that morning, her one hope was to reach this sanctuary.

She had only just managed to fling herself into the hole at the foot of the oak tree.

The beast's hot, putrid breath was blasting across her neck and, as she slithered into the burrow, she heard powerful jaws clashing together and felt several strands of her hair wrenched from her scalp.

Now sprawled on the ground, Dimsel was exhausted and quaking, but she was not safe yet.

At once a huge snout thrust its way into the hole and the mouse maiden jumped back to avoid its frenzied questing.

The den was not large, but she could stand against the furthest earthen wall without fear of being caught, or so she believed.

Recovering slightly, she watched the ugly snout push and squeeze against the entrance, snapping and biting the soil.

'Eat dirt!' Dimsel yelled, feeling very much braver. 'You'll not be devouring me today.'

The snout shoved down one last time. The dribbling, mottled lips slid back and rows of cruel, yellow fangs were instantly revealed.

A blast of evil breath filled the burrow and Dimsel covered her mouth as she coughed and gagged.

'You filthy beggar!' she cried and, picking up the besom that Lily had used to clean the den, went on the offensive.

With a defiant roar she charged and lashed out, ramming the broom straight up one of the huge glistening nostrils.

There was a yelp of pain, followed by a rumbling growl of fury and the snout was quickly withdrawn.

'Don't mess with the Dimster,' Dimsel declared, with a rude gesture and a wicked grin.

But she had maddened the monster beyond reason and suddenly its immense claws came scrabbling at the entrance, gouging out the earth in great clumps.

Dimself threw the besom away. 'Not clever,' she berated herself.

Soil and dirt choked the air and the entrance was ripped apart, growing ever larger.

The savage claws raked more of the ground away. Then the snout drove inward, plunging deeper into the den than before. Almost all of the vicious muzzle twisted and pushed its way in and Dimsel saw a glimpse of two large eyes glaring down at her. They were filled with anger and malice and she knew her time was up.

It was then that Iris had come strolling from the meadow.

Even in the burrow, Dimsel heard her friend scream. The monster's jaws instantly pulled back and daylight flooded the den as the creature whirled around to see who had shrieked so shrilly.

Outside, Iris had taken one look at the horror, then run back into the meadow. A chilling growl vibrated on the air as the fiend bared its fangs. Should it pursue her? Should it lope after her and hunt the squealing victim down?

'Run, Iris!' Dimsel bawled. 'Save yourself!'

Stifling her own terror for her friend's sake, she crept forward and peered up through the torn earth.

'Hey!' she shouted. 'You come back here and finish

what you started. You bog-breathed dung guts!'

A deep shadow fell across the demolished entrance and Dimsel hurled herself back just in time, as the beast came in for another attack. Why pursue that other prey when this one was caught already?

Dimsel pressed herself against the wall and the brutal, champing jaws came reaching for her.

The vile stench flooded her senses. The soil-clogged snout gaped open and a thick, drizzling, red tongue unrolled, to smear itself across her.

Dimsel turned her face away. She hoped that Iris had managed to find safety.

The slobbering maw moved in for the kill.

Young Whortle and the others reached the oaks but could not believe what they saw.

At the base of a great tree, with its head buried in the ground, was an enormous four-legged beast. It was covered in spiky, black and grey fur and, beneath that coarse coat were taut, powerful muscles.

'Look at them claws,' Hodge gasped. 'They're massive.'

'And lethal lookin',' added Samuel.

A blizzard of soil was blowing around the hidden face as the nightmare gouged and tore at the earth.

'Dimsel must be down there,' Figgy said. 'What if we're too late?'

Young Whortle lifted the spear to his shoulder. 'No we ain't,' he said. 'We're in the nick o' time. But we got to lure that brute away from there right now.'

Before anyone could stop him, the small fieldmouse charged forward. He remembered the stirring speech Captain Fenny had given the woodlanders before they attacked the evil worshippers of Hobb and, in honour of that heroic warrior, called his name like a war cry.

'What's he doing?' his startled friends spluttered. 'Come back!'

'Fenny!' Young Whortle yelled, running fearlessly up to the hind legs of the massive beast. Using both paws, he jabbed the point of his spear deep into the tough, hairy flesh.

The terror yowled and staggered sideways – fetching its head from the ravaged ground and swinging it about, to glower at the assailant.

At the edge of the meadow, the others gazed at the monster's awful head and cried out in shock

'I . . . I . . . it can't be,' Todkin muttered.

'It's what you painted.' Hodge gawked in disbelief. 'Come to life.'

'A wolf,' Figgy murmured. 'A real, live wolf.'

The hideous creature was an exact manifestation of the fanciful, and wildly inaccurate, animal that Todkin had drawn on the sign. But this was real – a snarling, vicious, baleful and breathing creation.

Its face was far more feral and pitiless than any genuine wolf. The jaws were monstrously wide and crammed with razor sharp, jagged teeth and fangs. Great pointed ears crowned the unwieldy head and a black, wrathful mask of fur surrounded the terrible ice-white eyes, whose pupils were small, sizzling circles of burning blood red.

'It ain't there,' Todkin whispered, willing the apparition to disappear. ' 'Tain't really there.'

'Yes it is,' Samuel said. 'And our Warty's in big trouble.'

'Right,' Figgy cried, raising his sword and springing forward. 'Let's finally earn our name – come on, you Wolf Killers!'

'Wait!' Todkin shouted. 'I got a plan.'

Young Whortle tugged on his spear to pull it from the beast's leg. It was stuck fast and, before he could twist it free, the wolf spun around. The weapon was wrenched from the fieldmouse's clutches and he was sent tumbling backwards, bowling over the ground.

The spear still lodged in its flesh, the monster rampaged towards him, its grotesque jaws intent on biting him in two.

There was no time for Young Whortle to scramble to his feet and escape and he saw his frightened face reflected in the bloody centres of those frost-ringed eyes as they bore down upon him.

'Fenny!' bawled a voice, as Hodge came haring to his rescue.

The bright sword went slicing through the underside of the wolf's chin and the brute skidded to a halt, stumbling over its forelegs in surprise and howling at the sudden pain.

Not waiting to strike again, Hodge hauled Young Whortle up and they ran clear.

The wolf thrashed its head, raking its tongue beneath its chin, then fixing them with its eyes.

In a flash it was after them.

'Up the oak, Neppy!' Hodge shouted. 'I can outrun this thing.'

'No Hodge!' his friend protested.

'Do as I say. I knows what I'm doing.'

So they ran close to the tree and Young Whortle raced up it in a twinkling.

The wolf snapped at his fleeting form, almost catching the tip of his tail. Then it rounded on Hodge and stampeded after him.

'Come on!' Hodge goaded. 'There's nothing can catch me.'

Running like the wind, he pelted between the trees, leading the monster round in a loop before tearing back once more.

He prayed it was enough time for Todkin and the others to have set their ambush.

It was.

Without warning, two fieldmice plummeted from the branches above. Screaming grisly battle cries, they landed on the wolf's muscular neck and clung on to the coarse fur as they raised their swords and began to hack and slash.

The beast bellowed in fury and slammed itself into the tree to shake them off, but Todkin and Figgy held

fast and continued to stab and wound.

Yammering, the wolf bolted to the open space between the oaks and instantly rolled on its back to crush the unwelcome riders.

Todkin was thrown clear but Figgy was not quick enough and the full weight of the beast squashed the breath from his lungs.

Gasping and dazed, he floundered on the grass as the fiend righted itself and turned to deal with him.

Todkin ran to his friend's side but Figgy was still winded and could not move. Then the wolf had them.

Its great head smashed Todkin off his feet and his sword went clattering from his paw.

Then the jaws opened and came shovelling along the ground to scoop them up.

'Good job I ain't fat yet!' Samuel Gorse trumpeted as he barged into view, holding the pikestaff at his side.

Before the wolf could dodge away, Sammy thrust the end of the pike, blade down, right through the monster's slavering tongue and jaw, pinning the creature to the earth. Then he flipped himself up, vaulting high over the astonished head, over the entire length of its body and landed beyond the destructive sweep of the lashing tail.

'Best jump yet,' Samuel crowed, punching the air and dancing around.

While the nightmare yowled and clawed at its tongue, trying to drag the pikestaff out, Todkin helped Figgy up. Then he scurried over to retrieve his sword.

Young Whortle clambered down the tree to join them and picked his spear from the grass where it had fallen.

There was a sharp yelp as the wolf tore itself free and the four friends stood together to face it.

Todkin and Figgy had their swords, Young Whortle had his spear and, while they were keeping the monster busy, Sammy thought he could easily get his pike.

The wolf squared up to them, its hooked claws scraping the earth as its bleak eyes stared down – at four little fieldmice with bitter weapons.

The shredded tongue lolled out and a repellent growl wheezed from its throat as a malevolent sneer curled its lips.

At least it would feast upon one mouse before those

blades and spikes could do their worst.

To the dismay of the fieldmice, the creature turned away and ran swiftly back to the oak where Dimsel's den lay.

'No,' Figgy yelled.

With the intention of lunging in and devouring the defenceless girl inside, the monster licked its fangs.

'Hoy!' a voice called some distance to the right. 'You don't think I'm still down there, do you? You dozy flea mountain!'

It was Dimsel's voice.

The wolf snapped its head aside and glared.

'Over here,' the girl cried, hooting with mocking laughter. 'What a crummy terror you turned out to be. Can't even kill a few tiny mice. You should be ashamed and kicked out of wolf school, or made to wear the stupid's hat every day!'

The frosty eyes narrowed. The voice was coming from the shadowy depths, under a clump of brambles.

Forgetting the other mice, the wolf ran in pursuit of that insolent girl. Swallowing her whole was far too pleasant a death for her.

Figgy and the others gave chase and Samuel grabbed his pikestaff on the way.

The brambles were a tangled, knotted thicket, formed from woody, thorny stems that grew across one other – creating a natural cave beneath. It was in there that Dimsel was hiding and jeering.

'You're useless!' she laughed. 'Worst wolf I ever saw.

I've seen bird droppings scarier than you – an' cleverer.'

Incensed, the monster cannoned into the thicket, snapping and rending at the shadows but catching only leaves.

As it whirled around, the thorns bit into its flesh and held it firm, cutting deep gouges. Oblivious, the wolf sought the mouse maiden in every corner but quickly became tangled in the woody stems until it was caught as surely as a fly in a web and the more it strove and resisted, the more tightly it was bound.

Desperately it began chewing at its thorny bonds, just as Figgy, Young Whortle, Todkin and Samuel came running.

'Where's Dimsel?' Figgy demanded brandishing his sword in the horror's face.

'Oh, Figgy!' the girl cried behind them. 'You does care – you're the bestest, most gorgeous brother in the world. I loves you and won't never be mean or 'orrible ever again.'

The fieldmice whisked around. This really was a day of miracles.

Seeing their incredulous faces, Hodge burst into giggles.

'You daft lummoxes!' he cried, still doing his Dimsel impression. 'I were only kiddin'. I still thinks he's a smelly waste of space with gormless pals who each need a good kick up the tail an' a Ratty Wrist-burn.'

The others didn't know whether to thump or hug him.

At that moment, the wolf finally bit and ripped itself free and, with a deafening howl, pounced upon them.

The fieldmice lunged with their weapons. Young Whortle wielded his spear, the three swords went slicing and Samuel's pike jabbed and spiked. It was a terrible, desperate battle. Figgy lopped an ear, Hodge cut the nose and then Samuel, bravest of them all, stood on the snout and drove the pike between the wolf's eyes.

There was a horrendous screech and the monster crashed to the ground.

Young Whortle staggered back, leaning on his spear and the others stumbled away, hardly daring to believe the beast was dead.

Then, before anyone could speak, the wolf's body began to twitch and quiver and they gripped the weapons again in readiness, although they knew they were too exhausted to continue.

But the wolf did not rise again. Something strange was happening to it. A breeze began to blow through the brambles and the creature rippled before it. As they watched, the wounds they had inflicted fluttered in the wind, becoming tears and rips in a large, painted paper shape that gradually lifted from the ground and shredded into a thousand tiny scraps before their goggling eyes.

For several moments it snowed paper, until the wind

gathered it up in a whirlwind of colour and swept the fragments through the trees and far away from Fennywolde.

The five friends stared after them.

'What just happened?' Hodge asked. 'What were that thing?'

'Todkin's painting,' Sammy answered.

'But it don't make sense,' Todkin murmured.

'Well I don't know much about art . . .' Figgy began.

Todkin stopped him. 'Don't say it,' he warned.

'How's about you stick to drawin' nice harmless daisies from now on,' Hodge suggested.

Young Whortle chuckled and clapped his paws.

'Them rascally water voles,' he declared. 'This is their doin'. Woppenfrake said he was goin' to give you lads summat special you'd remember. Wait till I tells him, he'll be tickled pink it went so well.'

Except for Samuel, the others gawped at him but, before they could fire off their questions, an annoyed, quarrelsome voice called out.

'How long were you plannin' on leaving me down that rat hole then?'

They turned and there, stomping from the ruin of her new den, was Dimsel. But not even she could dampen their spirits that day. At long last, they really were the Wolf Killers – even if it *was* only made of paper.

14

Beneath the Flames

The disappearance of the wolf monster was tricky to explain.

Todkin knew that no one would believe what had really happened. He didn't believe it and he had been there. So he simply said that he and the others had fought the brute so fiercely that it had ran off with its tail between its legs and would be too afraid ever to return.

Dimsel found that difficult to swallow but what other explanation could there be?

Grudgingly grateful, she showed them where she had hidden the *Silver Hare* but warned them nothing had changed. Just because they had rescued her, she wasn't going to back out of the Fennywolde Games. She still intended to win them.

The five friends had managed to conceal their weapons from her, for she would have certainly grabbed them. Placing them under a pile of leaves on their recovered raft, they were about to carry it back to their den when Iris Crowfoot arrived with a band of the stoutest fieldmice, brandishing sticks and pitchforks.

Isaac Nettle and Mr Woodruffe were at the forefront and a huge fuss was made of the Wolf Killers when their version of events was told – much to their embarrassment.

When the praise had died down, Mr Woodruffe became grave.

'In spite of what these brave lads believe,' he announced, 'we can't be certain this horror won't return – and what if there are more of them roaming the country? Now the Games are more important than ever. Sentry duty can no longer be mainly a pleasant pastime. It is our first defence against such marauding creatures.'

Isaac Nettle was regarding the Wolf Killers suspiciously. He could sense they were not telling the whole truth but he could not guess what that might be.

'A service must be held,' he proclaimed. 'To give thanks to the Green Mouse for delivering these youngsters from that evil, for surely it was His doing. Tomorrow morning we shall gather in the Hall and offer our prayers unto Him.'

'Can't it wait till after the Games?' Mr Woodruffe asked.

Mr Nettle glared at him. 'Most certainly it cannot!' he snapped. 'Did He tarry in His divine intervention? No He did not, thus we must be just as swift in our thanks and adoration.'

When Mr Nettle was in this mood there was no denying him, so Mr Woodruffe agreed.

Young Whortle and the others were treated as heroes and even Dimsel was praised. Their families insisted on making absolutely sure they were unharmed and they had to repeat the tale many times before they were left alone.

Midday had come and gone before the friends were allowed to return to their den with the *Silver Hare*.

Figgy collapsed on the ground. 'I don't know which was worse,' he groaned. 'Fighting that wolf thing or being mauled by relatives – ugh!'

'Only one day left before the Games commence,' Todkin said. 'And there'll be another wasted morning tomorrow. We'd best get painting this raft straight away. And Young Whortle, I reckon it's time you told us more about those water voles of yours!'

Young Whortle grinned.

The afternoon crept into evening. The *Silver Hare*'s timbers became a beautiful green colour and, after telling his friends as much about the inhabitants of the Grelffit Houm as they could accept, Young Whortle went off with Sammy to have another practice at pole-vaulting. When dusk was falling, he had managed two half decent jumps and was feeling more confident about the Games than ever.

When it was time to return to their nests, the Wolf Killers were not sure what to do with their weapons. They couldn't take them home because of the questions that would be asked if they were seen, so they hid them behind their hut, in case Dimsel came sneaking around again.

'Suppose you'll be going to the still pool again

tonight?' Figgy asked.

Young Whortle replied enthusiastically. 'Can't wait to tell them how we did,' he said.

'And none of us can come with you?'

'That's what Woppenfrake told me.'

'How about we hide and watch what happens?' suggested Hodge.

Young Whortle looked at them sadly. 'I'm real sorry,' he said. 'They'd know you was about and not show themselves at all. Why don't you wait till the Games are over, then I'll try askin' for you again?'

They could see how miserable he was with the situation, so they changed the subject and Hodge made them all laugh with his impression of Twit, who had arrived with Iris and the other Fennywolders carrying a cheese sandwich on the end of a stick.

''Tis for temptin' monsters away, see,' he said in a high, preposterously hopeful voice. 'Cos everyone do like cheese.'

Sentry duty passed quickly that evening and the barleycorn was thronged with fieldmice. All of the older brothers and many of the fathers took to the stalks to keep a look-out for nightmarish wolves. Even some of the girls broke the habit of a lifetime and climbed up to see why it was so interesting, but none of them stayed up there very long. Once more the five friends found themselves besieged with questions and were glad when their shift was over.

Young Whortle ran to the still pool as fast as he could. When he reached the water he stared at the island of the Grelffit Houm. The entrance was open and the light of the candles inside shone out across the pond like a shimmering golden path.

Diving in, he swam across and was soon peering down the painted tunnel.

'Hello?' he called. 'Is you down there?'

His voice echoed around the walls but there was no answer.

''Tis me, Young Whortle!' he shouted.

Still no answer came. So, recalling Woppenfrake's words, that he was always welcome, he made his way down.

The great burrow was deserted. Buckets and pails were dotted around the floor catching slow drips from the flooded pond far above. In that cavernous space, their relentless plops were amplified and formed a staccato percussion that jangled his nerves and made him uneasy.

'Woppenfrake?' he called. 'Firgild, Willibald?'

Again there was no response, so he wandered through the burrow and ducked behind the tapestry, hurried to the end of the passage beyond and entered the weapon hoard.

Apart from the countless axes, swords, spears and arrows, it was empty.

Young Whortle nibbled his lip thoughtfully.

'Where are they?' he asked aloud.

Returning to the main burrow, he sighed and looked around.

Other tapestries were hung on the walls and he wondered if they, too, concealed doorways and tunnels.

His forehead crinkled. Between two of the stoutest pillars was perhaps the most beautiful yet simple tapestry of all. It was woven in shades of grey and silver, blended with pale, muted blues.

At first, the fieldmouse could only see a subtle mingling of shadowy flecks, but the more he studied it, he found that there were shapes and symbols worked into the cloth. Then with a shock, the vague, indistinct images translated into one great picture that filled the whole canvas.

''Tis a hare!' he breathed. 'A leapin' hare. There be its long legs an' up there's the ears, all wild an' flowin' and – that there's the crescent moon he's a-jumpin' through.'

It was a ravishing, gorgeous work and Young Whortle stepped closer to touch the silken threads.

'Todkin would love to see this,' he murmured.

Curious, he drew the edge of it aside and sure enough, another chamber lay beyond.

Young Whortle passed inside and whistled through his teeth.

Although it was nowhere near as huge as the main burrow, this place was still impressive. The ceiling was arched and the far end was cloaked in darkness; but close by in the centre of the chamber, was a large stone trough, brimming with water, across which brilliant green flames burned steadily.

The fieldmouse marvelled at the spectacle. Then he realised that the curved walls and ceiling had been left unpainted – except for a section directly above the magical fire.

Bathed in the vivid, eerie glare, he moved forward with his head tilted back.

Painted up there were two panels, bordered by colourful images of leaves and flowers. The larger was filled with a scrolling script but the other was blank and Young Whortle suddenly remembered Firgild's words – one part of his great artistic labour remained unfinished.

He did not pause to try and guess why, for he tried to read the words painted overhead. After a while he gave up. It was a language unknown to him.

'What do it mean?' he muttered.

Looking around, he saw a low table draped in a green cloth. On that lay a sword in its scabbard, a small, silver badge in the shape of a hare and, propped against the table, was a shield bearing the same symbol.

The fieldmouse recognised them at once.

'*Ratbiter!*' he exclaimed, staring at the sword. 'An' that's his shield and that's his brooch and that cloth be his cloak!'

Young Whortle's skin tingled and his whiskers stiffened. The uncanny feeling that he had stumbled into something far greater than anything he had yet seen, began to creep over him. He knew he should not be there. If the water voles had meant for him to see this place, they would have shown him. He had felt as though he was prying into some ancient and holy secret – and the answer to it was within the stone trough.

Swallowing nervously, he moved closer, but he was like one in a dream. He was drawn to that deep, long vessel, almost as if it was controlling him, forcing him to look inside. He was unable to resist, there was a compelling power at work, forcing him to see.

Catching his breath, Young Whortle placed his paws upon its near corners and gazed down.

The emerald flames dazzled and danced before his eyes but beneath the crackling fire, lying on the bottom

of the trough, under that cold clear water, was a figure.

The fieldmouse spluttered and his eyes bulged.

'Fenny!' he cried. 'Fenny!'

With his arms folded across his chest, was the body of Captain Fenlyn Purfote.

Young Whortle staggered back, his mind in chaos. He did not know what to do or think, but he knew he had to get away.

Captain Fenny had died many hundreds of years ago but his corpse showed no sign of decay or corruption.

'What's going on?' Young Whortle wept. 'What's them water voles a-doin' with his body?'

He whirled around to run, to flee from the Grelffit Houm as fast as he could and not stop until he was safe in his nest. It was too much for a simple fieldmouse to understand.

He was just about to dart back through the tapestry when he heard voices. Young Whortle halted.

Woppenfrake and the others had returned. They were descending the winding entrance tunnel and would be in the main burrow at any moment.

'Finally,' Willibald's voice came echoing. 'All is prepared and ready.'

'Yes,' Woppenfrake answered. 'The time is almost upon us. How strange it will be.'

'Strange indeed, but our duties are clear,' said Firgild. 'We are but servants and must follow our master. That is our true purpose.'

'And yet,' Woppenfrake sighed. 'My heart is heavy.

There are those I shall miss.'

'You speak of the rimpi-too,' Firgild said. 'You have grown too fond of him. Such friendships are not for us.'

'I know that well, but you know why – you know what awaits him.'

'Yes, and we also have great liking for the fellow, for all the rimpi-toos of Fenlynfeld – but we are forbidden to save any of them.'

Listening behind the tapestry, Young Whortle was anxious not to be found.

'I can't let 'em see me,' he breathed. 'Where can I hide?'

He glanced back to the end of the chamber, where all was in darkness and a moment later he was racing towards it.

The gloom surrounded him and he pressed as deeply into it as he could, before blindly bumping his nose against the wall.

If he could only stay hidden until the water voles fell asleep, then he could creep out and return home.

'But what if they don't nod off?' he murmured to himself. 'They might never kip.'

Feeling small and wretched, he shuffled nervously towards the corner. Then he stopped. The wall behind him was not made of rock – it was wood.

The fieldmouse turned to face it and ran his paws over the surface.

'I wonder . . .' he whispered.

With searching fingers, he soon found what he had hoped was there, a long crack, running from the floor to higher than he could reach. Eagerly, he continued the search and there it was, a little above his head height – a metal handle.

' 'Tis a door,' he sighed in relief. 'Oh, Neppy, if this be the back way out then you're the luckiest mouse that ever was.'

With his heart in his mouth, he gripped the handle with both paws, turned it and pulled.

In well-oiled silence it swung open and a cool breath of musty air wafted through his fur. But it was not the air of the outside. It was the stale atmosphere of a huge underground cavern.

Timid and wary, the fieldmouse stepped through into absolute blackness. It was so completely dark that his eyes ached and he clasped his mousebrass to calm his nerves.

'Bless me,' he muttered softly and to his horror, the whisper went bouncing across the vast invisible space, reverberating round and around.

Whatever this place was, it was far bigger than the main, painted burrow.

If only he had brought a lantern with him. The thought of groping and stumbling around in this massive cave panicked him. There might be pits and ledges and all kinds of hazards, and where did it lead? He could be lost down here for ever and die alone in the grim darkness.

No, he wasn't about to risk that, and he shifted his feet, to return to the chamber he had just left.

And then he heard it – a deep, rattling breath and he knew there was something else in there with him.

His first instinct was to run, but he somehow conquered it and in a feeble, timorous voice, asked, 'Hello, who be there?'

The question sailed through the black space, rebounding many times before dying into silence.

Then the breath rattled again and Young Whortle could tell it was an animal of enormous size.

He edged back towards the door and then, with a sonorous rumble, the unseen creature spoke.

'Welcome,' it said, and the great sound was warm yet cracked with age.

'Welcome, Young Whortle Nep – son of Fenlyn's folk,' it continued. 'Long has it been since I have enjoyed the company of your kind.'

Young Whortle fidgeted nervously.

'Who . . . who are you?' he asked. 'How'd you know my name?'

A sighing laugh filled the cavern.

'I am . . . Oldest,' came the cryptic reply.

'Oldest what? Are you the magic spirit of our pond? Oh – beg pardon! Not our pond, your pond?'

'I am not. I am his guest only, but after he has departed I shall still be here.'

'Are you hidin'?'

Once more gentle laughter crowded the darkness and Young Whortle's lingering fears melted away to hear it.

'Perhaps I am.'

'So am I.'

'Have no fear of Virianna's sons,' the voice told him. 'Tender and noble are their hearts and they have cared for me these many ages.'

'I wants to believe them kind and good,' Young Whortle said. 'But I be so confused. They're higher'n any of my notions so I just don't know, but why is Cap'n Fenny's poor body out yonder, a-pickled in a stone coffin with fires burning over it? Don't look right nor respectful to me.'

'Ask that of them,' the voice said. 'They will tell you why my trusted Captain lies out there. He used to guard me when I dwelt beneath the forest mound and now he guards me here beneath the pool. May the Green keep him and may He keep you also. Listen now to my prophecy and you shall be safe. I say unto you – beware the straw that walks.'

The fieldmouse scratched his head. 'I don't understand,' he said. 'Straw don't walk – an' why're you down here in the dark? A candle or two would lift this heavy gloom.'

'Not for me, my eyes are blind. Yet the night holds no terrors for one who danced in the hollow void before the first leaf opened and sang at the first moonrise.'

''Ere,' Young Whortle insisted. 'Just who are you?'

Before the voice could answer, a paw touched Young Whortle's shoulder.

Startled, he leaped up in surprise.

It was Firgild.

'Little rimpi-too,' he said, tutting with concern. 'What are you doing here? You must not disturb our guest.'

Young Whortle was stammering an answer when the voice spoke from the darkness.

'Peace, my friend. My rest was not disturbed – he was expected. The valour and honour of the woodlanders still runs through his veins. He has the right to be here. From such stock shall the victors of the final battle arise.'

Firgild bowed.

'My pardon, Ancient,' he said reverently.

'With every dawn that rises, that dread day is nudged a little closer. My long waiting shall soon be over and the darkness foretold will come – spreading over the land, blotting out light and bringing suffering.'

'Then may the other prophecies also hold true.'

'We can only have faith that they do. Faith is all we have now, faith in the strength of the small, faith in the purity of their hearts. As it began with mice, so shall it end. That is the wisdom of the moon-sent angel. My blessing upon you, Young Whortle Nep and remember my warning – beware the straw that walks.'

The voice fell silent and, presently, the sonorous rumble began once more. The fieldmouse wondered if the creature had fallen asleep. Very gently, Firgild led him back through the doorway.

After the absolute night of the great cavern, the roaring green flames that crackled over the stone trough pained his eyes at first. Woppenfrake and Willibald were there and they nodded to him in greeting.

'Who were that?' Young Whortle asked, as Firgild carefully closed the door.

'If you cannot guess,' Firgild said, 'then I must say only this. You have been greatly honoured, more than you know. Save my brothers and myself, you are the only one in this world to have been granted an audience with him. But the time of his entombment is nearly over.'

Young Whortle pressed his paws together and bit his thumbs. He had no idea what was happening or what the baffling words meant. It was far too complicated and confusing for a humble fieldmouse. However, there was one thing he had to know the answer to.

'What you doin' with Cap'n Fenny?' he demanded. 'Why weren't he buried decent? Why is he in that there water, like a dead stickleback in a bucket? 'T'ain't no way to treat no one, never mind he!'

Firgild looked at his brothers and they chuckled mildly.

'Nowt to laugh at!' Young Whortle ranted. 'Makes me angry, it do!'

Woppenfrake held up his paw.

'Come here,' he said kindly, 'Look down at your

captain. What do you see?'

Young Whortle shuffled forward and stared down into the flaming water once more.

'I sees Cap'n Fenny's poor dead body,' he said.

Woppenfrake shook his head. 'No,' he corrected. 'You do not. Now look up at the ceiling and what do you see?'

'Lot of scribbly words I can't make head nor tail of.'

'I would not expect you to,' Firgild broke in. 'It is an archaic language, seldom spoken anymore. I believe there are some bats still learned enough to read it, but this is what those words mean in your speech.

> *'When evil comes and despair is all*
> *He shall rise from sleep's long thrall.*
> *When hope has failed and great is need*
> *He shall awake for one last deed.*
> *Call him thrice and ye shall know*
> *The one he answers is writ below.'*

Woppenfrake smiled sadly. 'When Mabb murdered Fenlyn Purfote, the spirit of the pool took pity on him and called his soul back from the shadows. Yet the Green Laws forbade him to walk again amongst his friends and people and so, here he lies, under enchantment and waiting – until the final days when his valiant heart and renowned sword will be needed again.'

'I can't believe it,' Young Whortle gasped. 'Cap'n Fenny is only sleepin'?'

'Until he is called,' Firgil said.

The fieldmouse gave a cheer and jigged around the trough, giggling and singing with bubbling joy.

The water voles laughed to see him.

'An' that's all it'll take to break the magic?' he cried. 'Shout his name three times?'

'We could call him a hundred times,' Willibald said. 'But the enchantment would not be broken. Only one voice will waken him.'

'Whose?'

Firgild gestured to the blank panel above. 'We do not know.' He shrugged. 'The name of the hero who ventures down here in the direst moment is a secret withheld from us. The Ancient will only speak his name on the night of our departing and only then can I complete the painting.'

'Gonna be a marvel an' a mighty sort, whoever it is,' Young Whortle declared. 'Oh I'm so happy I could—'

Suddenly he stopped dancing and his face fell.

'What do you mean, your departing?' he asked. 'Is you off someplace?'

The brothers wore sad smiles.

'Yes,' Woppenfrake told him. 'We are leaving Fenlynfeld. The spirit of the Glinty Water must find a new abode. The filth of the modern world will soon trickle and ooze into the pond and he must be gone ere that happens, or perish. Few places are left where he can dwell, but one has been chosen and we must journey with him to find it.'

'But, you won't be going just yet, though?' Young Whortle asked hopefully.

'In three nights' time,' Willibald said.

'When the moon is round and ringed by fire,' Woppenfrake added.

Young Whortle's eyes began to sting.

'You can't go,' he whispered. 'Not now, there's so much I wants to ask and so much I wants to tell. Why, I haven't even mentioned the wolf monster today. Brilliant that were, the lads loved it. They'd say so themselves if they could.'

'They cannot meet us,' Firgild said flatly. 'We are searching for a new home, in a far country. The sons of Virianna must be forgotten.'

'I won't forget you – not never!'

The water voles looked at him sorrowfully, then led him through the tapestry and back into the main burrow.

'It is time for you to return to you field,' Woppenfrake said. 'I will walk with you as far as the entrance.'

'I'll be back tomorrow night,' the fieldmouse promised.

'You will not find us,' Willibald answered. 'We must fast and meditate in seclusion before the ceremony.'

Young Whortle struggled to control his tears.

'Is . . . is this the last time I sees you, then?' he stuttered.

Woppenfrake squeezed his paw. 'On the third night,' he said. 'We are to summon the spirit of the pool from the depths and he will guide us away from this place. That is when we shall bid you farewell. Do not be late, look to the moon and come to us. Bring no other with you and tell your friends none of this until we are gone.'

'I promise.'

The two of them walked slowly up the tunnel to the outside world.

Firgild watched them sadly.

'I fear it was a mistake to befriend him,' he said.

'No,' said Willibald. 'Do not regret knowing the rimpi-too. He reminds us why the battle must not be lost. Whilst there are grains of gold such as he in the world, darkness must never be allowed the final victory.'

'And yet I fear for our brother. This parting will grieve him.'

'Foresight is ever painful.'

'The folk of Fenlynfeld will have much to mourn.'

'But not yet, not this summer. Let them enjoy this last year of peace, untouched by sorrow.'

'Yes, one last year – before the evil comes.'

As he led Young Whortle to the threshold of the Grelffit Houm, Woppenfrake tried to cheer him.

'And you say the wolf hunt went well?' he asked.

The fieldmouse nodded. 'Made me and the lads

proper heroes,' he answered, but there was no enthusiasm in his voice. 'Real famous in our field, we be.'

'Cherish your friends,' Woppenfrake told him. 'I wish I could have known them and shared such days, but it is not to be.'

'You'd have liked 'em, them's good lads. Figgy loves his ugly insects and Hodge would be doin' impersonations of you in no time. I bet Todkin knowed some stuff even you don't and as for Sammy . . .'

'What of Sammy?'

'Oh nowt, he was just hopin' you could magic him fat. He can't do it on his own. But that's not the real reason he'd like to meet you. My best friend is Sammy an' it feels wrong, him not sharing these times I've had – and now he'll never get the chance and won't know how much he's missed an' . . . what I'm goin' to miss.'

The conversation faltered and failed and when they passed out of the entrance and reached the water's edge, it was in an uncomfortable silence.

'In three nights' time,' Woppenfrake reminded him.

Young Whortle scowled. 'I wasn't gonna forget,' he said tetchily.

He waded into the pond and Woppenfrake watched him swim away, admiring his easy movement through the water.

'Most proficient,' he murmured proudly.

When Young Whortle reached the far bank, he

glanced around but the entrance stone had already slid shut.

Crying silently, he made his way back to the cornfield.

15

Gifts from the Grelffit Houm

The last morning before the Games was grey as a bruise.

Not wanting to incur Isaac Nettle's displeasure, everyone gathered in the Hall of Corn for his service of thanksgiving. Standing before them as they settled down, the mousebrass-maker looked even more austere and grave than usual. It did not bode well, and they feared he was going to turn the service into one of his scathing sermons. They were not wrong.

After the first Green Hymn had been sung, Mr Nettle spoke of the wolf that had crept through Fennywolde the previous day as a symbol of the evil of the times. The holy laws were constantly flouted and the visitation of the wolf was surely an embodiment of everybody's sins. The Green Mouse had shown His anger, it was a warning and they must change their ways. There were those in this field who were behaving no better than painted rat drabs and when he said that, he glowered straight at Alison Sedge. The girl was about to blow him an insolent kiss when her mother jabbed her in the ribs and hissed for her to behave.

Continuing, he told them to abide by the Green scriptures and not stray into folly and wickedness.

Tomorrow the Games would commence and he had heard talk of decking the ditch with flags and bunting – even garlands of flowers. Such idle vanities were the road to damnation. The Green's own creation was beauty enough and any who sought to add to it was surely guilty of criticising His perfect design. The Games were not to be used as an excuse for frivolity and woe betide any he found partaking of the blackberry ferment.

The service went on in this vein for simply ages and by the end of it everyone was restless and resentful and very hungry. When it was finally over the fieldmice shambled away, muttering and despondent, rubbing their numbed bottoms.

Isaac watched them depart and permitted himself a bitter smile. It looked strange and lost on his vinegary face. Then he called to his son. Jenkin hurried over and they left the Hall together.

Mr Woodruffe let out an audible sigh of relief and lamented the sour temperament of Fennywold's mousebrass-maker.

'Not even he can take the fun out of the Games though,' he told himself.

Young Whortle and his friends hastened to their hut to check on the raft. The paint was dry and she looked splendid. Figgy wanted to practise with his sword, but when he went to fetch it, the weapons were gone.

'Dimsel!' he groaned. 'Why can't she leave our things alone?'

'I don't think it was her,' Todkin called from within the den. 'Come and look.'

The Wolf Killers hurried inside.

Four bags of dark blue velvet, tied at the neck with golden thread, were arranged on the ground. Each had a large label with a name written on it.

Todkin read them out. 'Figgy, Hodge, Sammy and me.'

'Where's Warty's?' asked Samuel.

'It's them water voles,' Hodge cried. 'They've took our swords and left us these instead.'

Young Whortle grinned. 'I bet it's Woppenfrake's idea,' he said. 'Just the sort of thing he'd do. Go on, see what's inside.'

The fieldmice took up the bags. They were all different shapes and sizes. They had not been this excited since the day they had received their brasses.

'One at a time,' said Todkin, 'Figgy – you first.'

Figgy reached in and brought out a small but beautiful silver lantern. Magical signs and symbols were chased in the metal and on the outside there were lenses of different coloured glass, hinged at angles that resembled an insect's open wings. There was another label attached to the handle and Figgy read it aloud.

'The Lamp of Rimanda. Can be used night or day and will attract whatever insect you desire by using the appropriate lens. It will also grant you protection from those with stings. Warning – the lamp's power is broken if any harm comes to the insects it attracts.'

Figgy burst into laughter, fascinated, and examined the lantern.

Todkin went next. He reached into his bag and took out a large, bark-bound book of many blank pages. The first had been inscribed with the words: *The Book of Todkin – a collection of lore and sketches.*

'It's just what I always wanted,' he said. 'I can write everything in here and paste in my pictures, no more loose bits of paper.' And he hugged the book to himself. Woppenfrake had not explained the gift's true virtue and it was only much later that Todkin discovered it. However much he wrote or drew, there were always empty pages left and although he kept the book his entire life and used it every day, he never filled it.

'Oh, Mighty Green!' Hodge declared, mimicking Mr Nettle. 'Bless my unworthy paw and may it pull out a frivolous vanity, that I may spoil myself most disgustingly and wallow in the fires of wickedness.'

Opening his bag he fished out a most unusual object. It was slightly conical in shape and made of beaten copper. The outside was polished and undecorated, but inside were etched into the metal strange words, that spiralled round and around.

Hodge inspected it doubtfully before reading the attached label. 'What can it be?' he murmured. 'Bit small for a hat. Or maybe it's a wide bracelet?'

'Look at the label and find out!' an exasperated and intensely curious Todkin told him.

Hodge cleared his throat. There were only two words written on the paper that dangled from his gift. He was about to read them in an Alison Sedge voice, but when he saw what was written, he was too thrilled to try. Immediately, he put the smaller end of the cone to his mouth.

Outside the hut, Dimsel's voice suddenly called out. 'Hoy you lot, I'm going to pull your den down with you inside!'

The fieldmice dashed to the entrance in alarm, but there was no sign of Figgy's bullying sister.

'Where is she?' Samuel asked, glancing around nervously.

Hodge fell to his knees, giggling and helpless. Then he put the strange copper object to his lips again and suddenly his laughter was coming from the ceiling, then the floor, then one of the seats. To Figgy's astonishment, his friend's voice abruptly hooted from inside his own tummy; in fact, wherever Hodge pointed the wide end of the cone, it projected anything he said or any sound he made.

It was all too marvellous and he rolled on the ground, laughing uncontrollably.

Todkin took the gift from him and read the label. 'Voice thrower,' he said.

'Imagine the fun I can have with that!' Hodge cried, wiping tears from his eyes. 'No one's going to be safe – the trouble I can cause!'

Everyone agreed that it was a wonderful present and they couldn't wait for him to try it out on certain individuals.

'What've you got, Sammy?' Young Whortle asked.

Samuel Gorse reached into his velvet bag but his friends muttered in disappointment when they saw what he took out. It was only a biscuit, a plain, baked biscuit.

There was no accompanying label, and they felt extremely sorry for him. It was no match for their incredible gifts.

Sammy however was far from down-hearted. He gave the biscuit an inquisitive sniff. It smelled of ginger and cinnamon and butter and he closed his eyes with rapture.

'What you so happy for?' Figgy asked. 'My mam makes 'em all the time and so does yours.'

Samuel looked at his friends and smiled. 'Don't you see?' he said dreamily. 'All your gifts are your heart's desires and so is mine.'

Young Whortle was the first to understand and he squeezed Sammy's arm.

'Oh how amazin',' he whispered.

Samuel opened his mouth to take a bite, then thought better of it and popped the biscuit back in the bag.

'Not till after the Games,' he said firmly.

Then Todkin understood. 'You think it'll make you fat!' he cried.

'Course it will!' Young Whortle said. 'I told Woppenfrake that's what Sammy wanted most of all. 'Tis a magic biscuit.'

'Eat me, Sammy, eat me!' the biscuit begged from inside the bag, but it was only Hodge playing with his voice thrower.

They were all delighted with their gifts but couldn't understand why Young Whortle hadn't received anything.

'I've had plenty already,' he said simply. 'I don't need nowt.'

'Soon as the Games are finished and you get them water voles to agree to us visitin' them, the better,' Todkin declared. 'I wants to thank 'em personally and ask them questions so I can put it all down in my new book.'

Young Whortle did not answer. He was not allowed to tell them that the water voles were leaving and these gifts were Woppenfrake's way of saying goodbye.

'I better get some trainin' done,' he said. 'Come on, Sammy.'

While he practised and did his exercises, his friends spent the rest of the day planning Operation Foul in more detail, and Figgy and Hodge realised just how useful their presents would be.

The last day before the Fennywolde Games drifted into the evening and, on sentry duty that night, they were all excited and nervous.

Later, lying in his nest, Young Whortle could not sleep. So much had happened in the past week that his head spun to think of it.

He wondered what Woppenfrake and his brothers were doing in the Grelffit Houm at that very moment. It really was very generous of them to give his friends those incredible gifts and once again he felt terribly forlorn at the prospect of their departure. After everything he had seen and done since meeting them, how could he return to his ordinary life? It would seem exceedingly dull and mundane.

Staring out of his nest, he gazed up at the night sky and gradually slipped into a deep sleep.

Out in the meadow, the rest of the Wolf Killers had met in secret once more and were putting the final touches to their plans.

'That's perfect.' Todkin said confidently. 'Young Whortle's sure to win his events tomorrow – nothing can go wrong.'

16

The Games Begin

The first day of the Fennywolde Games finally dawned.

Every mouse rose early and made their way to the meadow, laden with food for picnics and chattering excitedly. It was going to be a fine, clear day. The sky was deliciously blue, with only a hatful of small white clouds sailing across it.

The Meadow Race was the first event and compulsory for every entrant. It was also the custom for any one else to join in, just for the pleasure of taking part, and so a great crowd of participants gathered at the start.

The route had been marked out the previous afternoon. The race was to begin by the oaks, traverse the meadow in great zigzags, reach the outlying trees by the still pool, then along the lower bank of the ditch until the Long Hedge, then diagonally back across the meadow to the oaks.

It was a test of speed and stamina and there were always plenty who did not manage to finish. Half-way along was a first-aid station, attended by capable mousewives equipped with splints and bandages, in case of broken bones due to carelessness, and reviving cups of berrybrew for those in need of refreshment. The fact that most of the runners who took part just for fun didn't get further than the first-aid station was not lost on Isaac Nettle and he viewed them with the contempt and scorn they so obviously deserved.

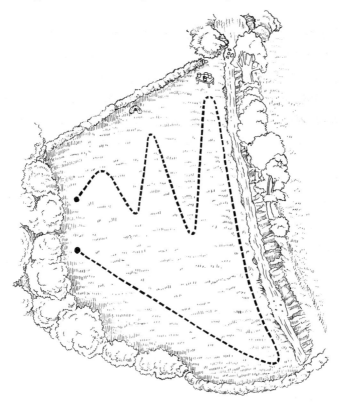

Young Whortle and his friends joined the throng of expectant runners. His friends exchanged knowing glances. Apart from Todkin, they were all going to take part in the race but had no intention of finishing. The atmosphere was excited, restless and hopeful. Young

Whortle performed some warm-up exercises and looked around happily.

Dimsel, Iris and Lily were at the front of the crowd and Figgy's sister was scowling threateningly at any who dared stand too close. The Burdock brothers were hopping up and down impatiently – they were still flecked with blue paint. Twit was stretching his short legs and touching his toes, Jenkin was receiving a stern lecture from his father, who then prayed for him, and Alison Sedge was lounging around at the rear, watching everything unfold with lazy and amused interest.

'Now just remember to pace yourself,' Hodge told Young Whortle. 'Don't dash off too quick straight away or you'll be out of breath and fall over by the time you reach the ditch and have nothing left for the homeward stretch.'

Young Whortle could hardly stand still to listen. He was ready and anxious to be off.

'Ain't you going to run next to me?' he asked.

Hodge coughed hastily. 'No, I want to see if I can beat Jenkin and Dimsel,' he fibbed.

'I'll run with you,' Samuel promised. 'As far as I'm able.'

Then Mr Woodruffe, the King of the Field, strode forward and, amid loud cheers, declared the Fennywolde Games open.

He held a bark drum in his paws. The Meadow Race would only start when he struck it. With great ceremony, he lifted it above his head and raised his arm

Just then two of the younger children ran on to the track, squealing merrily and had to be retrieved by their parents.

Everybody chuckled but the laughter was forced and the tension electric.

Mr Woodruffe grinned. This was his favourite time of the year. He looked at all those eager, anxious and optimistic faces, aching to prove themselves, and remembered back to when he had taken part in the Games. He had won the title of Head Sentry for three years running, so he knew just how much it meant to them.

Every eye was upon him, so he wasted no more time and called out. 'On your marks . . . get ready . . .'

He banged the drum.

With a tumultuous yell, the fieldmice charged forward and steamed into the meadow.

Hodge and Dimsel shot ahead of the rest almost immediately, but Jenkin and Figgy were hot on their tails.

Young Whortle was surrounded by other runners. The ones in front were either so wide or so tall that he couldn't see where he was going. Remembering what Hodge had told him, he jogged sensibly along and bided his time. Sammy ran next to him but was constantly looking around, seeing who looked like serious competition.

Dimsel, Figgy, Hodge and Jenkin were still in the

lead. The first of the zigzag's sharp corners was approaching and Figgy sprinted away from the others to be the first around it. Behind him his sister laughed unkindly. Nobody could keep that speed up for the entire race – he would never make it all the way around the course. But winning the event was the last thing on Figgy's mind.

Todkin's face suddenly appeared through the tall grass ahead, and Figgy dived aside to join him.

Hurriedly, Todkin passed him a straw cage and he took up another. Then with a gleeful cackle they thrust them out over the track, opened them and shook out the contents.

Out tumbled the ugliest insects Figgy had ever caught. He had spent several hours last night with the Lamp of Rimanda and had been overjoyed at the frightful specimens that had buzzed and droned towards the lantern.

There were devil's coach-horse beetles, the sexton and ground beetle and, for good measure, several dozen earwigs.

Flailing their legs and buzzing angrily, they fell on to the track. Some of them opened their wings to fly away and at that moment Dimsel and Jenkin came racing around the corner.

One of the beetles flew straight into Jenkin's face and he called out in fright as it clung to his nose and the antennae beat upon his ears. With a wail, he stumbled and fell over, before the beetle whirred away. Dimsel saw the other insects crawling and swarming in her path but merely hopped aside and ducked clear of those that were flying. She had grown up with Figgy's collections, so such creatures didn't bother her at all.

Hearing Jenkin's yowls, Hodge knew what had happened and he rounded the corner fully prepared to leap and jump over whatever was in the way.

Moments later the fieldmice who were behind him encountered the insects and many of them squealed in dismay. Iris and Lily squeaked the loudest and darted right and left, abandoning the race completely, with earwigs in their hair.

By the time Young Whortle reached that part of the course, most of the beetles had flown off or crawled into the long grass, so he didn't realise anything out of the ordinary had happened.

The group surrounding him had thinned out: several had fallen behind, others had moved ahead and a surprisingly high number had tripped over Samuel's feet when they had attempted to run past. The next corner was reached and then the next, and Young Whortle was still as fresh as when he had started. All those exercises and training sessions were now paying off.

Meanwhile, Todkin and Figgy had not been idle. Cutting across the meadow, they hurried to their next ambush site and waited.

Dimsel and Hodge made it to the trees by the still pool and the first-aiders cheered them on with blackberry-flavoured enthusiasm.

Hodge was enjoying himself. He could easily beat Dimsel if he wanted to, but knew what was going to happen next so he was content to merely keep up with her as they ran alongside the ditch.

Young Whortle's group thinned out more and he actually started to overtake a few of them. When he passed the first-aiders, eight of the runners who had been in front were already sipping their refreshment and obviously had no intention of continuing.

He glanced quickly at the trees beyond and thought of the water voles far beneath the ground there.

A cry from Twit who was close behind brought him sharply back to the race. Samuel had stumbled and fallen in a sprawl, just as Twit had tried to overtake Young Whortle, and had brought Master Scuttle down with him. It was most unlucky for Twit, but he was more concerned for Sammy's well-being than his own chances of winning. Young Whortle hesitated and was going to turn back and help, but Samuel urged him on and assured him he was fine – which he was.

Dimsel Bottom ran with long, determined strides and her arms pumped like pistons. Her face was set and her mouth tightly closed. She could not believe her brother had put such a great distance between them. He was nowhere to be seen, but he simply couldn't have made it to the Long Hedge already and be running the straight diagonal stretch to the finishing line. He must have tripped and was now nursing a scraped shin or twisted ankle somewhere in the grass and clover. The thought kindled a triumphant glow inside her and she smiled as she ran.

The ditch sped by on her left and the Long Hedge drew closer. Before reaching the cow parsley, the track veered right and Hodge allowed himself to fall back a little. Dimsel had to be first around that corner.

The girl raced on and turned it nimbly. Too late she saw the great webs strung across the path and she ran headlong into them.

Figgy had discovered just how remarkable the Lamp of Rimanda really was. When he had put the violet-coloured lens in front of its candle, all the spiders in the vicinity had come scurrying towards it and immediately began spinning their nets. So, he had let the lantern flicker there for most of the night and now the cobwebs were as thick as cream, hanging across the track like dense foggy curtains in great sticky swathes.

Hiding in the tall grasses, he and Todkin fought to keep silent and not explode with laughter as the bullying mouse maiden came bounding blindly into their trap.

Straight into the heart of the draping webs Dimsel blundered, and they ripped and tore around her. Her face was covered in a clinging veil and she had to claw at it with her fingers in order to see where she was going. Yet it cost her only moments. She was soon through and clear of the cobwebs. At a ferocious pace, she hurtled along the track.

'Didn't think that'd stop her,' Figgy grumbled.

'Was worth it to see the look of disgust on her face, though,' Todkin hooted. 'It's still in her hair and she's trailing webby strands all over.'

Suddenly Hodge appeared, leaping through the holes that Dimsel had made.

He looked searchingly in the grass for his friends and Todkin leaned out to pass him his voice thrower.

'She's all yours now,' he cried.

'My pleasure!' his friend answered, and he pelted after Figgy's sister.

Dimsel could see the finishing line in the distance. This race was hers for the taking – everyone would know how brilliant she was. Those insects and webs had been peculiar but even she didn't suspect her brother was responsible. Nothing could stop her now, or so she thought.

And then, to her horror, she heard that terrible, savage growl again – the wolf monster had returned.

It was in front of her, somewhere in the long grass, probably crouching down to pounce as she ran past.

The memory of the terror she had known in her den as it tried to dig her out came flooding back. The growl became a horrendous snarl and she heard the great teeth snap together in those evil jaws.

It was the only thing that had ever frightened her. Howling, she tore back along the track.

'It's here!' she yelled wildly. 'The wolf is back!'

As she fled past Hodge she didn't even notice that he was shaking with laughter.

Running alongside the ditch, Young Whortle was feeling very pleased with himself. Only the Burdock brothers, Shrubby Raggit and Jonah Vetch were in front of him now.

Little by little he caught up with Jonah until they were neck and neck and then he was out-running him, leaving only the three others in front. Then a very strange thing occurred.

Dimsel Bottom came shrieking around the corner by the Long Hedge, covered in cobwebs and, how peculiar – she kept on running – into the cornfield. What could have happened?

Shrubby was the first around the bend and skidded when he saw the tattered webs strung across the way. Instead of putting his head down and barging clean through them, he slithered to a stop and became horribly entangled. The more he wriggled the worse it became. He whirled around and the cobwebs wrapped about him as surely as thread around a bobbin.

The Burdock brothers gave him astonished glances as they raced past. They were doing better than they had hoped but each was desperate to beat the other.

Abihu Burdock edged out in front and did his best to stay there.

Behind him, Uriah Burdock heard him call.

'That Dimsel Bottom do fancy you. I heard her tell Lily Clover.'

'No she don't!' Uriah bawled. 'Don't you say such!'

'She wants to kiss you and love you and make you speak poetry to her.'

'No she don't. You take that back!'

Uriah huffed and strained and finally caught up with his brother. They were extremely close to finishing but Uriah shoved Abihu with his shoulder and sent him toppling sideways.

'Ow!' squealed Abihu, 'What's that fer?'

Uriah leaped on top of him and started pummelling him with his fists.

'Dimsel Bottom don't like me,' he ranted. 'You was lyin! Tell me you was lyin'!'

'Oof – ouch!' cried Abihu. 'I never said nowt about Dimsel Bottom and you.'

'Yes you did!'

'No I never!'

'Yes you did!'

And they rolled across the track, biffing and bashing each other while Hodge leaned back in the grass and patted his new and treasured gift.

Young Whortle was now in the lead.

He called on his last reserves of strength and sped along as fast as he could.

Figgy, Todkin and Hodge cheered him as he dashed by. He was nearly there, nearly at the finishing line – he would be the first mouse across.

And then, from seemingly out of nowhere, Jenkin Nettle sprinted up behind, and with only a tail's length to go, he charged past Young Whortle and won the Meadow Race.

The crowd roared and jumped up and down. Jenkin was hoisted onto shoulders and paraded around in victory. Alison Sedge watched him with great admiration and flung buttercup petals in the air.

Young Whortle sank to his knees and lay panting on the grass.

His parents hurried over and congratulated him on doing so well, but his friends uttered dismal groans and blamed one another for not nobbling Jenkin properly.

Gradually the other runners came haring and in some cases, limping, over the finishing line. The first-aiders were delighted to find so many in need of their attention this year. Never had there been so many bruises and sprains.

And so the first event was over. Jenkin was praised and he looked to his father. But Isaac Nettle showed no sign of pride and the rejoicing smiles faded from his son's face.

In spite of being pipped at the post, Young Whortle was far from discouraged. He had never dreamed he would come second and he thanked his friends as soon as he had his breath back.

But there was no time to linger and chat, for the Fennywolders were already moving off to where the next event was to take place.

It was the Barley Swing.

Young Whortle was not entered for this event so he wanted to take his time strolling to the cornfield. But Samuel said he was particularly interested in it, so they made haste and got there just in time.

'If Jenkin wins this one,' Sammy whispered to Todkin, 'Warty will have a dreadful job trying to catch up.'

'Don't worry,' Todkin reassured him. 'Everything's been taken care of.'

The Barley Swing was a race through the top of the corn, leaping and swinging from one ear to the next across the great field, keeping to a route that had been marked out by coloured threads that wound through the barley. It was an extremely tiring competition and the winner was the one who travelled the furthest, for few ever reached the field edge.

The taller mice had a definite advantage, for their arms were longer, so the smaller entrants always sat it out.

Five fieldmice were tackling it this year: Jenkin, Shrubby, Lanky Brommock, Ned Rattle and Dimsel.

Dimsel was nowhere to be found. Nobody understood why she had run away during the Meadow Race, for she was the only one who had heard Hodge's wolf impression.

So only four were left. Shrubby had managed to rid himself of most of the cobwebs but he still shuddered when he thought about it.

He and the others lined up beneath the corn stalks where the ends of the threads were tied and waited for Mr Woodruffe to hit the drum again.

Then, up they climbed and were soon swinging their way forward, lunging across, grasping the next ear of corn then leaping over and doing the same with the other paw.

Watching them from the ground, the assembled mice saw them lurch away. Jenkin pulled out in front immediately and was so adept at it that he seemed to be flying and the barley barely rustled around him.

'He's ever so good!' Young Whortle exclaimed.

Samuel pulled an anxious face but Todkin mischievously jiggled his eyebrows at him.

The spectators moved through the field with their

eyes fixed upward. Shrubby had already fallen behind and Lanky Brommock was a little ahead of Ned. Jenkin had put such a distance between them, though, that they would never catch up with him.

Just as Shrubby was about to give up hope, there came a startled yell and the cornstalks that Jenkin tried to catch hold of, collapsed under him and he came tumbling down, landing with a bump in a heap of straw.

'Oh dear,' Todkin declared. 'The downpour we had the other day must've rotted the stems, how unlucky!'

'Good job that straw was there to break his fall,' added Figgy innocently.

The Barley Swing continued and was won by Shrubby Raggit, Ned came second but poor Lanky Brommock suffered the same ill fate as Jenkin. Fortunately there was a lot of straw where he fell, as well.

'What a shame,' Young Whortle said, oblivious to the smirks on the faces of his friends.

Isaac Nettle walked away without uttering a word.

And so the time came for the Tail Hang.

Twelve fieldmice were entered in this event; Twit was one of them and he wished everyone else the very best. Competitors could choose their own corn stalks and piles of moss were quickly pushed beneath them. The Burdock brothers were also taking part and they selected two stems far enough apart to avoid any accidental collisions but close enough to keep an eye on each other. Jenkin had decided against entering and so he joined the crowded audience and waited for the event to commence.

Young Whortle flexed his tail in preparation, curling and uncurling it, then strode up to his barley stalk and climbed quickly to the top.

'Barley wranglers take your places!' Mr Woodruffe cried.

Twelve senior and very responsible mice strode to the base of the stalks and listened for their cue.

'Blanketeers ready!' called Mr Woodruffe.

Six pairs of stout husbands with blankets gripped in

their paws, toddled into position beneath the stems and stretched the strong cloth taut between them. If any mouse missed the mossy padding, then they were there to catch them. That was the theory, but they generally missed and ended up crashing into one another.

Young Whortle and the other entrants wrapped their

tails tightly about the top of the barleycorn, just below the ripening ears.

Mr Woodruffe held up his paw.

'Entrants, commence the hanging!'

He banged the drum once and Young Whortle and the others fell forwards. Their stems bobbed down and they dangled in the air.

Isaac Nettle, Mr Woodruffe and Old Todmore stared upward and scrutinized them. They were the judges and awarded marks out of five for technique and quality of suspension.

'Abihu Burdock don't look like he'll cling on long,' Old Todmore muttered. 'But then, neither do his brother.'

'Verily, those two stick-at-naughts fail at most things,' Mr Nettle said sourly.

'But look at Twit!' declared Mr Woodruffe. 'I never noticed how skilled he is afore.'

'What use is such skill in the tail of a simpleton?' sneered Isaac. 'The fool should not be permitted to take part in these Games – his presence is a mockery and an insult.'

Their deliberations were interrupted by Tiddly Crowfoot – Iris's brother. With a woeful squeak, he slipped from his stalk and dropped on to the moss below.

'A shameful attempt,' Isaac snapped.

'Some of them others don't look too steadfast,' Old Todmore added with a shake of his head.

'But look at Young Whortle!' exclaimed Mr Woodruffe. 'It's as if he's a part of that there barley.'

'The next test will tell,' said Isaac, but they awarded the full five points each to Twit and Young Whortle.

Mr Woodruffe strode forward.

'Barley wranglers,' he announced. 'Commence your wrangling!' and he started to beat the drum slowly.

The mice at the base of the stalks gripped them with both paws and began shaking in time to the rhythm.

Young Whortle grinned – this was easy. The barleycorn dipped and swayed and he could not help gurgling with pleasure.

Abihu Burdock let out a shriek and fell off almost right away. He was promptly followed by his brother and as soon as they picked themselves up from the moss, the two squabbled about who had beaten who.

The drum thumped a little faster and the barley wranglers increased the force of their shaking.

Twit laughed and giggled, and waved at his parents down below.

The stalks jiggled more wildly and three more entrants were flung from their places. One of them missed the moss completely but for once the blanketeers were ready and caught him neatly, much to everyone's surprise. Watching from the crowd, Grommel rubbed his back and scowled.

The drumbeat became even faster. Two more fieldmice toppled down and then another.

Only Young Whortle, Twit and Jonah Vetch remained – and Jonah was already making groaning noises.

Admiring murmurs spread through the spectators. The Tail Hang had never taken this long before. And still the speed of drumbeats increased.

For the three competitors the world was spinning and rocking and it was too much for Jonah. His tail unwound from the barley and he was sent flying into the field.

Two sets of blanketeers charged after him but they both missed and he landed so heavily on his right foot that it turned badly and he had to withdraw from the Games altogether.

All eyes were trained on Twit and Young Whortle. Their small figures were revolving blurs and both of them were burbling. Mrs Scuttle covered her eyes, unable to watch her son in such a plight, but her husband was overwhelmed with pride.

'That's it, my boy,' he whispered. 'Hold on there.'

Young Whortle's parents were too transfixed to do anything and stood like wide-eyed dummies, unable to blink until it was over.

Figgy, Hodge, Todkin and Samuel had not reckoned with Twit being so good at this event and Todkin blamed himself for not foreseeing it.

'Young Whortle has to win this,' he breathed. 'He has to.'

Suddenly there was a shriek and one of the mice was

thrown clear. The crowd gasped and then burst into cheers and applause.

The Wolf Killers were jubilant – Young Whortle had won.

They dashed forward and looked up at him as the corn stalk ceased its violent motion.

'Well done, Warty!' Samuel yelled.

'Neppy?' called Hodge. 'Are you . . .?'

'Look out!' Figgy hollered.

But it was too late and for the third time they were covered in Young Whortle's breakfast.

17

The Completely Brilliant
Dimsel Bottom

With all the cornfield events completed, the late afternoon was taken up with the Wrestling and the Pebble Lift. Unfortunately Dimsel Bottom returned just in time to take part in both of them.

She had run all the way into the adjoining field and was halfway through the rows of young cabbages there before she stopped and thought she had better turn back and see what had happened to everyone. What if the wolf had murdered them all? Feeling guilty, she hurried homeward, cuffing a couple of young rabbits around the ears on the way, just for the sake of it.

When she realised that there had been no wolf at all and the Meadow Race had continued without her, she was furious. Everyone knew how clever Hodge was with his impersonations so only he could have made those snarls and growls; but she could not understand how he had contrived to make them come from in front of her when he was some distance behind.

Angry but confused, she glowered at her brother's friends and was even more vexed to discover she had also missed the Barley Swing.

In the shadow of the yew tree, the fieldmice gathered to watch the Wrestling. Dimsel was in such a foul temper that no one stood a chance against her. Even the burliest of mice were nervous of her and she won each bout easily.

Then came the Pebble Lift and she proved herself the strongest mouse in Fennywolde by holding the heaviest stone above her head for longer than anyone ever had before.

Todkin and the others were aghast. In one afternoon Dimsel had won two events. If she won just one more she could become the main champion of the Games.

Only one event was left that day – the Tree Climb.

It was early evening when everyone assembled over by the oaks and formed a wide circle beneath the tallest.

Young Whortle stepped forward with the other competitors. The Tree Climb was a favourite with everybody and so all the hopefuls had entered this event. Thirty-two fieldmice stared up at the distant branches right at the top and most were confident they could beat the others.

To Young Whortle's surprise, Figgy and Hodge had decided to enter this one as well.

'It's just a bit of fun fer us,' Figgy explained. 'Besides, I want to see if I can beat our Dimsel.'

'You'd better,' Todkin whispered to him.

'Where's Sammy?' Young Whortle asked. 'Not seen him since just after the wrestlin'.'

'I sent him to guard the raft at the den,' Todkin lied blithely. 'No telling what Dimsel will do now.'

The fieldmice limbered up and blew on their paws. Twit had recovered from the Tail Hang and was perky as ever and the Burdock brothers were eyeing one another belligerently. Jenkin was silent and brooding, Dimsel was still on the warpath and the rest were raring to go.

Young Whortle gazed up and simply wished he could be first.

With the drum in his paw, Mr Woodruffe stood in front of the massive oak and was about to strike it when Isaac Nettle barged in.

'A prayer to the Green!' he demanded. 'Before these impious ruffians go rampaging up one of His venerable creations, let us beg His pardon and ask for His blessing.'

To humour him and get it over with, the crowd bowed their heads, but standing at the back, Alison Sedge was sniffing a tormentil and humming something definitely unholy. Mr Nettle's eyes glinted at her with disdain but she merely shrugged and tossed her head.

When the prayer was over, Mr Woodruffe raised his paw once more.

'Now for the popular Tree Climb!' he proclaimed. 'May the best mouse win!'

He banged the drum and all the competitors darted to the tree. In a trice they were scrambling up the bark and the race had begun.

On the ground, Todkin crossed his fingers.

Up the oak the fieldmice dashed. They were all agile climbers so for the first few moments everyone was equal. Then the main leaders started to emerge. Young Whortle was an early contender: he whizzed up the oak as though Hobb himself was after him. But Dimsel and Jenkin were never far behind and it was soon impossible to tell who was winning, for the positions changed with every moment and each new branch that had to be navigated.

Figgy and Hodge kept close to the leaders but their sole aim was to hinder and hamper Young Whortle's rivals at every opportunity.

Just when they reached the halfway point, Figgy made his first move and grabbed Jenkin's tail, yanking it hard. The boy yelped and had to dig his toes and fingers into the rough bark to prevent himself falling. He threw Figgy a contemptuous look when the other boy climbed past him.

'Sorry about that,' Figgy shouted. 'Didn't mean to.'

That didn't fool Jenkin but it made him more determined to win than ever and he was soon hurrying by him again.

Without warning Figgy caught up and pushed roughly into him, pretending it was an accident and Jenkin had to swerve aside.

'Are you mad?' he cried, avoiding another reckless shove. 'You almost knocked me clean off.'

'Oh rubbish!' Figgy answered rudely. 'The Green Mouse wouldn't let anything bad happen to you – your dad would never let Him hear the end of it! He'd go on and on and on, like he always does – the dreary old droner.'

'Shut up about my dad!'

Figgy was delighted. Jenkin's devotion to his father was his weakness and he continued to hurl insults about Isaac Nettle until the boy could bear it no more.

'Stop it!' Jenkin bawled. 'You don't know what he's like! You got no idea. He's the brass-maker – the voice of the Green Mouse here in our field. How dare you say such things! Shrivel in the darkness, that's what you're goin' to do. You'll be struck down an' blighted!'

'Blight yourself, and your dad can go blight his miserable head as well and shove it up . . .'

That was too much. Jenkin reached across and tore Figgy from the tree trunk, throwing him down on to a branch and leaping after him with his fists at the ready.

Figgy skipped away, laughing. There was no way Jenkin could beat Young Whortle now. He took hold of a leafy twig and swung across to the neighbouring bough, then scarpered – his part in the sabotage of the Tree Climb achieved.

Quivering with rage, Jenkin stood on the branch glaring after him. Then he realised he had lost his chance of winning the race and uttered a cry of bitter disappointment.

'What'll Father say?' he cried in despair.

Meanwhile, Hodge was finding it difficult to catch up with Dimsel to ruin her chances.

He had heard Figgy taunting Jenkin and tried to do the same.

'Enjoy your run before?' he asked.

Above him, Dimsel only grunted.

'You should've seen your scared face!'

Again she ignored him and concentrated on her climbing.

Hodge began to snarl and growl like the wolf monster.

Dimsel heard him and clenched her teeth. Someone was due for a thumping and she promised herself that pleasure, as soon as the event was over.

Young Whortle did not understand what Hodge was going on about. He had also heard Jenkin's heated yells but thought the argument about the other night had flared up again. Bit silly, he thought, to do that in the middle of the race.

He loved climbing trees and this oak was one of his particular favourites. The evening was warm and he was relishing every moment of the race. Just then Dimsel was a little ahead of him but he put his back into it and hurried past her.

The girl's ears flattened against her head as she strove to climb faster. The top-most branches were already in view and the cheers of the crowd far below had grown very faint. With sweat trickling down her generous brows, Figgy's sister overtook Young Whortle for the last time.

'Dimsel,' she told herself. 'You're completely brilliant!'

Falling behind, Hodge knew she was going to win. There was nothing he could do. Only one chance remained . . .

High in the oak tree, sitting inside an old dusty hole in one of the tallest branches, Samuel Gorse peeped out and waited for the right moment. He had been there for ages and had struggled with his conscience about what Todkin had told him to do. Yet the oath he had sworn could not be denied and so there was no way out.

Peering out again, he saw Dimsel clambering closer – it was now or never.

Feeling horribly guilty, he reached out and threw down the object he held in his paw. It was something Figgy had been saving for several weeks.

Dimsel Bottom had no warning. The first she knew was when the wood pigeon's rotten egg smashed on her head and the putrid contents splattered down her face and ears and were dripping from her whiskers. The stench was horrendous and she almost choked straight away.

Baulking and coughing, she sat on the nearest branch and desperately tried to scrape the foulness from her fur.

Samuel pulled his head in sharply, in case she or anyone else should see him, and hid under a pile of dry leaves. He felt incredibly cruel, but the sight of her astonished face, crowned by the broken shell and the vile gunk that was running down her cheeks was the most sublime sight he had ever seen and it was one he always conjured in later years, to cheer himself up.

Outside, Young Whortle was so surprised at what had happened that he almost stopped to help Dimsel, but she pulled such a terrifying grimace at him that he left her alone and hurried upward.

'Go on!' Hodge yelled from below. 'You're nearly there, Neppy.'

Almost bursting with happiness, Young Whortle pushed his way through the leaves at the top of the oak.

He was about to give a whoop of victory when a chirpy voice said to him, 'Nice up here 'innit?'

And there was Twit, sitting in the fork of a twig, swinging his legs from side to side – his foolish face split by a great glad grin.

'How . . . how did you get here so fast?' Young Whortle spluttered.

Twit beamed at him. 'I likes climbin', I do,' he giggled. 'I done climbed up round the other side.'

The unexpected result of the Tree Climb confounded everybody, not least the Wolf Killers, but they took the optimistic view that at least neither Dimsel nor Jenkin had won it.

When everyone made their way home through the meadow, most of the Fennywolders regarded Twit with suspicion. How had such a tomfool managed so amazing a feat? He had always been a figure of fun and ridicule, so they found it almost impossible to see him in any other light. Elijah and Gladwin Scuttle, however, were the proudest mice in the whole countryside that night.

Young Whortle decided that a good sound sleep was what he needed, so he climbed into his nest early and thought about what had happened that day. He was not down-hearted. He had longed to be first at the top of the oak tree but the best fieldmouse had undoubtedly won, there was no denying that. Who would have thought silly Twit had that sort of speed and skill in him?

He sighed. Was it still possible for him to achieve his dream and become Head Sentry? He was not so certain now, but he had never guessed the Games would be so exciting. Even the older fieldmice who normally poured cold water on the achievements of the young had to admit it was turning out to be one of the best and most closely-run tournaments they had ever seen.

Puffing on his pipe in a corner of the Hall, Old Todmore was repeating the results to himself in order to commit them to memory. He knew that his listeners would want to hear about these Games long after they had finished.

'There's still a chance,' Young Whortle told himself. 'Nowt's decided yet.'

And very softly, he began to snore.

Later, when it had grown dark and Samuel thought it safe to descend from his hiding place in the tree, he met the other conspirators in their den and discussed everything that had occurred and what was needed for the following day.

'Young Whortle's got three events left,' Todkin told them by the light of the candle. 'The Raft Race, the Ditch Swim and the Ditch Vault.'

'The vault is in the morning,' Hodge said, 'the rafting is last in the afternoon and the swim is the morning after.'

'So that's most of his events done tomorrow,' Todkin muttered. 'But still plenty of time for Dimsel or Jenkin to win another few and be outright champion.'

'Well, Dimsel's already done four of her six,' Samuel reminded them. 'So she's only got the raft and one other left.'

'Probably the swim or the high jump,' Figgy said. 'She's good at both of those.'

Todkin mulled it over. 'And Jenkin's entered in

exactly the same ones as Young Whortle,' he added.

'Warty'll need a lot of help to win the pole-vault,' Samuel said glumly.

'I've thought of that,' Todkin replied. 'But it's the swim what worries me. He didn't get that minnow wiggle right and he never got a chance to practise on the *Silver Hare* cos of Dimsel pinchin' it.'

Hodge snickered and rubbed his paws together. 'I think Figgy and me should pay a visit to all them lovely rafts down by the Long Hedge,' he said. 'An' do some, ahem – slight modifications.'

'Oh that's sneaky!' exclaimed a shocked Sammy. 'Ain't that goin' a bit far?'

'Too late to say that now,' Todkin said. 'Besides, we swore to play every dirty trick we could. Now, if only we knew where Dimsel's stowed her raft as well.'

No one had any idea where that unseen craft might be hidden and so there was nothing more to discuss. Leaving Todkin and Samuel to guard the *Silver Hare*, Hodge and Figgy left the hut and made their way to the Long Hedge where, under cover of darkness, they set to work, fraying ropes and removing nails.

18

The Savage Goddess

Young Whortle whimpered in his sleep. He was dreaming, but his dreams were frightening and unpleasant. He was in the meadow with Sammy and they were running for their lives. A sinister shadow came swooping from the sky with out-stretched talons and he felt a terrible pain pierce his shoulder.

He rolled over in the nest and the dream changed. He was alone in the cornfield, a mist was rising and curling about his waist. He was lost and afraid and something evil was pursuing him, rattling and creaking through the barley.

'No!' he cried, arching his back before slumping down once more. Now he was cold and everything was dark. The blackness of the void enveloped him and he drifted through the emptiness until at last, a point of light appeared. He was lifted up, green flames leaped around him and he felt the warmth and pulse of life return.

In his ears a gentle, caring voice said, 'And this, my little rimpi-too, is my gift to you.'

A bright light shone and sunshine streamed into Young Whortle's eyes.

With a jolt, he awoke – breathless and shaken.

'Bless us!' he gasped, staring wildly around.

It was morning and a dazzling wedge of the glorious day was slanting into his nest.

Rubbing his eyes, he let out a sigh of relief and the horrors of the night melted and were forgotten.

'The Games!' he shouted, springing out of bed and clambering to the ground. 'I'm late!'

The Ditch Leap was the first event of the day. It was being held near the Long Hedge, where the ditch was narrowest and the opposing banks were roughly level. The aim was to jump from one side to the other and whoever leaped the furthest out of their three attempts was the winner. It seemed simple enough but usually only the tallest fieldmice went in for it.

When Young Whortle came hurrying, the crowd had already gathered and Lanky Brommock was just about to start his run-up.

Todkin and the other Wolf Killers greeted Young Whortle with friendly smiles. Around their necks, the mousebrasses were shining brilliantly, for Todkin had instructed everyone to give them a good polish.

'How's it goin'?' Young Whortle asked.

'Not bad,' said Figgy. 'Lanky will win this, no problem. The good thing is that neither Jenkin nor Dimsel are in it, so we don't have to worry.'

In four great strides, Lanky went charging towards the ditch. At the last moment he leaped from the bank. Everyone held their breath and he sailed through the air – landing on his heels, far over on the other side.

'No one will beat that,' Todkin observed.

'Who's next?' asked Young Whortle.

His friends chuckled. 'You'll never guess,' they said.

When the applause for Lanky had subsided, the next entrant stepped forward.

The crowd roared with laughter. It was Twit.

'Mornin' all!' he called, waving both paws.

'But he's smaller than I am,' Young Whortle exclaimed. 'What's he think he's a-doing?'

'He's showin' us just how crackers he really is,' Hodge said.

'Winnin' the Tree Climb must've cooked what teeny brains he had,' Figgy tittered.

A curt voice behind them made the Wolf Killers turn around.

'Twit's doing it because he wants to,' the voice said – and there was Jenkin Nettle. A fresh bruise blackened his eye and the five friends winced when they saw it.

Jenkin regarded them coldly and shot Figgy a reproachful look.

'There's other reasons to enter these Games,' he told them. 'It's not just for the glory of winning. Twit is trying his very best and puts every ounce of his little heart into his events, because he enjoys them so much. Isn't that more important? He does the best he can the whole time. He wants to join in and be a part of it but all you lot do is laugh and sneer. He's worth a hundred of you, and more.'

With one last disgusted glance at them, he pushed

his way forward and joined Twit's parents, to add his encouragement to theirs.

The Wolf Killers stared at one another un-comfortably.

'Maybe we should be nicer to Twit,' Young Whortle mumbled.

The others thought of the oath they had sworn. 'All right,' agreed Todkin. 'But let's get the Games over with first.'

'Did you see that shiner Jenkin had?' Samuel whistled. 'Never seen one as ugly as that before.'

'Clumsiest mouse in Fennywolde,' Hodge said with a shrug.

'As for that "taking part" rubbish,' Figgy scoffed, 'that's what losers always say – they want to win, same as the rest an' probably more.'

Any further speculation was drowned out, for Twit began his run-up. With a hop, sprint and a skip, he dashed at the bank and jumped. His pink tail twirled madly behind him and his arms whirled like windmills but he only succeeded in leaping halfway across the ditch and landed with a splash, up to his middle in water.

'Good job it weren't no deeper,' he called out happily. 'I can't swim.'

But his words were swamped by the laughter of the crowd and his father and Jenkin paddled in to fetch him.

The other competitors took their turns. Everyone

managed to reach the other bank with ease but, on each of his two remaining attempts, Twit could get no further than halfway and on the last jump fell face down.

Lanky Brommock won the Ditch Leap by a wide margin.

'I could've beat him,' Sammy tutted.

It was still a while before midday and the Fennywolders moved along the ditch to the gap between two elms. Here the water was deeper and the far bank higher. This was where the Ditch Vault was to take place.

The poles were stacked to one side and Samuel went to fetch Young Whortle's.

Six mice were taking part in this event: the Burdock brothers, Young Whortle, Lanky, Jenkin and Twit. Only one attempt was permitted, and if it went wrong there were no second chances.

'It's Jenkin and Lanky we have to worry about,' Samuel whispered to Todkin.

'No we don't,' came the suave reply.

Young Whortle looked across the ditch and balanced the pole in his paws. This was his weakest event but he was determined to try and use everything Sammy had taught him.

Mr Woodruffe stood on the far bank with the drum.

'And now the Ditch Vault!' he announced. 'Competitors must use their poles to flip themselves up on to here. Not an easy task.'

With a bang of the drum, the event commenced.

Abihu Burdock was first in line. He took up his pole and, with a superior look at his brother, ran to the ditch. Deftly he thrust the pole out and down – into the centre of the flowing water – then launched himself up into the air. There was a loud snap and the pole broke beneath him. Abihu shrieked and crashed into the ditch.

'Oh dear,' Todkin muttered dryly but no one heard him because Uriah Burdock was hooting with glee.

It was Twit's turn next. His pole seemed a little too large and heavy for him but he carried it resolutely at his side and charged forward. He was just about to push it into the centre of the ditch when it slipped from his fingers and fell sliding to the ground, and Twit fell on top of it. An instant later saw him astride the pole, unable to get off, and its momentum sent it rushing into the water – tipping him sideways into the drink.

Twit thrashed and spluttered and once again he had to be rescued. Covered head to toe in mud, he trudged to his mother with the guffaws of the Fennywolders filling his ears. For the first time in his eager, innocent life, he appeared hurt and dejected.

'I had nothing to do with that!' an earnest Todkin mouthed to Sammy.

Next up was Uriah. Giving his still-soaked brother a snooty glance, he ran to the bank and pushed down with his pole. The same snapping sound of splintering wood occurred when he was in mid-air and the pole broke in two places.

Yowling, he hurtled across the water and thudded comically into the side of the far bank, arms and legs spread wide around him.

As he peeled away and tumbled down the slope into the ditch, he was heard to warble, 'I beat you Abihu!'

When Lanky went to run at the ditch, he never got as far as using his pole. He slipped on some of the mud that had fallen from Twit and with one long leg waggling in the air, went slithering into the crowd.

It was Jenkin's turn. He looked over at the Wolf Killers accusingly, then examined the pole he had been given and called for a replacement.

Todkin pretended not to comprehend and signalled to Figgy and Hodge to follow him as he moved closer to the front. Then he shielded his eyes and squinted at the sky. The sun was resplendent and blazing, just as he had hoped.

When he was satisfied that his new pole had not been tampered with, Jenkin held it correctly and took large paces back to ensure a good run-up.

Todkin and the others absently toyed with their mousebrasses.

With a shout, Jenkin ran forward and Sammy could tell it was going to be a perfect vault.

Suddenly Jenkin cried out. Searing lights flooded across his eyes and blinded him. His thrust went wide of the mark and he was wrenched into the air before he could stop himself.

He clamped his eyes shut but they were still stinging and tiny suns were popping and flashing behind the lids as he flew over the ditch. Then he crashed against the far bank but, unlike Uriah, he had the presence of mind to clutch at the grass and haul himself over the edge.

The onlookers clapped half-heartedly. What a poor performance, they grumbled. Isaac Nettle was amongst them and he turned away, not bothering to see if his son was unharmed.

Winded and rueful, Jenkin blinked and his vision returned to normal, just in time to see his father stride off.

Todkin, Figgy and Hodge were elated but they had to wait until Young Whortle had his turn before they could celebrate.

'Now don't let go of the pole until you're in the air,' Samuel was telling him. 'You got nowt to worry about and very little to beat.'

Young Whortle nodded at him but was concentrating far too hard on what lay ahead to hear what was being said.

Solemnly, he lumbered towards the bank.

'Push down, leap up, push down, leap up,' he repeated to himself.

The pole shot out and into the middle of the ditch. Watching from the crowd, Samuel held his breath. It was the best that Warty had ever done. The small fieldmouse rose into the air in a graceful arc and then . . .

A huge groan issued from the Fennywolders and the Wolf Killers smacked their foreheads in disbelief.

The pole was sticking vertically in the ditch's thick mud and there, stranded at the very top, dangling with a mournful expression on his face, was Young Whortle. He had forgotten to let go.

'Oh you stupid Neppy,' he scolded himself and slithered down, thoroughly ashamed and blushingly embarrassed.

So it was judged that Jenkin had won the Ditch Vault, but it was the sorriest competition that any of the fieldmice had ever witnessed.

As it was lunchtime, a great picnic was held in the meadow. It was perfect weather. The scent of hawthorn blossom mingled with the sweet perfume of wild flowers and, combined with the delicious heat of midday, it was a potent spell. Everyone wanted to lounge in the long grass for as long as possible and nibble their favourite dishes, in between contented dozes. The only other event that day was going to be the Raft Race, so the picnic was a very leisurely and agreeable affair.

While the Wolf Killers ate their lunch, they tried to look on the bright side. It wasn't easy.

'You've got to win everything from now on,' Todkin instructed Young Whortle.

'And Dimsel mustn't win anything at all,' Figgy added. 'Nor Jenkin. They're both one up on you now.'

Sheepish as he was about his vaulting performance, Young Whortle still had hopes. He was certain no one would beat him in the swimming tomorrow and the *Silver Hare* really was a fabulous craft.

The afternoon crept languidly by and slowly the fieldmice began to stir and pack away the picnics.

It was time for the Raft Race.

Every newly-built vessel was brought to the ditch. Those by the Long Hedge were carried down and floated on the water. Most of them had been brightly painted and possessed gaudy sails and were decorated with home-made flags and pennants. Flowers festooned many prows and Ned Rattle's *Sunny Sunbeam* was bedecked with buttercups and daisies and a great dandelion was tied to the top of the mast, looking like a blazing sun.

The ditch was a riot of vibrant colour and Isaac Nettle viewed the florid flotilla with undisguised contempt.

He had forbidden Jenkin to paint his raft and it looked impoverished and drab compared to the others. Mr Nettle had named it the *Humble Servant* and was even critical of the seat that his son had attached to it, deeming it a luxury.

The Burdock brothers' pretty blue crafts were

identical to one another except that the flags were no longer red. Abihu's now flew a white one and Uriah had chosen yellow. Sitting aboard their vessels they ignored each other and drummed their fingers on their paddles.

Twit's *Scuttleboat* was one of the best. He had painted it a cheerful crimson and a crisp white sail was furled on the mast. He was immensely proud of what he and his father had built together. Whistling a lively tune, he stood on the deck and imagined he was on a huge, sea-going ship. He never dreamed that one day, he was destined to be aboard such a marvel.

With great ceremony and a chorus of howling, the Wolf Killers brought forth the *Silver Hare* and the Fennywolders marvelled at her.

Todkin's design really was elegant and he had worked very hard on the tablecloth sail. It was now dyed green and a leaping hare was painted in silver across it. When Young Whortle saw it he gasped, immediately thinking of the tapestry in the Grelffit Houm and what lay beyond.

' 'Tis . . .'tis just right,' was all he could stammer.

'Why, that's worthy of the Green Mouse Hisself!' called out a fieldmouse who had enjoyed too much berrybrew with his picnic.

Isaac Nettle's corrosive glance quelled any further blasphemous compliments and he watched the five friends manoeuvre the raft on to the water with the sourest face he had ever worn.

Only one more raft was still absent – Dimsel's.

As the would-be sailors prepared themselves and Young Whortle clambered on board the *Silver Hare*, a strange noise sounded over the meadow.

It was the slow clacking together of hollow sticks. They were clonking out a funereal rhythm and, amid that doleful beat were voices, chanting the same words over and over.

'The Savage Goddess is here, the Savage Goddess is here.'

The fieldmice muttered anxiously and looked to Mr Nettle for guidance.

'What is it?' they cried.

Acid-faced and cold, Isaac stared into the meadow. Already something could be seen moving through the tall grasses.

'Looks like feathers,' Mr Woodruffe declared, just as baffled as the rest of them.

Sitting on the *Silver Hare*, Young Whortle had a moment of panic. Could this be Mabb? Had the pagan goddess of the rats returned to Fennywolde, to finally wreak the vengeance of the Raith Sidhe upon its inhabitants?

'Not in bright daylight, surely?' he murmured.

Then all was revealed. The obscuring grasses parted and out strode Dimsel Bottom, banging together two large sticks.

Iris and Lily were directly behind her, chanting the words and between them they were carrying their leader's raft. It was a sturdy, well-built vessel of Dimsel's own devising and appeared capable of good speed, as well as being a menace to any other craft that sailed too near.

Todkin's face fell when he saw it.

The raft was painted black and straight twigs, whittled into spikes, speared out on all sides while, at the stern, the girls had fixed long pheasant feathers that reared up in a spreading fan shape.

It looked like a heathen craft from some barbaric legend and, to emphasize the theme, Dimsel had drawn thick charcoal lines across her face and wore a necklace of smaller feathers. There were more at her elbows and ankles and a crown of woven straw was jammed on her head.

Bashing the sticks together one last time, she threw them down and Iris and Lily called out, as they had rehearsed, 'All hail the Savage Goddess!'

There was a stunned silence.

Slowly every eye was drawn to Mr Nettle to see what his reaction would be, but he was not the first to speak.

'Pooh – what's that awful whiff of rotten eggs?' Alison Sedge said loudly from the crowd.

Dimsel ignored her.

Then Isaac raised a trembling finger and pointed at her charcoal-streaked face.

He was struggling to control himself and in a cracked, furious voice, declaimed, 'What new, wanton vileness is this? I say unto thee, insolent and graceless maid, the Almighty Green shall suffer thy sacrilege no longer! He shall smite thee and His retribution will be terrible. Thou shalt be accursed and the weight of His wrath shall not be lifted till thou repenteth a thousandfold!'

He whirled around and glowered at the rest of the fieldmice. They had never seen him this angry before and some of the younger children began to snivel and cry.

'Impious and profane thou art,' he bellowed. 'All are guilty. Thou hast turned away from the Green Laws and thy festering sins stink in His face. Indulge thy avarices and sail thy vainglorious boats, but I shall not stay to witness it!'

With fire in his eyes, he spat at Dimsel's feet then marched through the assembly, and everyone jumped aside to let him pass.

On the *Humble Servant*, Jenkin put his head in his paws.

Dimsel Bottom stood proud and haughty. She had not dared to hope her appearance would inspire such a dramatic effect and a conceited smile twitched on to her face.

Mr Woodruffe walked over to her. He was not impressed. 'Poorly done,' he told her. 'Where would we be without our mousebrass-maker? I don't care what your opinion of him is – you will show Mr Nettle the respect he is due.'

Dimsel was about to object but he held up his paw.

'No arguments,' he said tersely. 'Another word from you and you'll be disqualified from the Raft Race, before your nasty little creation even touches the water.'

That silenced her but she stared back at him mutinously.

The King of the Field waved her away and Dimsel told Lily and Iris to take the *Savage Goddess* to the ditch.

Todkin shook his head miserably when he saw how buoyant it was and how steadily it floated.

'Young Whortle don't stand an earthly,' he muttered.

Figgy and Hodge groaned; if only they had been able to sabotage Dimsel's vessel.

'That's it then,' Figgy said. 'Might as well award the

Head Sentryship to my sister right now and cancel the other events. She's as good as won.'

Samuel looked at the *Savage Goddess*, then the *Silver Hare*. There was no doubt about it, Dimsel had the better raft and he knew she would not scruple to barge by and ram her rivals or merely scare them off with those brutal spikes. Poor Young Whortle, he had so ached to win. Even now his little face was still trying to look hopeful and intrepid, but Sammy could tell he was afraid he had lost before the race had begun.

And so Samuel Gorse made a decision, for friendship's sake.

The Fennywolders spread themselves out along the ditch and some even went to the still pool to bag the best views for the finish.

When everyone was ready, Mr Woodruffe returned to the high bank where he could look down on the race, and took up his drum.

The rafts were lined up and anyone not intending to compete was told to leave the water.

Figgy looked around him. 'Where's Sammy gone?' he asked. 'He'll miss the start.'

'No he won't,' Hodge said in surprise. 'There he is – he was talking to your sister!'

Samuel hurried back to them, strangely silent and downcast.

'What were you doing with her?' Figgy demanded suspiciously.

Samuel avoided his eye. 'Just making a sacrifice to

the *Savage Goddess*,' he replied.

Figgy and Hodge scowled but clever Todkin realised what he had done and knew how dearly it had cost him.

'Green love you, Sammy,' he said.

Mr Woodruffe's voice cut through Figgy and Hodge's puzzled questions.

'Let the Raft Race commence!' he cried from the far bank and, with a flourish, he struck the drum.

With his back against the mast, Young Whortle plunged his paddle into the water on the left, drew it back then repeated it on the right.

Whether it was the excitement or his new love of the water, he did not know, but he no longer felt seasick and the *Silver Hare* shot into the lead straight away.

Squatting cross-legged on the *Savage Goddess*, Dimsel Bottom gave a yell of challenge and paddled furiously.

Ned Rattle's *Sunny Sunbeam* was closest to her and those cruel spikes were soon heading right for him.

Fretting, he steered his raft away but crashed into the *Scuttleboat* on the other side and Twit yelped as he endeavoured to keep his vessel steady.

The *Sunny Sunbeam* took on water and promptly sank. Ned swam ashore and stared back miserably. The dandelion that had adorned the mast had bobbed to the surface and was now floating there like a wreath.

Dimsel cackled and drove the *Savage Goddess* out into the centre of the ditch, scattering the other competitors to the edges, where they were forced to bump and scrape along in the shallows.

The Burdock brothers had started well but were already in difficulties. The mast of Abihu's craft was teetering and wobbling and Uriah's deck had sprung a leak.

As they strove to counter these calamities, they neglected to watch where they were going and so the two blue rafts smashed into one another. With a glug and a plop, they both sank and only their flags remained above water, fluttering sadly. The brothers made it to dry land, where they instantly started scrapping and had to be pulled apart.

'Three down,' Figgy mumured.

Jenkin was determined to beat Dimsel. He paddled fearlessly close to her vicious spikes and the brazen girl tried to push him away with her paddle.

'Hey!' Jenkin shouted, knocking it aside with his fist. 'That's against the rules.'

'Stuff them!' Dimsel laughed, doing it again. 'And stuff you!'

This time the flat blade of her paddle smacked him across the ear and Jenkin blazed with fury.

'Nobody hits me!' he bawled, and to Dimsel's dismay he grabbed her paddle and wrenched it from her, hurling it into the crowd on the bank.

'No!' Dimsel shrieked. 'How am I supposed to paddle now?'

The grim-faced Jenkin made no reply and the

Humble Servant pulled away from her, closing in on Young Whortle's raft.

In the audience, Hodge and Figgy cheered. Now Warty had a chance.

But Dimsel was not so easily hindered. The *Savage Goddess* drifted aimlessly along, twirling helplessly in a circle but she was far from beaten.

Twit was loving every minute of being captain of the *Scuttleboat*. The unfurled sail was now billowing gently, filled with the warm breeze and he was singing a jolly song his mother had taught him.

Shrubby Raggit's raft was almost level with his own and Twit gave him a happy wave.

'How do, Shrubby!' he called. 'B'ain't it grand?'

The other mouse returned the salutation, then they had to steer around the sunken Burdock vessels and were soon sailing closer to the sinister shape of the *Savage Goddess*.

'You go left, I'll go right!' Twit shouted to Shrubby and they carefully navigated around the ugly craft, ducking out of the way of the spikes.

Standing on deck, her face twisted with impotent rage, Dimsel looked quickly at the pair of them and chose the most likely.

To Twit's surprise and alarm she jumped from the *Savage Goddess* and landed heavily on the *Scuttleboat*. The crimson raft tipped and yawed and Twit almost slid off the stern.

'I'll have that!' Dimsel commanded, snatching the

paddle from the astonished fieldmouse.

'That's mine!' Twit cried. 'Give it back!'

Dimsel snorted and leaped back to the *Savage Goddess*.

'It's wasted in your paws anyway – you dim mongrel,' she spat.

Everyone on the shore was horrified at what she had done and at her spiteful words. They began to boo her.

Dimsel merely scoffed in answer and made rude signs to them. She was going to win. When they awarded her the title of Head Sentry she would take enormous delight in telling them all where to stick it.

Guffawing, she used the *Scuttleboat's* paddle to bring the *Savage Goddess* around and set off in desperate pursuit of Jenkin and Young Whortle.

Adrift on his raft, Twit did not know what to do. He could not swim to the bank and Dimsel's hateful words throbbed in his head like a gong. Why was she so nasty? Why did they all pick on him? He only wanted to be friends. Suddenly the *Scuttleboat* tipped once more but this time it was serious. The ropes that bound the branches of the deck together were unravelling. Someone had loosened the knots.

'The rotten bullies,' he wept. 'Why for they wanna do that to me? My lovely raft! Oh, help – help!'

The *Scuttleboat* split apart beneath him and all that remained was a collection of crimson sticks.

Twit squealed and thrashed wildly in the deep water.

To their shame, the Fennywolders laughed at his frantic efforts.

'Look at silly Twit!' they giggled.

'What a barmy performance!'

'Shame there's not a prize for best idiot – he'd win every year!'

Twit's father pushed his way though them.

'My boy's drowning!' he yelled.

Elijah Scuttle leaped into the ditch but he wasn't a strong swimmer either and soon he, too, was in trouble.

At once Figgy and Hodge dived in and swiftly brought them both safely back to the bank, where Mrs Scuttle hugged her husband and son and kissed them anxiously.

'Oh, Mam,' Twit wept in her arms. 'I can't stay here no more. I got to get me away.'

Gladwin pressed him close to her and he collapsed in desolate sobs. Then she turned to thank Hodge and Figgy for saving them. But they had already slunk back into the crowd, consumed with guilt and remorse for having sabotaged Twit's lovely raft.

Further along the ditch, Shrubby was also in difficulties. When the *Savage Goddess* came thrusting past, his vessel had sprung three leaks and he was sitting in water.

Dimsel mocked him and continued paddling. Jenkin was not far away now.

Using her considerable strength, she ploughed on and the ditch churned and frothed in her wake.

They had entered the final stretch and the gap was
closing between them.

Young Whortle was still in the lead. His eyes shone
and although he was tiring, he was not going to stop
paddling until he reached the finish, in the centre of
the pond.

He had not looked back since the race began, so he
knew nothing of Twit's problems or Dimsel's cruelty
but now, feeling confident, he chanced to glance over
his shoulder.

The *Savage Goddess* was almost parallel with the *Humble Servant* and their captains were shouting insults at one another. Behind them he could see only the few ramshackle rafts that remained afloat, for Shrubby's was already at the bottom of the ditch.

Chortling happily, he faced the front again and continued, shuddering as he passed beneath the cold shadow of the Hanging Tree.

The pool was almost in sight.

Todkin's voice came calling to him from the bank and Young Whortle saw his friend running along the shore, pointing and jumping up and down.

'Hello!' he shouted back and, tilting his head, he did the gang's wolf howl.

Too late he saw the water bubbling and foaming in his path and understood what Todkin had been trying to warn him about. He had completely forgotten the great rocks that lay before the pool mouth.

Young Whortle panicked and paddled madly, trying to turn aside and steer between them. There was a grinding crunch and the *Silver Hare* ran aground.

'No!' he cried.

Quickly he jumped onto the rock, and pushed and heaved with all his might to free her.

Jenkin and Dimsel were still hurling insults at one another. The *Savage Goddess* swung dangerously close and the spikes grazed Jenkin's side.

'Keep back!' he told her.

'What are you goin' to do if'n I don't, brassy boy?'

she crowed. 'Set yer dad on me? Some threat that be, for every Green lecture he throws my way, I'll make his whiskers curl with summat worse! His stupid Green Mouse don't frighten me no more.'

Jenkin stared at her, aghast. 'Don't say such things!' he cried.

'If your Green Mouse is as powerful as you think,' she snapped, 'then how come I'm going to win these Games?'

'Who says?'

'I do! And He can't stop me.'

Both of them strained at their paddles. They saw Young Whortle struggling with the *Silver Hare* on the rock and Dimsel shrieked with glee.

But for Jenkin it was all over. His raft was coming apart – just like Twit's and Shrubby's had.

There was nothing he could do and the *Humble Servant* broke up and he was tipped into the water.

Dimsel's raucous, gloating laughter was horrible.

'Don't worry, Jenky! Alison Sedge will give you the kiss of life – it's what she's always wanted. Now, make way for the Dimster, best mouse in the whole of Fennywolde and beyond!'

The *Savage Goddess* sailed away, towards the rocks where Young Whortle was still grunting and shoving.

Jenkin swam to the shore and glared after her. 'I pray my dad is right,' he muttered. 'And you get punished good an' proper.'

Young Whortle gave one further push and, to his

relief, his raft started to budge. He gave it another and it broke free of the rocks.

Rejoicing, he leaped on board again and took up the paddle, just as Dimsel came ramming behind him.

The prow of the *Savage Goddess* slammed into the *Silver Hare* and the deck rail cracked in two.

Everyone on the bank gasped in horror.

Young Whortle was flung backwards and he hit his head on the mast.

Dimsel roared with callous laughter and, using Twit's stolen paddle as a weapon, gave her rival's raft an angry blow that set it rocking violently.

'Hoy!' Young Whortle shouted, rubbing the back of his head with one paw and clinging on with the other.

Ignoring him, Dimsel paddled relentlessly and the *Savage Goddess* cruised past.

Young Whortle was about to give chase when one of those spikes caught his sail. Todkin's beautiful work was torn from the mast and hung from Dimsel's horrid, wrecking vessel, trailing limply in the water behind.

She had nearly reached the still pool. Young Whortle could see it glinting and shimmering ahead as shafts of sunlight glowed through the trees.

'No you don't, Dimsel Bottom!' he fumed. 'You ain't gonna take this from me.'

More determined than ever, he dredged his paddle through the water.

Dimsel forced her way through the reeds and out on

to the brimming pond the *Savage Goddess* went sailing. Almost there, almost at the finish – it was the most wonderful feeling.

Throwing up her paws, she gave a triumphant cry – then coughed. The breath wheezed in her lungs and she started to feel dizzy. She thought she was going to faint and was furious with herself for being so weak. Only a few more paddles and she would shoot across the pond's surface and be victorious.

Feeling giddy, she dipped the paddle into the water then screeched in horror when she saw her paws. They were puffing up like balloons and so were her toes!

Dimsel howled – what was happening?

Her feet swelled and the bands of feathers she wore snapped from her ankles. Then her legs grew heavy and each one inflated to the width of her shoulders. Her arms burgeoned and sagged until she could no longer hold them up and they swung at her sides. A deep rumbling sounded in her stomach and three rolls of flab avalanched across her belly and her tail became a stout sausage. She felt her necklace tighten and break as her jowls expanded and her cheeks grew round and blubbery.

Oblivious of her transformation, Young Whortle came darting from the rear on the *Silver Hare* and paddled like a mouse demented, until his raft rushed over the pool and past the centre. He had won!

Suddenly Dimsel screeched.

'I'm fat!' she bellowed. 'I'm fat!'

The *Savage Goddess* lurched and buckled under her weight, then capsized and she was pitched into the water.

Young Whortle rose and stood on the deck of his raft.

'Oh, Sammy,' he whispered. 'What have you done?'

19

Amnemsis

Young Whortle paddled quickly back to where Dimsel was labouring in the water and towed her great bulk to the bank, where she beached herself and lay gasping.

The Fennywolders gathered around her in awe and amazement.

''Tis a judgement,' they muttered.

'Serve her right.'

'What did Mister Nettle say? The weight of the Green Mouse's wrath, that's what!'

'And that's some weight!'

'The power of the Green Mouse has been shown.'

'Well, I never saw anyone so huge in all my days. She won't fit in a normal nest.'

Dimsel tried to move but she was too heavy and she sobbed piteously.

'I'm too fat!' she howled.

Alison Sedge knelt down and patted her large head.

'Tush now,' she cooed. 'You ain't fat, Dimsel – you're gigantic.'

Dimsel blubbed even more and Alison capered lightly away. This was the best day she could remember and she went in search of Jenkin. But young Master

Nettle had already left to find his father.

The other mice continued to tut and stare.

'She won't pop, will she?' someone asked.

Several of the bravest youngsters crept forward and gave Dimsel's bloated tummy a tentative prod. Her ample flesh undulated and rippled around her.

'She's like a jelly puddin',' they trilled.

Most of the crowd grew fearful. Although it was fascinating, such shocking displays of vengeance from their Green Mouse were unheard of and they hurried home to offer up prayers and swear that they were faithful.

When Figgy saw his sister, huge and helpless, he couldn't stop laughing but his parents were more practical and did their best to comfort her.

The *Savage Goddess* was rescued from the pool and, once the spikes were removed, wheels were fitted underneath. It took five burly fieldmice to roll Dimsel on to it, for she was far too big to move unaided and then, straining their backs, they trawled her to the Hall of Corn.

After that, Dimsel was never the same malicious bully. She had learned her lesson and no longer doubted the Almighty Green. Her colossal weight took over a year to shed and with it went her pride and arrogance. It was a much gentler mouse maiden who eventually emerged from those mammoth layers, but she and Alison Sedge still never saw eye to eye.

★

Young Whortle had stayed by the pond to help retrieve the *Savage Goddess* but as soon as that was done, he went in search of his friends, for even Figgy had disappeared by that point.

When he reached the den he was very agitated and angry. He stormed inside.

His fellow Wolf Killers were giggling and greeted him warmly.

'It's the winner of the Raft Race!' Hodge declared.

'Captain Neppy!' Todkin cried. 'Whale catcher!'

'You didn't say the new password,' Figgy laughed. 'From now on it's "barrel of lard"!'

Hodge sprawled on his back and in a big, lazy voice moaned, 'I can't blink, my eyelids are too fat to shift.'

Todkin and Figgy collapsed into each other and tears rolled down their faces.

Young Whortle stood before them with his arms folded. He stared crossly at Samuel, who was wringing his paws and looking awkward.

'I did it for you, Warty,' he explained. 'I didn't mean for her to guzzle down the whole biscuit – she grabbed it off me.'

'Did it for me?' Young Whortle snapped and the outrage in his voice caused the others to stop laughing.

'So you could win,' Sammy burbled wretchedly.

'I could've won on my own,' Young Whortle shouted.

'No you couldn't!' Todkin retorted. 'Dimsel was out to win by any means and deserved what she got.'

Young Whortle rounded on him. 'It don't matter if she did deserve it!' he yelled. 'Sammy givin' her his biscuit makes me a cheat as well.'

'So?' Figgy cried.

Todkin kicked him and in that instant, Young Whortle understood.

'You've been fixing everything all along, haven't you?' he muttered. 'The poles that snapped, the stalks that collapsed, the rotten egg . . . what else have you done?'

They cast their eyes down and shifted awkwardly.

'Did you help me win the Tail Hang?' he demanded.

'No!' Todkin insisted. 'You did that all on your own – I promise!'

Young Whortle shook his head. 'But there's more I don't know about,' he guessed shrewdly. 'I wanted to win the Games to prove summat, to be summat good and fine – not be the cheatin' mouse with liars and dirty tricksters for friends. How could you?'

The others said nothing.

'And you, Sammy!' Young Whortle exclaimed. 'I'm disappointed in you, most of all.'

'What are you going to do?' Todkin asked.

'I'm going straight to Mister Woodruffe.'

His friends stared at him pleadingly.

'What are you going to tell him?' Hodge murmured.

Young Whortle drew his paw over his face. 'Oh stop worrying,' he said. 'I'm not going to rat on you. I'll just say that I doesn't want the Raft Race to count and we should all be given another chance at summat else tomorrow.'

'Tomorrow?' Todkin squeaked. 'But you're already entered in the swim and that only leaves the High Jump and . . .'

'And the Slingshot,' Samuel said.

'Then I'll take my chances,' Young Whortle barked. 'And don't any of you dare try to cheat fer me again, do you hear me?'

His friends nodded and Young Whortle stomped from the den to find Mr Woodruffe.

Todkin gave a forlorn sigh. 'He's lost, then,' he said flatly.

The King of the Field was in the Hall of Corn when Young Whortle found him. Mr Woodruffe was organising a huge domed nest to be built on the ground for Dimsel.

When he heard Young Whortle's plan he thought about it for several moments then agreed, clapping the boy on the back for being so considerate and fair-minded.

Feeling neither, Young Whortle took himself off for a walk through the barley, deep in thought.

He wasn't even sure he wanted to continue with the Games. Knowing his friends had connived behind his back hurt him deeply and he felt resentful, betrayed and foolish.

The evening wore on and he spent his sentry duty in

a different part of the cornfield, away from the others.

When he returned to the Hall, Dimsel's new home was complete and they were wheeling her inside.

'Don't you fret now,' her mother was saying. 'We'll be close by if you need anything – so long as it's not a pie.'

The girl could only weep in answer and, with her famous want of tact, Grandma Bottom remarked that even her tears were fat.

After the excitement and wonders of the day, Fennywolde went to bed early. Around the Hall of Corn, the lanterns were extinguished and the nests were lost in darkness.

It was a fine cool night, the stars were white and clear and, when Young Whortle clambered into his own small nest, he glanced sleepily up at the moon. It was full and milky bright, but shimmering around it was a halo of fiery colours.

The fieldmouse's mouth dropped open. How could he have forgotten?

Leaping back to the ground, he raced from the Hall – wide-awake and exhilarated. The Games and the hurt were banished from his mind and he rushed to the still pool, faster than he had run in the Meadow Race.

Tearing along the track by the ditch, he saw flickering lights through the trees ahead. Pushing through the undergrowth, he caught his breath and drank in the sight, wishing with all his heart to remember it exactly as it was – in every detail.

The still pool had never looked so beautiful and enchanted. Now he could understand why the water voles revered it. Hundreds of torches had been pushed into the banks, forming an unbroken ring of fire, but the flames were as white as frost and crackled with tiny stars.

From the overhanging branches of the surrounding trees, lamps of emerald glass were suspended from silver chains. The surface of the pond mirrored every scintillating gleam and scattered the bouncing reflections, so that the very air was aglow and trembling with lustrous light.

It was the most enchanting, magical vision Young Whortle had ever seen – so unreal and ravishing and yet no dream.

With fire sparkling in his eyes, he turned his gaze and looked across the water to the island of boulders. The entrance to the Grelffit Houm was open and two tall posts topped by ornate lanterns stood either side of it.

He was just about to swim over when he saw his own raft come sailing around the great stones and, standing upon it, was Woppenfrake.

The water vole was dressed in a long, cream-coloured robe, embroidered with golden thread. On his brow the silver band gleamed and glittered and he appeared more noble and magnificent than Young Whortle had ever guessed.

Gracefully, and without the use of any paddle, the

Silver Hare floated towards him and bumped gently into the shore.

Woppenfrake smiled and bowed.

'You are most welcome,' he said in a soft whisper. 'My brothers and I have fasted these two days below ground, retreating into ourselves and meditating on the journey that awaits us. It lightens my mood to see you again, but tell me, what has been happening on the Glinty Water? When we left the Grelffit Houm this evening, all was in disarray, I found pheasant feathers floating over yonder, a tablecloth with a hare painted upon it over in the reeds and I discovered this delightful craft, which could have been built by the Green Himself.'

Young Whortle laughed, a great carefree laugh and he realised just how much he had missed his mysterious friend.

Woppenfrake stepped from the *Silver Hare* and the two walked around the pond as he checked the torches and made certain everything was in order.

Quickly Young Whortle told him of the Raft Race, what had happened to Dimsel and how his friends had conspired to make him win.

'And is it their usual nature to be so deceitful?' Woppenfrake asked, when he had finished.

'No,' Young Whortle answered. 'That's what's so awful, them's good lads normally.'

The water vole laced his fingers across his chest and looked him straight in the eye. 'Then you can count yourself blessed,' he declared. 'For to help you, misguided though they were, they were willing to do dreadful things and in so doing, injure their selfs. Once again I regret not knowing them.'

'Well, they've put me in a right pickle now. I got to choose one more event to do tomorrow after the Swim and there's only the High Jump and the Slingshot left.'

Woppenfrake peered down at him.

'Your size would make jumping any height a difficulty,' he observed. 'But what of the other? How is your aim?'

'You might as well ask me to lift Dimsel,' Young Whortle laughed. 'I be the worst at the Slingshot in the history of Fennywolde. I'm downright dangerous with one of them there things – everyone knows that.'

He shrugged his shoulders in resignation.

'I'll just do the Swim.' He sighed. 'If only the lads hadn't been so daft – never mind. Oh, but they'll be awful sorry to hear you've left us. Do you really have to go?'

'You know I must. The world's veins are clogged with sickness. The spirit of the Glinty Water will not survive if he tarries. But be not sad at heart, for this night you shall meet him.'

Young Whortle stared at the pool and the countless lights danced and glittered before his eyes.

'What's he like?' he asked nervously.

'He has many aspects,' Woppenfrake said. 'Old and young, solemn as a louring sky, deadly as the storm or merry as birdsong. Once there were many of his kind and each possessed great powers. Through him, my brothers and I have outlived the centuries and it was his enchantments that called Fenlyn Purfote from death's darkness. One of the mightiest spirits of old is he who dwells within the Glinty Water.'

A shiver of anticipation ran through Young Whortle. 'How will he appear tonight, then?' he asked. 'Solemn or deadly?'

'Have no fear,' the water vole said. 'When my brothers and I summon him, we shall call upon his joyous side, for this night is a celebration – a festival of farewell to the land his presence has hallowed since this world was shaped.'

'And he won't mind me bein' here?'

Woppenfrake chuckled. 'Of course not!' he exclaimed. 'You are our honoured guest. Besides – a son of Fennywolde has the right to be present. The rimpi-toos have been his neighbours for many—'

He paused and an idea seized him.

'Master Nep,' he said quickly. 'How are you with needle and thread?'

Young Whortle started at him blankly. 'Never tried,' he answered.

'But no doubt you could manage to stitch three small things together?'

'I suppose – so long as nowt fancy's wanted.'

The water vole clapped his paws and excitement gripped him.

'There is yet time,' he cried. 'The ceremony will not begin till Firgild has completed his work in the Grelffit Houm. The Ancient has kept his promise and told to us the name of the valiant hero who will come to awaken Captain Fenlyn when the great evil darkens this land. My brother is painting that name in the empty panel as we speak and Willibald is preparing the incense for tonight's invocation. Hurry, before their tasks are done!'

Young Whortle grinned to see him so animated and eager. 'What do you want me to sew?' he giggled. 'Have you ripped yer frock?'

'The oaks!' Woppenfrake said urgently. 'The oaks beyond the meadow. You are familiar with them, you climb them often, do you not?'

'All the time,' came the amused answer. 'You got a magic needle that sews trees together then? What good's that?'

The water vole ignored his frivolity.

'Climb up and up,' he told him. 'To the topmost sprig and fetch back three perfect new leaves.'

Young Whortle thought he was joking. 'One for each of you?' he asked. 'Wouldn't you rather have a nice cheese pasty?'

'Hurry,' Woppenfrake insisted. 'Before the ceremony begins!'

The fieldmouse was baffled. It sounded like absurd nonsense but the inhabitants of the Grelffit Houm were above his understanding and if Woppenfrake needed three oak leaves, he was not going to argue.

'I'll be fast as I can,' he promised. 'Don't start your party without me.'

And he hurried off towards the meadow.

'Be swift my friend,' Woppenfrake murmured. 'You do not know how important this task shall prove for you. A year hence, your very life will depend upon it.'

Young Whortle reached the oaks in no time and scaled the very one he had climbed on the first day of the Games.

Cool night breezes rustled through the leaves which shimmered like pale silver under the moonlight. Within moments the fieldmouse was at the highest point, and sitting in exactly the same spot as Twit had.

With only the starry heavens above him, Young Whortle looked around for the newest leaves. Then he took a sharp breath, in wonder.

Fennywolde looked lovely. Basking in the moon's pearly splendour, his home really was the most hauntingly beautiful land. From that dizzy height every corner of the meadow was spread beneath him and, beyond that, the ditch was a ribbon of quicksilver. He gazed at the great cornfield in the distance, foaming with ghostly, wan shadows, and smiled.

The clump of trees around the still pool was glowing with magical light. It was as though luminous waters had poured down from the moon and filled the pond. Impatient to get back, Young Whortle set about completing the task he had been given.

Reaching out, he selected three of the newest, freshly unfurled leaves and pinched them from their twigs. Clamping them between his lips, he began the downward climb.

When he was only a third of the way from the ground, Young Whortle halted and pressed himself close to the trunk. He could hear voices.

Down there, in the oak's vast shadow, two figures were speaking. They were too far away for him to see who they were and the voices were low and indistinct. He scowled in annoyance. Who could be wandering about at this time of night? Whoever it was, he did not want to meet them and have to answer any awkward questions about his own comings and goings, so he crept on to a branch and waited for them to pass by.

Gradually the figures drew closer to his tree and he saw that one of them was taller than the other. One of the voices rose in anger and Young Whortle grew uncomfortable – they were having an argument.

Removing the young leaves from his mouth, he

wondered if he should cover his ears and not listen. Then the tall figure began to shout and with a shock, he knew who it was.

'Mister Nettle!' he breathed.

All thoughts of stopping his ears were forgotten and he leaned forward for a better view.

Sure enough, the taller figure was Isaac Nettle. Young Whortle strained his eyes to make out the other – it was his son, Jenkin.

'But Father!' Jenkin was pleading. 'I've tried my hardest. I've won two events and I can't fail to win another tomorrow.'

'Thou shouldst have won them all!' Isaac snapped back. 'If thou hadst been a true servant of the Green, then thou wouldst already be Head Sentry! He would have given thee victory over that godless rabble.'

'I'm sorry! But so many things have gone wrong. It weren't my fault the barley collapsed and the raft disintegrated.'

'Then what of the Tree Climb?' his father yelled, thumping his strong fist against the oak that Young Whortle was sitting in.

'That . . . that was my fault,' Jenkin confessed. 'I was to blame, I could have beaten Twit.'

'Thou didst let an imbecile beat thee! Why dost thou insult me so?'

'I'll do better.'

Isaac rounded on his son. 'For what reason did my beloved wife, thy mother, die giving thee life? None

335

that I can see – a wastrel and a disappointment thou hast ever been.'

'Don't say that, Father. You don't mean it. I will become Head Sentry – I swear by the Green I will.'

To Young Whortle's horror, he saw Mr Nettle grab Jenkin by the hair and hurl him roughly against the tree.

'How dare thee call on Him as witness to thy vain promises!' Isaac raged.

He raised his paw threateningly.

'Didst the fate of Dimsel Bottom not inspire thee with dread?' he thundered. 'The Almighty Green hath proven His anger and shown His power. Why dost thou never listen? When I look at thee, I see not a son – but the instrument of my wife's death. I hate thee with a heat fiercer than any I can stoke in my forge! I wish thou hadst never been born.'

Jenkin cried out to hear those vicious words and Young Whortle finally understood the origin of that outburst, when he and Sammy had found him weeping at the still pool. Jenkin was merely repeating what he had heard his father tell him, time and time again.

'Please, Father!' Jenkin begged. 'I only want to make you proud of me.'

'Proud?' Isaac screeched. 'Of thee? All thou bringeth me is shame and loathing!'

Young Whortle saw the fist fly down and, before he could stop himself, he cried out.

'NO!'

Mr Nettle stood back and stared up.

'What was that?' he snapped.

Shaking, Jenkin held his throbbing face. 'I . . . don't know,' he stuttered.

'Someone is there,' Isaac declared. 'Come here, whoever thou art.'

Young Whortle wanted to race down and tell Mr Nettle exactly what he thought of him, but he knew the mousebrass-maker would only take it out on Jenkin.

So much was explained now. All those knocks and bruises that Jenkin had claimed were due to his own clumsiness . . . he wasn't clumsy at all.

What could he do? Holding his breath, Young Whortle hid in the leaves.

'Who is it up there?' Isaac shouted.

Jenkin stood timidly by him and gazed up at the oak.

'Perhaps it was an owl?' he suggested.

His father snarled.

'There are no owls in Fennywolde!' he spat and, turning on his heel, he strode into the meadow.

'Yet what a grievous misfortune that is!' he called back. 'For, by the Green, I wish one would swoop down and carry thee off, that I might never see thy sickening face again.'

Jenkin made to wipe his eyes, but they were dry – he had no tears left. His face stinging, he saw his father vanish into the tall grasses and, with a heart almost too heavy to carry in his chest, he went stumbling after him.

In the oak, Young Whortle was consumed with anger and pity. As soon as the Games finished tomorrow he would tell Mr Woodruffe what he had seen and heard. The King of the Field would know what to do about it.

'Poor Jolly Jenkin,' he muttered. 'I wish he'd have told us.'

Remaining in the tree for as long as he thought it would take the Nettles to return to the cornfield, he put the harvested leaves back in his mouth and clambered down.

From the ground, he was relieved to see that the glimmering lights of the still pool were hidden from view. Good – Isaac Nettle would not be venturing there to ruin what was happening that night.

But Young Whortle had wasted enough time already, so he hastened back across the meadow.

Rushing through the undergrowth, he hurried beneath the trees around the pond and the shimmering light enveloped him.

By now Firgild and Willibald had joined their brother and they, too, wore long robes. Standing side by side on the shore, their arms were outstretched over the water and in their paws they each held a shallow silver bowl.

They were reciting strange words in their own antique language and Young Whortle felt suddenly humble and shy. He saw the water voles for what they were – mystical beings from a forgotten legend. He did not belong there.

'Just in time!' Woppenfrake called out to him abruptly. 'We had almost given up hope that you would return. Do not loiter there, come hither.'

Bashfully, the fieldmouse stepped forward and joined them.

Firgild and Willibald bowed in greeting.

'And you have the leaves!' Woppenfrake declared. 'Most excellent. Now, Firgild, loan him one of your needles.'

Firgild had it threaded and ready, and passed it over.

'What do you want me to stitch, then?' Young Whortle asked.

Woppenfrake stared at him in astonishment. 'Why, the leaves you have gathered, of course!' he exclaimed as though that was obvious. 'You must sew them together, and quickly, before the spirit of the Glinty Water appears.'

'We were just about to invoke him,' Willibald added, showing Young Whortle the incense that the silver bowls contained, as if that explained everything.

The fieldmouse looked at the three leaves and scratched his head. 'I know I'm only a simple rimpitoo,' he began. 'But just what am I supposed to make from these?'

'Why – a hat!'

'Yes, a hat! What else?'

'A jaunty little hat for the journey.'

Young Whortle fixed them with a suspicious scowl. 'You pulling my tail?' he asked.

The water voles chortled at his disbelief.

'We assure you we are not,' Woopenfrake told him. 'The spirit will appear to us in his most child-like aspect. He will delight in any gift made by your own paws. Trust me, Master Nep, if you do this – you shall earn his blessing.'

'And maybe more besides,' Firgild said mysteriously.

The fieldmouse shrugged. 'If it'll keep you all happy.' He grinned and, sticking his tongue out for extra concentration, he sat on a stone and began sewing the leaves together into a very rough hat shape.

The three brothers exchanged meaningful glances.

'It will suffice,' Woppenfrake whispered. 'The boon will be granted.'

Willibald nodded. 'Then let the ceremony commence,' he said.

Taking up one of the burning torches, he held it aloft and called out.

'As it was written, this night the flame is around the opal moon and so the time is upon us. Thus the Millagaroo, the sons of Virianna are here. I, Willibald of the Gilded Dawn, summon you.'

Firgild took up another torch and, as it flared and crackled above his head, shouted, 'The time of our leaving is here, arise from the deeps – I, Firgild, Guardian of Forgotten Secrets, summon you.'

Woppenfrake held up a third torch.

'The journey begins this night,' he called. 'Come – be amongst us, let us bid this sacred place farewell and grant a final blessing. I, Woppenfrake, Minister to the Glinty Water, summon you.'

As one, the brothers lowered the flaming ends of their torches into the silver bowls. The incense within spat and sparked and three streams of different coloured smoke began to rise and filled the air with a delicious honey-sweet scent.

Young Whortle finished sewing his ridiculous hat and tried it on for size. It slipped over one eye.

The water voles had returned the torches to the ground and were lifting the silver bowls high.

Golden smoke burned from the one Willibald held, sapphire blue poured from Firgild's bowl and Woppenfrake's was a brilliant green.

'Amnemsis, Amnemsis,' they exhorted. 'Arise from the far reaches – this final time.'

Stooping, they placed the bowls upon the water, waved their paws through the rising smoke and stood back.

To Young Whortle's delight, the three bowls quivered as unseen forces gripped them and they were drawn out over the pond. When they reached the centre, they revolved around one another in a circle and the smoke coiled in the air above, forming a billowing spiral of colour.

'Amnemsis,' the water voles cried. 'We welcome you.'

Young Whortle could not believe his eyes. Deep down in the pool, a soft radiance was flickering – the spirit was ascending.

The supernatural light grew steadily stronger, rising up beneath the spinning bowls. The smoke above had formed a pulsing, foggy cloud and suddenly from its heart a gentle rain began to patter down. The middle of the pond splashed and sizzled and the light welled up.

Woppenfrake turned to Young Whortle.

'Your gift,' he instructed. 'Place it upon the water, with the crown uppermost.'

The fieldmouse obeyed and at once the ludicrous, leafy hat sailed from his fingers and went scooting towards the centre, where the magical rain drummed down upon it.

There was a deep rumble and a flash of lightning seemed to burst beneath the water. For an instant the whole pond was a dazzling sheet of intense white flame, then Young Whortle's hat jiggled and his amazement increased when it started to rise up into the air.

'Now I seen it all,' he whispered, astounded.

For beneath the hat was a face.

'Amnemsis!' the water voles called reverently and they bowed as low as their stout bodies permitted.

Young Whortle did the same, but he couldn't help sneaking a peep at what was happening.

The being that rose from the still pool was the strangest he could ever have imagined.

He had expected the spirit of the pond to be an immense and powerful apparition, but the shape that emerged was only a fraction larger than himself – and the hat fitted perfectly.

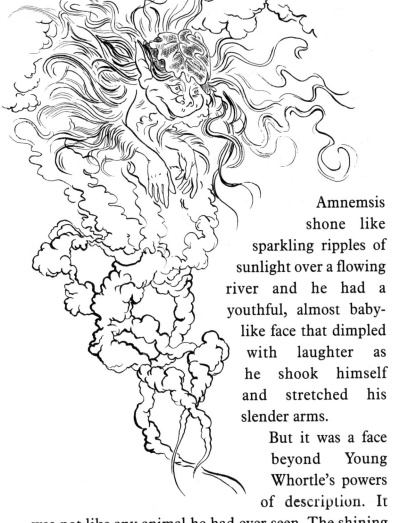

Amnemsis shone like sparkling ripples of sunlight over a flowing river and he had a youthful, almost baby-like face that dimpled with laughter as he shook himself and stretched his slender arms.

But it was a face beyond Young Whortle's powers of description. It was not like any animal he had ever seen. The shining skin was smooth as a frog's. Long pointed ears were wiggling under the rain and the nose was small and upturned above a wide, smiling mouth.

Young Whortle knew that it was a good and supremely noble face and he had nothing to fear.

Revelling in the splashing water, the spirit spun around. Iridescent droplets cascaded from his limbs and trembling rainbows flashed and faded around him.

Beneath the hat, his hair was silver and fine as spider silk. It not only covered his head in a luxuriant gossamer mane, but fringed his arms and flowed down his scaly back. When he moved, it streamed and swirled around him in strange slow waves, as if he were still beneath the pool.

Thrilled to the marrow of his tiny fieldmouse bones, Young Whortle could not take his eyes off him. The incredible spirit gambolled and cavorted in the magical rain, floating above the water as lightly as a flake of snow, buffeted by the wind.

His voice was as uncanny as the rest of him. It gurgled and trickled, gushed and babbled – filled with the music of clean rushing water. Young Whortle could have listened to it all night long. It was such a happy, pure sound that spoke of mountain rills, clear blue seas, glacial rivers and sprinkling summer showers.

Beaming indulgently, the water voles watched their Master's sprightly play as he ducked and weaved in and out of the smoke. They worshipped and venerated him in each of his aspects, but this merry spirit child was their favourite.

Amnemsis's bubbling joy was bottomless and infectious and Young Whortle was soon laughing with him. Tears rolled down his furry cheeks and when he wiped them with his paws and looked up again, he found that Amnemsis was staring straight at him.

The spirit's eyes were shining into his. They were two points of wintry light, as old and profound as the heavenly stars yet also benevolent and, at that moment, curious.

'Lord of the Hallowed Waters,' Woppenfrake addressed him. 'This is Young Whortle Nep – a most valiant and true friend of the Grelffit Houm.'

'Rimpi-too,' Amnemsis cried, the remarkable, shining face wreathed in glad smiles.

'Yes,' Firgild said. 'He is a descendant of those who journeyed hither with Fenlyn Purfote, whom you called back from the grave and wrapped in sleep till he is needed once more.'

Woppenfrake cleared his throat and added, 'Master Nep is the one who made that delightful hat which suits you so well.'

The spirit's eyes flashed at the water vole and Woppenfrake gave the slightest of nods as if an unspoken question had passed between them.

Amnemsis looked back at Young Whortle. The cloud above billowed forward and he floated closer.

'Evenin', Your Holiness,' the fieldmouse ventured, not sure what else to say to such a powerful being.

The white eyes glittered and a momentary chill passed through Young Whortle. He gasped in surprise. It was as if a cold tide had flooded his heart, but he sensed it was nothing to be afraid of; and when it passed, he felt lighter and the burden of the recent days was lifted.

Amnemsis reached out an elegant, glistening hand and touched him lightly upon the forehead. His dimpling smile widened and he turned to the water voles, uttering something in their archaic tongue. Whatever it was, it pleased them immensely and Woppenfrake was profuse in his thanks.

Young Whortle was desperate to know what was being said, because whatever it was sounded marvellous. They were all so jovial. Then Woppenfrake saw his questioning glance and begged his pardon.

'Our Lord, Amnemsis, is aware of your plight with the Games tomorrow,' he explained. 'Your gift has pleased him as I hoped it would and so he will grant unto you one more wish, the very last drop of magic from the Glinty Water. But first . . .'

The spirit gurgled and held out both hands.

The fieldmouse raised his paws and Amnemsis clasped them. The sweet-smelling smoke twisted about Young Whortle's waist and suddenly he was lifted off the ground.

Amnemsis sang out, his voice splintering into many notes and the fieldmouse was drawn up into the air, then out over the still pool where the spirit loosened his hold on his paws and released them.

Young Whortle thought he was going to fall and

thrashed his arms and legs, only to discover that he was as light as a feather.

'I'm floatin'!' he gasped. 'Like a soapy bubble!'

Amnemsis grinned and swooped down over the water, signalling for him to follow.

The fieldmouse somersaulted and pointed his nose downward. With a whisk of his tail he shot after him. It was the most fantastic sensation – he was flying. He could hardly believe it but here he was, darting through the drizzly cloud like a giddy sparrow.

A sudden squirt of water spouted up from the pond and hit him in the face. He looked around and Amnemsis was pointing and laughing.

Young Whortle pulled a pretend scowl. 'Oh no you don't!' he said and chased after him.

Happy as children they flew across the pond, diving low then soaring up and weaving in and out of the leafy branches.

On the shore, the water voles watched them playing and remembered when they were young. Amnemsis had taken care of them when they were orphaned and they would never leave him.

'It is good the rimpi-too is here,' Firgild said. 'I fear I am far too old for such games.'

Woppenfrake raised an eyebrow at Willibald and, with mischievous chuckles, they pushed him into the pool.

Young Whortle rushed upwards after Amnemsis until they were higher than the trees and sitting on the top of the cloud. Bobbing gently up and down, the spirit surveyed the surrounding countryside and his radiance dimmed.

The fieldmouse understood.

'You been here a long time,' he said. 'Must be real hard to leave.'

Amnemsis only sighed in answer and they floated together in silence for a time.

Then the spirit's humour returned. He would make one last inspection of his age-old home. So, jumping up, he flew off, away from the smoke and the trees and over the cornfield.

'Wait for me!' Young Whortle shouted and, kicking his legs, he raced after him.

Like a streaking meteor, Amnemsis went tearing across the barley, tracing a bright path through the darkness.

Laughing all the while, the fieldmouse pursued him and the corn ears tickled his tummy as he scooted over the rustling surface. Then down they plunged, zooming between the stalks, and into the Hall of Corn where Amnemsis delighted in peeping into every nest.

The sleeping Fennywolders mumbled in their dreams and some drowsily asked for the lantern to be snuffed out. Grandma Bottom was the only one still awake and, when the spirit's face appeared at the entrance to her boudoir, she squealed and pulled the blanket up to her nose.

Amnemsis giggled at her funny face and reached in

to touch her, but she slapped his hand and sent him
cartwheeling backwards.

'Go haunt someone else!' she scolded. 'You should
be ashamed.'

Then the spirit was off again, hurtling towards the
ditch and the meadow beyond.

Ned Rattle and Shrubby Raggit were on sentry duty.
They had been discussing the disastrous Raft Race
when the unearthly, gleaming shape had come flaring
over the field and gone nipping in and out of the corn.
For the entire time it lingered in the Hall, they
remained stunned and stonily silent and only when it
went rocketing past them, causing their stems to sway,
did they turn to one another with their mouths
gawping.

But before either could utter a word, Young Whortle
Nep went scudding by, flying over the barley with his
feet in his paws and his tail dangling down.

'How do, lads!' he called.

Ned and Shrubby watched him disappear into the

distance and solemnly vowed never to drink berrybrew while on duty again.

Amnemsis and his new playmate flew over the meadow, scattering moths and bolting through the wild grasses, until at last they returned to the still pool, following the course of the ditch.

Three sopping water voles awaited them and Amnemsis shone brighter than ever.

'It is time,' Woppenfrake announced gravely and he held up his paw to call Young Whortle to him.

The fieldmouse floated down to the bank. As soon as

his feet touched the ground, he felt the magic leave him and he knew it was over.

He searched for something to say. How could he possibly thank them for everything they had done? Forcing a smile, he said, 'Pity you ain't going tomorrow night instead, I'd win the High Jump for sure if I could fly like that.'

Woppenfrake steepled his paws beneath his chin and looked beyond the torches to where a large stone jar stood.

'Amnemsis has still not granted you his final boon,' he declared. 'When we have departed, reach into there. What it contains is for you, with his and our blessing.'

'What's in there? 'Tis almost as tall as me.'

'You will discover that for yourself,' Willibald said.

'And what you do with it,' Firgild added, 'is up to you.'

Woppenfrake stared at the stars and sniffed the air.

'We must leave now,' he said. 'Our tenure is over at last.'

Young Whortle did not know how to say goodbye. Everything he thought of seemed clumsy and inadequate, so he threw his arms around Woppenfrake and hugged him desperately.

'Won't I ever see you again?' he muttered thickly.

'Perhaps,' the water vole replied softly as he returned the embrace. 'My brothers and I must go now. The journey must begin, our new home awaits us.'

Sadder than he had ever been, Young Whortle

looked up into his whiskery face.

'I wish I'd met you sooner,' he said, trying not to cry. 'But then, I'm just so glad and downright lucky to have knowed you at all. The luckiest mouse in the whole world, that's what I am.'

'It is we who are lucky,' Woppenfrake told him, and he meant it.

The fieldmouse sniffed and wiped his nose, then ran to the others and hugged them, too.

Flying back to the centre of the cloud, Amnemsis sang a mournful song and the water voles stepped out onto the pool. The spirit's magic upheld them and they walked over the shimmering surface to stand beside the three silver bowls.

'The Glinty Water is now yours,' Woppenfrake called. 'Be sure you take care of it.'

'I promise,' Young Whortle shouted back. 'For as long as I live.'

The brothers looked at one another sadly then raised their paws in farewell.

Above them, Amnemsis removed the leafy hat and bowed. His silver hair blew thickly about him and his eyes glittered.

The incense in the bowls crackled loudly and the smoke that poured from them sputtered and turned a snowy white. Soon the colourful cloud had transformed into a bank of dense white fog that flowed down, obscuring the sons of Virianna until they were grey silhouettes.

A strong wind suddenly blustered through the trees and ripped around the pool. Every torch was extinguished and the lamps were torn from the branches and fell into the water. With a grinding of stone, the entrance to the Grelffit Houm slid shut and the only light was the vague shape of Amnemsis floating within the fog.

Then the thick white mist began to lift. It rose from the pond and moved slowly over the trees.

'Goodbye,' Young Whortle whispered.

And from what seemed a great distance, he heard Woppenfrake's voice call out, 'Always remember, my brave little rimpi-too – travel your own best way.'

The cloud ascended, melting into the night sky and the still pool was in darkness.

Young Whortle waited until the last smudge of mist had vanished from sight. Then he looked around.

The torches were gone and the lanterns that had stood outside the Grelffit Houm were no longer there. Every trace of the water voles had been removed – except one.

Looking very out of place was a tall stone jar on the bank behind him.

Wondering what it could possibly contain, the fieldmouse walked up to it and peered inside.

It was half filled with water but something else lay at the bottom.

Curious, he dipped his right paw in and had to stand on one leg to lean all the way inside.

The thing was soft and small. His fingers closed around it and he prepared to fish it out.

Suddenly his arm tingled and tiny silver stars fizzed and prickled through his skin.

Young Whortle jumped back and stared at his right arm. The fur was bristling and, as he watched, a pale flame flickered up to his shoulder. Then it spluttered and was gone.

'What were that?' he breathed fearfully and he smacked his arm just in case any more fires were about to erupt there.

Then, in the moonlight, the fieldmouse examined what he held in his wet paw.

It was a strip of leather, tied into a loop and wide in the middle.

'A slingshot!' he exclaimed. 'From the woodlanders' weapon hoard. That were kind, but it's no use to . . .'

Gripped by realisation and sudden excitement, he foraged for a small stone and fitted it into the wider part. Then he cast around for a target. The fallen branch that jutted out over the pond had a twisted twig poking from it, bearing a solitary dead leaf, but it was too far away and he shook his head sceptically.

'I could never . . .' he murmured.

Despite his doubts he started to whirl the sling around, fully expecting it to go whizzing in the opposite direction and knock some poor bird from its nest in the trees. With a grunt of effort, he released the stone.

An instant later the leaf was sliced clean off and the

stone went whistling into the shadows on the far side of the pool.

'Oh, Warty,' he marvelled. 'You're going to be Head Sentry after all.'

20

The Head Sentry

Hidden behind cloud, a pale sun climbed over the horizon to herald the final day of the Fennywolde Games.

Yawning and blinking, the fieldmice rubbed the sleep from their eyes and clambered from their nest.

Grandma Bottom told everyone who would listen that some sort of sparkly ghost had definitely looked in at her during the night, but that was such a preposterous notion, no one took her seriously. Who would want to look in on her, anyway?

Shrubby and Ned said nothing about what they thought they had seen and never mentioned it to each other ever again. Such things were impossible.

Many concerned well-wishers dropped by Dimsel's enormous dome to see if she was still huge and came away more than satisfied that she was.

Sitting in his favourite corner, Old Todmore was smoking his first pipe of the day. He couldn't put his finger on it, but something had changed. The atmosphere of the field was different, the change was almost imperceptible but it was there. He rubbed his paws together. A chill draught was sighing through the barley.

'An ill wind,' he mumbled to himself.

Young Whortle slept deep and long and had to be woken by Samuel and the other Wolf Killers who called up to him from below.

'Time to get ready for the Ditch Swim,' they said.

Young Whortle popped his head out of the nest and beamed at them.

'Mornin' lads!' he greeted them chirpily.

His friends looked pleased. 'Is you still speakin' to us, then?' Samuel asked.

'Course I am!' he replied. 'Now let's get goin'. I don't want to miss the start.'

Everyone was gathered at the ditch and Young Whortle noticed at once how much quieter and subdued the Fennywolders were.

'What's up with them?' he asked Todkin.

'They really do believe the Green Mouse visited a terrible retribution on Dimsel,' Todkin told him.

'No one's goin' to believe it were just my biscuit,' Sammy put in.

'So Mister Nettle is everyone's favourite misery-guts again,' mused Hodge. 'They'll do anything for him now to keep in the Green's good books, and stomach all the sour sermons he throws their way.'

Young Whortle scanned the crowd for the mousebrass-maker. Isaac was standing a little apart from the rest and grimly enjoying the awe and deference being shown him.

'He's nowt but a bully,' Young Whortle said. 'Much

worse than Dimsel ever was. And after the Games I'm going to let everyone know just how horrible he is.'

'You'd better get in the water,' Figgy advised. 'The race is about to start. Do you remember what I told you about the minnow wiggle?'

His only answer was Young Whortle's laughter.

Due to the voiding of the Raft Race result, those who had taken part and were not already entered in the Ditch Swim were allowed to participate. So there was quite a throng in the water by the time Young Whortle went wading in to join them.

Lanky was there, as were Ned, Shrubby – the Burdock brothers were already arguing and, staring up the rippling course, was Jenkin.

The Nettle boy did not want to talk to anyone. He had walked right past Alison Sedge earlier and she gazed sorrowfully at him from the bank, pulling petals from daisies in distraction.

His black eye was a livid purple and his lip had swollen again.

Young Whortle knew why.

'Mornin' Jenkin,' he called.

There was no response, but he expected that. Now that he understood what was going on, he would do all he could to help – and so would the rest of the Wolf Killers once they knew.

The day was not the warmest and the competitors were very relieved when Mr Woodruffe held up the drum and gave it a loud thump.

Young Whortle dived forward and the race began.

Up on the high bank, his friends could only gape and stare as he sped through the water.

'He's not wigglin'!' Figgy exclaimed.

Sammy danced up and down. 'No!' he cried. 'But he's winnin'!'

No one could keep up with Young Whortle Nep. He sliced through the water as fast as any fish and faster – and all who saw him gawked in astonishment.

The other entrants were left far behind and his friends ran along the bank to cheer him on, but even on foot they could not keep up with him.

Soon he was swimming through the cold shadow of the yew tree and then the rocks that had almost cost him the Raft Race appeared.

A twist of his hips and a flick of his legs and that obstacle was left behind.

Then, wending through the tips of submerged reeds, he entered the still pool.

Once again the finishing line was the centre of the pond but Young Whortle ceased swimming and trod water.

He gazed on the ancient home of Amnemsis and remembered the adventures he had had there. On that far bank, he had met Virianna and she had protected him from the fury of Mabb. This was the very pond in which Woppenfrake had turned him into all manner of creatures and up there, in the trees, he had flown with the water spirit.

Then he looked over at the sloping boulders that reared up out of the pool.

'The Grelffit Houm,' he murmured.

A group of mouse children had sailed across to it on the *Silver Hare* and were now sliding down the stones and splashing in the water below – squealing and shrieking.

Young Whortle was almost angry, but how could they know what a fantastical place lay beneath them? Down there were the treasured weapons of the woodlanders, the swords and shields that had vanquished the evil Hobbers in the war of long ago. Down there a mysterious, great creature was still crouching in the darkness, waiting for the final battle between Light and Dark and, most important of all, down there – Captain Fenny was sleeping.

'Hey, Neppy!' Figgy's voice broke into his thoughts. 'You've not won yet. You have to get to the middle!'

And so the fieldmouse cast off his memories and returned to the present.

Moments later the Wolf Killers sent up a group howl and they leaped in the air at his victory.

The banks quickly filled with applauding spectators and Young Whortle made his way to the shore, where Hodge and Figgy lifted him onto their shoulders.

'That was incredible!' Samuel announced.

'The other swimmers aren't even at the rocks yet!' Hodge hooted. 'How did you do it?'

'Same as everything else,' he replied with a fond

glance back at the island. 'My friends helped me.'

'I must be the best teacher ever!' Figgy cried.

When Jenkin came second in the Ditch Swim, most of the crowd had already followed the Wolf Killers into the meadow, where a scrumptious breakfast was laid out on a long row of tablecloths.

Meagre and desultory applause greeted him and he looked around for his father. Isaac had left with the others.

Wearily Jenkin trudged ashore.

Young Whortle sank his teeth into the best breakfast he had eaten for over a week. No more raw diced carrots or whole broad beans for him. He tucked into marmalade pancakes followed by a large strawberry dipped in cream and washed down by a wheat cake smothered in honey.

Groaning with pleasure, he lolled on his back and patted his full stomach.

Samuel out-matched him but he still showed no signs of putting on any weight and he wished he had only offered Dimsel half of that magical biscuit.

Hodge was staring up at the sky and trying to decide who should be the next victim of his voice thrower. He was pretty certain it was going to be Alison Scdgc's mother – she was ripe for a bout of tormenting. There were a few others he could toy with as well.

Figgy was peering through the different coloured lenses of his lamp and wondered what the pink one was for, while Todkin was making notes in his book and sketching some of the mice eating their breakfasts.

'So,' he said, without looking up from the page. 'Now you've got two fabulous wins under your belt. What shall we do the rest of the day?'

'Such a shame you didn't make Head Sentry,' Hodge said idly. 'But at least you'll have more time on your paws.'

Young Whortle sat up smart.

'Who says I'm not going to be Head Sentry?' he demanded.

'But there's only two events left,' Figgy said. 'And you're rotten at both.'

Hodge let out a pained groan. 'Don't tell us you're going to do the Slingshot!'

Assuming an air of injured dignity, Young Whortle rose. 'I'll see you lot after,' he said. 'I'm off to get some practice.'

And he stomped towards the cornfield.

His friends looked at one another with ghastly grimaces.

'We'd best run and hide,' Samuel said. 'Nowhere's safe from him with one of them things.'

'I know one place that's perfectly safe,' observed Todkin thoughtfully.

'Where?' they asked.

'Anywhere near the target.'

Hurrying back to his nest, Young Whortle took up the

slingshot that he had been given the previous night. It was dry now and he wanted to go and see if his new skill had stayed with him.

Preferring to be alone, he made his way to the Long Hedge and put the sling in his right paw. His skin tingled and tickled once again and he knew the gift was his to keep forever. Chortling to himself, he chose random targets to aim at: some close, some far away, some small, some large.

Each one suffered a direct hit. The snowy tops of cow parsley were shot clean through, a dandelion was obliterated with an explosion of gold, a stack of wood left over from raft-building was sent toppling, a spray of hawthorn blossom was made into confetti and a worm cast was sliced in two.

He just couldn't miss and even when he tried to throw badly, the missiles still found their targets.

Eventually he plopped himself down on the grass and stared at his right paw.

'You're a deadly weapon,' he proclaimed. 'Quite fright'nin', that is.'

A breathy, musical laugh made him start and he spun around to find Alison Sedge rising from the high grass a little distance away. Her large brown eyes were filled with amusement and she flicked her bunches over her shoulders as she regarded him.

'H . . . how long you been there?' he stuttered.

'All the time,' her soft voice said. 'Who'd have

thought it, Young Whortle – a dead-eyed flower slaughterer.'

For some unaccountable reason, the boy hastily hid his paw behind his back, which amused Alison even more and his ears turned scarlet.

'I reckon you'll win that there event,' she told him. 'An' if you does, I'll let you take me for a walk after – if you want.'

Young Whortle burbled that it would be a pleasure and, laughing lightly, she sidled away.

Pulling out his paw, he chewed his fingernails and watched her saunter into the cornfield, then jumped to his feet. It was time for the Slingshot.

When he returned to the meadow, Young Whortle discovered that the High Jump had been won by Lanky Brommock and the area for the next event was being cleared.

All competitors had to stand on the high bank of the ditch and hit three targets in the meadow opposite. They were woven straw globes, like miniature versions of their nests, and were balanced on poles hammered into the ground. They were all the same size but placed at staggered distances further into the meadow, so that the first target was very close to the far bank but the third was so far away that only the strongest arm could fling a stone to reach it.

'Where've you been?' Samuel asked, when Young Whortle rejoined his friends.

'Don't do this,' Figgy begged him. 'You're likely to knock someone's block off.'

But Young Whortle would not listen to them and at that moment Mr Woodruffe struck the drum and the event commenced.

Shaking their heads, the Wolf Killers backed away.

There were five entrants in the Slingshot: Young Whortle Nep, Shrubby Raggit, Jenkin Nettle and the Burdock brothers.

Shrubby was first up to the mark.

He whirled his sling about his head and let fly.

The first target stubbornly refused to be hit, as did the second and his stone never even reached halfway to the third.

Then came Abihu Burdock. He stuck his tongue out at his brother and ceremoniously loaded his sling.

Hopping up and down he whizzed the stone round and round. When it was loosed, it struck the pole that the first target was balanced on and the straw globe wobbled and fell off.

The crowd applauded. Although, technically, he had not hit the target, it was still a very good shot.

Uriah sulked on the sidelines.

Abihu went for the second target. His stone glanced across it and the globe spun wildly around but did not fall off.

More applause and Uriah's scowl deepened.

Feeling confident, Abihu swaggered to the pile of stones, selected a suitable one and ambled back to the mark, whistling tunelessly.

Uriah wanted to smack him.

Abihu swung the sling around and around and then . . . he toppled over and fell down the bank, bumping all the way down and landing with a great splash in the water below.

Everyone gasped and Uriah dashed to the edge to make sure his brother was unharmed.

Abihu was sitting in the ditch with the empty sling draped across his ears, a clump of grass in his mouth and mud over his face. He was bruised and dishevelled but the only hurt he'd suffered was to his pride.

Uriah exploded with laughter and collapsed on the ground helplessly. He was so overwhelmed by the comical spectacle of his brother that he could not stop and, without warning, he wet himself.

Mortified, he rushed through the crowd and ran home, too humiliated and ashamed to leave his nest for a whole week.

The Burdock brothers never had another argument.

Isaac Nettle's vinegar face was enough to quell any hilarity at these occurrences. The Fennywolders were taking their lead from him now. Watching the proceedings from the back, Alison Sedge narrowed her eyes and saw it all. She tutted under her breath: life was set to change in the cornfield. It would be much less fun.

Next up was Jenkin.

He flexed his arm then fitted a stone. His own face was set like granite as he concentrated on the nearest target. The sling whined over his head as he spun it around and then the first straw globe was knocked from the pole.

The fieldmice cheered and, without pause, Jenkin loaded up another stone.

Moments later the second target went bouncing into the meadow grass and the spectators yelled their cheers.

Jenkin did not relax his concentration for an instant and he put the third stone into his sling.

Alison bit her lip. She could not bear the tension and

found herself praying silently to the Green Mouse, or whoever else was listening and could help her.

'Let my Jolly Jenkin do this,' she whispered. 'Please, please, please.'

She looked over at Mr Nettle and, to her amazement, saw that he, too, was looking anxious; the hard lines around his eyes were softening and an expression of affection was beginning to form.

Alison had to stare at him to make sure. Not only was there affection – but there was pride as well.

Everything depended upon this final throw.

'For Jenkin's sake,' the mouse maid implored, and she crossed her fingers, held her breath and shut one eye tightly.

Jenkin stepped up to the mark.

The sling swished over his head but, before he cast the stone loose, he caught sight his father's face. He had never seen him look like that before.

It startled him and his concentration was shattered. He tried to recover but the stone hurtled out over the meadow and missed the third target.

The audience groaned in disappointment and Jenkin's heart sank. He looked over to his father and despaired when he saw that the unfamiliar expression had gone.

Alison wanted to go over to him, but *her* love was not what he needed and she hung her pretty head.

Mr Woodruffe strode out and shook Jenkin's paws vigorously.

'Two excellent throws!' he told him. 'No one will beat that. Why – this is your third win of the Games, one more than anyone else. That makes you Head Sentry!'

'Wait a minute!' a voice cried out. 'I ain't had my turn yet.'

Young Whortle stepped forward and many of the onlookers gave frightened squeaks.

'Don't let him throw!' Iris Crowfoot objected. 'Nearly splattered me he did, last time he used one of them things.'

The crowd agreed with her. In fact some of them were already looking for cover.

Mr Woodruffe puckered his brows. 'You don't really want to enter this, do you?' he asked.

'I got me one more event left to do,' Young Whortle stated flatly. 'An' this be it.'

'But you don't stand any chance of beating Jenkin,' the King of the Field warned. 'You'd have to knock down both of the first two targets and at least hit the third in order to beat him. It's impossible.'

Young Whortle folded his arms adamantly.

'Let me throw,' he demanded.

Mr Woodruffe could see there was no dissuading him.

'Very well.' He shrugged and banged the drum for attention. 'Young Whortle Nep is about to throw,' he called out. 'I suggest you all seek shelter.'

More of the Fennywolders hurried away and only a

few of the most courageous and the most stupid remained. The Wolf Killers were in neither group. It was their loyalty to their little friend that anchored them there. Alison Sedge was another who lingered, but she knew what no one else did about Young Whortle's prowess and could not help but grin at the scared faces of those who were running away. Even his own family was making a bee-line for the elm trees to hide behind.

Jenkin and Mr Nettle were also present. Isaac had never run from anything and certainly wasn't going to flee from a foolish young dreamer like the Nep boy. And so he remained, glowering and bitter, and Jenkin stood by him.

Mr Woodruffe, however, was already scurrying away with his paws over his head.

Young Whortle watched them go with a wry smile. His right paw was tingling again and he fitted a stone into the sling.

Out in the meadow the targets were being reset by Ned Rattle's father. He had been taking refuge in a strong wicker hut specially built for the occasion but when he saw who was now standing on the high bank he thought it must be a joke. He didn't think it worth balancing the straw globes back on the poles but he did. Then, instead of returning to the hut, he sat in front of it, lazily chewing a piece of grass – feeling perfectly safe.

In the time it took for the targets to be reset, Young

Whortle found himself reflecting on everything that had happened to him. His adventures had been incredible and he had embraced each and every one of them.

The water voles had gone but now something new was beginning. He was about to become Head Sentry. It was a dream he had always ached for and today it was going to be a reality. Those mice who had just scarpered would soon learn a thing or two. He would show them not to underestimate him. He might be small but he was capable of amazing things.

He swung the sling and the stone zinged through the air.

The first target burst apart and Ned Rattle's father let out a horrified shriek, then flung himself back into the hut.

Everyone who was still watching uttered cries of bewilderment and the Wolf Killers roared in jubilation.

'Warty!' Samuel yelled. 'You're glorious!'

Jenkin stared across the ditch at the remains of the target. How was it possible? He looked up at his father and saw only coldness and disappointment.

Jenkin squeezed his eyes closed and turned away.

Young Whortle readied himself for the second throw. By this time some of the cringing spectators were re-emerging from their sanctuaries with astounded looks on their faces.

The little fieldmouse chuckled. He was showing them. He was proving himself.

He paused. But hadn't he already proven everything? Hadn't he fought Hobbers and killed a wolf and weren't his friends the best that anyone could ever hope for? Besides, wasn't winning this way, using this magical skill – just the same as cheating?

'Neppy,' he muttered. 'You're crackers. Things couldn't be better than they are right now. You don't need to be Head Sentry no more.'

And as he realised it, he beheld Jenkin's desolation and knew precisely what to do.

'Righty-ho, Woppenfrake,' he shouted, to the surprise of those around him. 'I hopes somehow you can see me. I'm travellin' my own best way – an' it feels grand.'

And, with a twinkle in his eye, he took the sling from his right paw and swapped to the left. Then he spun it around him in a blur and flung the stone through the air.

The crowd behind him screamed and threw themselves to the ground.

The stone went soaring over the cornfield.

A piercing howl, far better than any the Wolf Killers could manage, even Hodge, resounded from the Hall of Corn.

Young Whortle had successfully hit Dimsel Bottom – on the bottom. But then, as it was currently such a large area, it was no great feat.

The fieldmouse still had one more throw but he decided it was best for everyone's health if he retired early.

Mr Woodruffe came scampering back once more.

'Then that definitely means Jenkin is the winner of the Slingshot!' he announced. 'And therefore, he's also the winner of the Fennywolde Games – he's our new Head Sentry for the coming year!'

The Fennywolders stamped their feet and shouted their cheers and congratulations.

The blanketeers had been standing by in readiness. They picked up the new champion and tossed him in the air, bouncing him on their blankets.

'Father!' Jenkin cried. 'I did it! I won – I'm Head Sentry.'

Isaac Nettle watched him fly up and down and the winter thawed from his face.

'Well done, son,' he said.

The Wolf Killers were about to go and commiserate with Young Whortle when they blinked and elbowed one another.

Alison Sedge had already strolled over – and was kissing him.

And, at that moment, a host of beautiful white butterflies descended and everyone cooed, except for Figgy, who said, 'So that's what the pink lens does!'

Finishing Lines

It turned out to be a golden summer for Fennywolde and Todkin was kept extremely busy writing everything down in his book. They did not know it, but it proved to be the last year the Wolf Killers would spend together. Yet they lived it to the full just the same, all six of them – they had asked Jenkin to join the gang.

As for Isaac, he finally showed his son respect and affection, but sometimes he lapsed back into his old horrible ways. When that happened, Figgy would send a plague of biting midges to torment him night and day and Hodge would use his voice thrower to make all manner of rude noises erupt from his vicinity during those long sermons, which scandalised and shocked everyone.

Young Whortle often returned to the still pool and sat wistfully before the entrance of the Grelffit Houm. He wondered where the water voles had gone and if he would ever see them again.

Once Figgy and Hodge tried to prise their way in with sticks but the great stone never budged.

And so the autumn came, the barleycorn fell before

the harvester and the Fennywolders moved into their winter quarters. Dimsel had lost enough weight by then to be able to walk, but one of the entrances still had to be specially widened. To his dismay, Sammy never got fat.

By the time ice and snow gripped the ditch and the still pool was frozen over, the Wolf Killers had forgotten all about the oath they had sworn – and that it had not been fulfilled. Thus the first shadow of evil fell upon their land.

But deep below the ground, beneath the flickering green flames, Captain Fenny slept on. Lit by that emerald fire, the name of the hero who would one day awaken him, was painted on the ceiling.

TWIT

More tales from the dark world of Deptford

The Deptford Mouselets
Fleabee's Fortune

The Festival of First Blood is approaching and
Fleabee, a young ratgirl, faces a difficult
choice: she must kill or be killed. This is the
will of Jupiter, Lord of all rats. But Fleabee is
unlike the rest of her kind. She is soft-hearted
and unable to harm anything. Then Madame
Akkikuyu foretells a different path for her.

Fleabee's destiny lies elsewhere – in a world
full of magic and peril . . .

More tales from the dark world of Deptford

The Deptford Mice
The Dark Portal

Robin Jarvis

The first book in the Deptford Mice series.

In the sewers of Deptford there lurks a dark presence, which fills the tunnels with fear: Jupiter, Lord of All.

Worshipped by the fearsome rats, Jupiter's evil dreams of conquest and domination could well come true. Until a small, frightened mouse wanders into this nightmare realm and the Deptford Mice are thrown into a world of horror and sorcery.

Can the mice survive this terror? Or have they lost the cosy world they once knew for ever.

'Bursting with action, danger, gruesome detail and some very narrow escapes . . . from a prolific storyteller who excels at anthropomorphic tales such as this one.' Riveting Reads: Boys into Books 11–14

More tales from the dark world of Deptford

The Deptford Mice
The Crystal Prison

Robin Jarvis

The second book in the Deptford Mice series.

An innocent young mouse lies murdered in a moonlit field as the screech of an owl echoes across the ripening corn.

The Deptford Mice have escaped the horrors of Jupiter's lair and sought refuge in the countryside. But once again they must face terrifying evil as they are embroiled in a series of horrible murders.

At first the simple country mice suspect Deptford newcomer Audrey – but the truth turns out to be far more sinister.

'Jarvis is a real story teller.' Carousel

More tales from the dark world of Deptford

The Deptford Mice
The Final Reckoning

Robin Jarvis

The final book in the Deptford Mice series.

The ghostly spirit of Jupiter has returned, more terrifying than before. Bent on revenge, he smothers the world in an eternal winter of snow and ice.

The Deptford Mice are worried: the mystical bats have fled from the attic, and a new rat army is gathering strength. With food short and no sign of spring the mice know there's a desperate struggle ahead.

Who knows how many will survive and at what cost?

'a great writer, in command of his intricate plotting.'
Scottish Sunday Herald